On the
Wave
of a *New*
Beginning

Happy Reading!
K.C. Leigh
John 1:1

K.C. Leigh

On the
Wave
of a *New*
Beginning

*A Chandler's Cove
Mystery*

On The Wave of a New Beginning
© 2019 by K.C. Leigh

Scripture quotations are taken from the New International Version (NIV) of the Holy Bible. Copyright ©1973, 1978, 1984, 2011 by Biblica, Inc.® Used by permission of Zondervan. All rights reserved worldwide. www.Zondervan.com. The "NIV" and "New International Version" are trademarks registered in the United States Patent and Trademark Office by Biblical, Inc ®

Any emphases in Scripture quotations are the author's.

This book is a work of fiction. Names, characters, places, and incidents are either the product of the author's imagination or are used fictitiously. Any resemblance to actual events, locales, business establishments, or persons, living or deceased, is entirely coincidental.

Cover Design and Editing by Jamison Editing
Interior Design and Proofreading by Jason Sisam | https://jasonsisam.com

ISBN 978-0-578-54456-4 (Print)

First Edition: 2019
10 9 8 7 6 5 4 3 2 1

Printed and bound in the United States of America

ACKNOWLEDGMENTS

I would like to thank Beth Jamison and Jason Sisam for helping me create a beautiful book, inside and out. I would also like to thank my Peachtree City writer's groups and my faithful beta readers for helping me hone my craft. Kudos to my friends and family for standing by me and encouraging me every step of the way. Most importantly, I give praise to my Heavenly Father for helping me use my words to glorify Him!

"We are tied to the ocean. And when we go back to the sea—Whether it is to sail or to watch it—We are going back from whence we came."

—John F. Kennedy

PROLOGUE

October, the Outer Banks

CAPTAIN NATHAN BEALL sat alone in the salon of the *C. C. Princess* nursing a nightcap and unwinding from a hectic day of deep-sea fishing. After hauling in a hefty catch of Yellowfin and Wahoo, he'd spent the afternoon cleaning the catch and putting it on ice. His evening had consisted of routine maintenance to the 48-foot Cabo Convertible's twin diesel engines. Tethered to the side of the dock, the *Princess* rocked back and forth as the ocean waves caressed her hull. The hypnotic creaking of the boat's dock lines echoed through the otherwise silent night.

Nathan finished his drink and placed the empty glass on the coffee table. He swung his long legs onto the tan leather couch and closed his eyes. He sighed, wondering if his sixty-five-year-old bones could keep going at such a grueling pace. The old-line fisherman knew first-hand that life on the sea was not for the faint of heart.

Beginning to relax, Nathan's mind wandered back in time. Visions of a beautiful wife and child came into focus. He smiled to himself, remembering the happy times the three of them had spent together. But that was another time and another place.

The sudden sound of activity on the docks jolted Nathan back to reality. He checked his watch. The midnight hour approached. Time to go home and get some sleep.

Yawning, Nathan stood up and stretched his weary body. A twinge of pain shot through his left hip, but he shook it off. Grabbing his keys, he turned off the galley light and locked up the boat for the night.

Heavy fog pervaded the late October evening, dampening Nathan's skin along with his spirits. Hearing raised voices, he scanned the dock in the direction of the noise, but the thick mist and dim dock lighting obscured his vision. He briefly hesitated, then stepped onto the dock. "I hope Jim's not in trouble again," he muttered under his breath. He knew that his fishing buddy, Jim Pritchett, liked to pick fights when he drank.

Nathan headed in the direction of his friend's boat and saw two figures in the shadows. Was one of them Jim? He couldn't be sure.

As Nathan approached the shadowy figures, a loud crack rippled through the still night, stopping him in his tracks. His senses went on alert. Was that a gunshot? Straining his eyes and ears for any sight or sound of movement, he gathered up the courage to breathe.

A hooded figure bolted toward Nathan. Cold, dark eyes pierced through him like a knife. The surreal specter dashed into the fog, leaving Nathan glued to his spot.

As the runner made his escape, Nathan caught a glimpse of a shiny object. Dazed, he opened his mouth to speak, but the words stuck in his throat. The distant sound of a foghorn brought him back to his senses.

Immediately following the foghorn's blast, Nathan heard the roar of a motorcycle engine speeding away from the docks. Beginning to feel his limbs again, he stumbled in the direction of the noise. A few feet away, Nathan glimpsed a dark mass lying on the dock. The next thing he saw made his stomach churn.

Sprawled out on his back, a man lay motionless. Crimson blood oozed from a gaping wound to his abdomen. Could it be his friend? Nathan took a closer look at the body. He didn't recognize the dark-skinned, dark-haired man who lay before him. "Thank God, it's not Jim!"

Unsure of what to do next, Nathan reached down to check for a pulse. The clamminess of the man's skin caused his stomach to churn again. Staggering to the side of the dock, he leaned over the railing and vomited into the water.

Retrieving a handkerchief from his shirt pocket, Nathan wiped his mouth. After inhaling a few deep breaths of the cool sea air, he regained his composure. He grabbed his cell phone out of the pocket of his jeans and dialed 9-1-1.

Within minutes, Nathan glimpsed red and blue lights swirling through the thickening fog. Police and rescue vehicles arrived on the scene. The paramedics discovered that the injured man did, indeed, have a weak pulse. As he clung to life, the rescue team loaded him into the ambulance and sped away.

Without warning, stars danced before Nathan's eyes and he struggled to breathe. Shivering in the chilly Carolina gloom, he staggered sideways, toppling onto a nearby bench.

Pull yourself together man, Nathan berated himself. *You don't want the police thinking you did this, do you?*

One of the arriving officers was Nathan's friend, Stan Phillips. The tall, muscular cop approached the bench with a blanket in his hand and a concerned look on his face. Noticing his friend's distress, he sat down next to Nathan, handed him the blanket, and coaxed him to slow his breathing.

Once Nathan calmed down, Stan encouraged him to remember what he'd seen and heard. Nathan's hands shook as he described the harrowing incident to his friend. He recalled first hearing raised voices followed by a loud crack, then seeing a hooded figure race past him into the fog. Seconds later, he remembered the sound of a motorcycle leaving the docks.

Stan continued to question Nathan for what seemed like an eternity. During that time, the crime scene unit gathered what little evidence they could find. After an exhausting hour, Stan told Nathan that it was time to leave the docks.

"We need to take you down to the station," Stan informed him. "You'll have to give a formal statement, and we need to perform a few simple tests."

Nathan grimaced at the thought. "How long will it take?"

"We have to follow police protocol. Hopefully not too long."

Nathan willed himself off the bench and accompanied Stan to the police station. Upon arriving, his hands and clothes were checked for gunshot residue and he was fingerprinted. Afterward, he was ushered into an interrogation room so that he could give a formal statement.

Time stood still for Nathan as he awaited any news, either good or bad. While he waited, he overheard another officer give Stan an update on the condition of the injured man. Following an arduous attempt at resuscitation, the John Doe had died from a gunshot wound to the abdomen.

In the wee hours of the morning, Nathan was cleared to leave the police station. Stan drove Nathan back to the docks, promising to touch base in a few days. Exhausted and on edge, Nathan sped home and remained there, anxiously awaiting Stan's call.

After several stressful days and sleepless nights, Nathan received word from Stan that the John Doe had been identified through a fingerprint scanning database in South America. The gunshot victim had worked as a migrant coffee bean farmer in Columbia, but U.S. Customs had no record of the man legally entering the country.

For weeks following the incident, Nathan couldn't sleep. He snapped at everyone around him and jumped at every loud sound. Over time, he stopped going out on the water altogether. Because of this, his business suffered.

Jim suggested that Nathan see a doctor, thinking that his friend might have PTSD. Nathan didn't know much about post-traumatic stress disorder, but he wasn't about to have a shrink poking around in his head.

By February, Nathan couldn't stand it any longer. He called Stan, frantic for an update. Stan informed him that the case had grown cold, and that the shooter's identity remained a mystery. The realization that a killer might be able to identify him was more than Nathan could handle. He had to get out of town, the faster the better.

Not knowing where to turn next, Nathan remembered Jim raving about a place called Chandler's Cove. Nestled in the center of the Gulf of Mexico, the quaint coastal town was famous for its annual fishing rodeo, as well as, its warmth, charm, and southern hospitality. This might be a good place for him and the *C.C. Princess* to hide. But could he risk going to Chandler's Cove now that his daughter lived there?

Deep-sixing any doubt, Nathan contacted the head of the Chandler's Cove Harbor Coalition and reserved a slip on the docks. Arranging for the *Princess'* transport, he began packing up his tiny apartment, donating his few pieces of furniture to the Goodwill. Within twenty-four hours, Nathan's black Ford F-150 was brimming with all his earthly possessions.

Before leaving, Nathan phoned Stan to apprise him of his plans, urging the cop to call him if he caught a break in the case. With that, he jumped in his truck and headed out of town, leaving his old life behind. Uncertainty reflected in his rearview mirror, but hope stretched across the horizon in front of him.

ONE

Summer, Chandler's Cove

IN THE DOWNSTAIRS foyer of Callahan Manor, the majestic grandfather clock chimed four times. Sitting at her roll-top desk paying bills, Caroline Callahan was reminded of a time around 1995 BC, before children, that is, when life was simple, and her wallet was fat. If she thought for one minute that her family could survive without cell phones, a satellite dish, or wireless internet, she would happily bid the technological money-grabbers adieu.

Caroline's number one motto had always been, "A penny saved is a penny earned." Conversely, Jason, her husband of twenty years, preferred the latest and greatest of just about everything. To be fair, if it weren't for Jason, they'd still be living in the 1980s.

Personally, Caroline liked the 80s. Those were the *good ole days.* Memories of Michael Jackson, leg warmers, and dance classes occupied the recesses of her mind. Back then, dance was her saving grace. It had carried her through many difficult times, like the dark years after her father abandoned her and her mother. Today, she was saved by God's grace.

Slapping a stamp on the last bill, Caroline set it on top of the stack and glanced down at the calendar on her desk. She'd marked the last day of July with a glittery gold star. Tonight, the family would be celebrating her mother's 65th birthday.

In all honesty, Roseann Whitmore had never needed an excuse to throw a party. Just being alive was cause enough for her to celebrate. Caroline closed her eyes, thanking God for his bountiful gifts and asking that he bless her mother's joyous occasion.

Jason hollered up the stairs. "Caroline, are you getting ready? The party starts at six thirty. We need to hurry." Always a stickler for punctuality, Caroline's handsome hubby did not take kindly to being late.

"I'm working on that right now," she hollered back.

Jumping up from her desk, Caroline strode to her antique armoire by the bedroom door and placed the stack of bills on top. She, then, proceeded to the bathroom, showered, and dried her pixie-cut tresses. She finished with a spritz of shine spray to enhance her hair's sun-kissed strawberry blonde pigments.

Hoping to find the perfect outfit for a summer soiree, Caroline rushed into the walk-in closet, wondering what to wear to beat the heat. Her coastal summer attire generally consisted of Capri pants, a T-shirt, and sandals. One would think that, after spending the past three years in a beach town, she would have grown accustomed to the hot, humid summers. But one would be mistaken. Hot and humid, was just that, hot and humid.

Caroline rummaged through her side of the closet, mentally kicking herself for not taking the time to shop for a new outfit. Grabbing a pair of floral print capris, she slipped them on, while sliding clothes hangers back and forth. Spotting a white eyelet blouse, she pulled it over her head, then stepped out of the closet to look in the mirror.

Caroline frowned. Too casual. Roseann would never approve. Giving up, she slipped out of her clothes, slipped into a robe, and returned to the bathroom to apply her makeup.

As Caroline preened, Jason entered the bathroom, grimy from having completed a brake job on his new but used truck. He gave her a quick kiss on her freckled nose as he squeezed past and headed to the shower. "Let me get cleaned up, then I'll be ready to go."

"You know that Mother won't be ready when we get to her condo," Caroline said matter-of-factly. "She likes to be fashionably late."

Jason's eyebrows shot up. "She won't be late to her own birthday party, will she?"

Caroline laughed. "No—that would never do."

Ten minutes later, Jason jumped out of the shower, towel-dried his short, chestnut brown hair, and trimmed his Van Dyke beard. "How do I look?" he asked.

Caroline put away her makeup mirror and stood. "Since you ask…" she said, coming over to stroke his beard, "When are you going to get rid of that gray, old man?"

Jason thought for a moment. "Don't you think it makes me look distinguished?" He strutted his distinguished self to the closet.

"No comment," Caroline rebutted as she scooted to the armoire, remembering the expression: like mother, like daughter. She was running late, too. She took out two sundresses and gave them the once over.

Presto chango. Like magic, Jason exited the closet donned in his favorite burgundy and tan Hawaiian shirt, a pair of khaki shorts, and sandals.

Caroline shook her head, wondering why she was making such a fuss. "I'm glad this party has a luau theme. You look appropriately Hawaiian." She displayed the dresses for Jason to see. "Honey, which one should I wear, the robin's egg blue or the emerald green?"

"Wear the blue one. It matches your eyes."

Jason came up behind Caroline, wrapped his arms around her waist, and kissed her neck. His beard tickled her skin.

Caroline giggled. "I thought we were in a hurry."

Jason gave her ear a little nibble. "I was just thinking about how sexy you'll look in that dress."

"Hold those thoughts until after the party, hot stuff. Mother will be miffed if we don't get her to her party on time."

Jason spun her around. He stood five inches taller than her 5'5" height. Looking into Caroline's baby blues, he held her gaze. The golden flecks in his hazel eyes sparkled. "Give me a kiss to hold me over."

She obliged.

They were interrupted by the ringing of the phone.

Jason released his hold. "It must be Princess Roseann. Only your mother has timing *that* perfect."

"I know. I'll tell Her Ladyship we're on the way." Caroline hurried to answer the phone. "Hi, Mother. Happy Birthday."

"Thank you, dear." Roseann sounded like a cheerful bluebird happily splashing in a birdbath with her friends. "Remind Jason to bring the video camera—and don't forget the guestbook and quill pen for the guest table."

"I've got everything in my tote," Caroline assured her, looking at the bedside clock. "We're leaving in ten. See you soon. Kiss, kiss," she added, hanging up the phone.

"I'll get the SUV ready," Jason said, leaving the bedroom.

Caroline threw off her robe and applied a quick dusting of Chantilly body powder, then put on the blue dress, accessorizing it with sapphire earrings, a matching necklace and bracelet, and jewel-strapped sandals. She sashayed down the long hallway and stopped at the top of the stairs. "Hey guys, are you ready to go?" Caroline called out to her sons, Evan and Max.

No response.

She repeated her request, adding a little more oomph this time.

"Just about" and "be there in a minute" came wafting down the hall. Evan, age eighteen, and Max, age nine, shot out of their rooms. The trio single-filed it down the stairs, wasting no time getting to the SUV. Evan stopped long enough to grab his bass guitar.

Jason, ready at the wheel of Caroline's garnet red Subaru Outback, motioned for everyone to hurry up. Caroline and Max joined him, while Evan placed his guitar in the back seat of his copper-colored Scion XB.

"Don't forget you promised to help Aunt Flo with the cooking," Caroline called out to Evan. "She's also asked if you could stay after the party to load up her station wagon."

Flipping his ginger bangs off his forehead, Evan rolled his cobalt-blue eyes. His nonverbal reply came through loud and clear. Caroline's number one son was on the verge of complaining, when she gave him her "don't fool with Mother Nature" look. When it came to nonverbal communication, she could give as good as she got.

"You know this job will look good on your resume for culinary school," Caroline reminded him.

"I know," Evan conceded as he slid behind the wheel of his Scion.

Caroline blew him a kiss. "Be careful—and don't be late."

"I'll be there on time," Evan promised as he sped away.

Famous last words, she thought. Evan and his Nana marched to the beat of their own drums.

TWO

JASON SLOWED to a stop at the entrance to Roseann's gated beachfront condominium complex, Sandpiper Shore. He rolled down his window, and Caroline waved to the guard on duty. "Hey Walt. We're here to pick up Roseann for her big birthday bash."

Walt Gaston greeted everyone with a Cheshire-Cat smile. Gray-blue eyes twinkled behind large black framed glasses that rested on his tanned bulbous nose. "I can't believe the big night has finally arrived. Roseann has been so excited all day. She called me twice, giving me additions to tonight's guest list."

Roseann's trusted friend snapped his fingers. "I almost forgot." He stepped into the guard shack, returned with a newspaper clipping, and handed it to Jason. "I cut out the birthday announcement that was in *The Village Times-Herald* today. I thought Roseann would like another copy for her scrapbook."

With his quick smile and easy-going personality, Walt held a special place in Caroline's heart. "Thanks, Walt. Roseann couldn't ask for a better friend."

A military veteran and electrical engineer by trade, Walt served in the U.S. Air Force for twenty years. Five years before retirement, he transferred to Fort Watson Air Force Base, located a few miles west on Koke Island. After retiring, he remained in Fort Watson and worked for a large electrical contracting company for several more years. Three years ago, after the death of his wife, Walt took a job as a security guard at Sandpiper Shore.

The pre-dusk humidity made the air feel like a sauna bath, and Walt was feeling the effects of the sticky heat. He took off his tan uniform hat and mopped his buzz cut with a handkerchief. Replacing his hat, he grabbed his clipboard and scanned the guest list. He stroked his gray handlebar mustache. "I count fifty names. Roseann hasn't added any last-minute guests, has she?"

"I wouldn't put it past her, Walt," Jason quipped. "But no worries, man. We dodged a bullet this time."

Caroline scrunched up her face. "Don't make fun," she chided, lightly punching Jason's arm.

Jason grabbed her hand and kissed her palm.

Walt chuckled. "I know it's not every day a princess turns sixty-five years young."

"Come join the festivities after your shift, Walt," Caroline urged. "I know Mother would want you to share in her special day."

Jason released Caroline's hand and turned his attention back to Walt. "Keep calm and carry on my good man," he said with a wink.

Walt waved in acknowledgment as Jason pulled away from the guard shack. Joke or no joke, Roseann's friends and family agree that she is, indeed, a princess. She even has the tiara to prove it. Thankfully, she was not so bold as to wear the dazzling head ornament in public. But to a birthday party? Stranger things had happened.

Jason drove around to the far end of the complex, winding his way past rows of wood-sided buildings the color of driftwood. The game plan was to get Roseann to the beach pavilion in time to oversee the finishing touches to the decorations. He pulled up to unit number 1012 and parked in front, keeping the motor running.

"I'll just run in and get Mother," Caroline said to Jason and Max. "We'll be out shortly."

"Remember to stay on task, darling," Jason shouted out the window as Caroline made her way up the front steps.

She chose to ignore the remark, knowing that Jason had good reason to reprove. Time grew wings and flew out the window when she and her mother got together.

Caroline let herself in the front door and shouted a welcome from the entrance foyer.

"I'm almost ready, dear," Roseann called from her bedroom.

Eager to see the results of her mother's recent redecorating efforts, Caroline strolled into the tidy kitchen with its new almond appliances. The pecan colored cabinets complimented the tile floor and granite countertops, which were a nice blend of earth tones. Off from the kitchen, a glass-topped wicker table and chairs with beige cushions sat in the cheery breakfast nook. A matching baker's rack filled with assorted recipe books, gourmet cookware, and a set of everyday china, stood across from the table.

She walked from the breakfast nook into the spacious den. New sandy-colored carpet lined the floors. A sleeper sofa with peach and blue accents rested against the mirrored wall at the far end of the room. A blue recliner and peach upholstered armchair were positioned to the left of the sofa. Two wicker tables flanked each end of the sofa. Dolphin lamps with taupe shades adorned each tabletop.

Continuing her tour, Caroline stepped down into the cozy sunroom. Along one wall, honeycomb blinds hung from three large windows. An ivory loveseat sat on the opposite wall. To the back of the room, a lace-covered French door led to a covered deck and the pool just beyond.

She sat down on the loveseat and surveyed the fruits of Roseann's labor. Resting her head on the comfy cushioning, Caroline closed her eyes. Her mind drifted back to the time her family first ventured to Chandler's Cove. Roseann and her step-father, Grant, had purchased a one-bedroom vacation home at Sandpiper

Shore in 1985. Surrounded by water on three sides, the Gulf Bay to the north, Chandler's Cove Harbor to the west, and the Gulf of Mexico to the south, the town has access to Koke Island via the Inlet Pass Bridge.

Every summer, the family would travel from Atlanta to the gulf to spend a week in the golden sun, white sand, and emerald surf. The rest of the year, Roseann rented out the condo for a week or a month at a time. In those days, the fishing village was home to a few motels, half a dozen beach houses, and a couple of condo complexes. The sandpipers and seagulls outnumbered the tourists ten to one on the secluded beach.

After Grant succumbed to esophageal cancer five years ago, Roseann decided to make Chandler's Cove her permanent residence. She sold the one-bedroom condo and upgraded to her current two-bedroom unit. Today, Chandler's Cove is no longer a sleepy little village, but has become a teeming town full of year-round residents, summer vacationers, and winter Snowbirds.

The distinct scent of Chloe perfume wafted through the air, rousing Caroline from her reminiscence. Roseann followed the scent into the sunroom and glided over. A shimmering purple object dangled from her outstretched hand. Lavender-tipped French manicured nails, sparkling with tiny rhinestones, adorned each digit. "Could you help me with this, dear?" Roseann asked, bringing an elegant, yet understated, amethyst necklace to her throat.

"I see that you found something to match your new lavender dress," Caroline commented, hooking the necklace's clasp.

"And earrings to match, as well." Roseann brought both hands up to give Caroline a better look at the dangling purple stones. Her emerald-green eyes sparkled with excitement. With her petite five-foot-two frame, she reminded Caroline of a fragile china doll that is never to be played with, only admired.

"That color looks good on you, by the way," Caroline said as they stepped back into the den.

"How do you like what I've done with the condo?" Roseann asked, opening her arms wide.

"Simple, but classy. Just what a beach house should look like. Your taste is impeccable as usual, Mother." Caroline checked her watch, then headed to the foyer. "We'd better go. Aunt Flo is expecting us."

Roseann took one last look at her reflection in the gold-framed mirror by the front door. She primped her short, wavy, salt and pepper hair, checked her passion pink lipstick, and grabbed her lavender purse. "Let the party begin," she lilted, her voice resonating like the sound of wind chimes blowing in the wind.

They stepped out the door and were on their way.

THREE

THE ENTOURAGE LEFT the condo complex and drove across the street to the beach pavilion.

"What's Aunt Flo doing?" Max asked, as Jason eased into an open parking space near the front entrance. Everyone looked up to see Caroline's aunt frantically waving her arms in the air. Exiting the Subaru, the group climbed up the pavilion steps to get a closer look.

Reaching the landing, everyone began to laugh. A dozen ducks haphazardly waddled all about the party area, and Aunt Flo was attempting to shoo them back down the ramp with a dish towel. As permanent residents of Sandpiper Shore, the curious little creatures were frequently found swimming in the lake, sitting on the golf greens, or halting traffic as they crossed the roads.

"Oh, good—you're finally here," Aunt Flo gasped, catching her breath.

Roseann assessed the chaos. "Goodness gracious, these ducks have *got* to go!" she exclaimed.

Flo wiped her forehead with the dish towel and pushed her

falling platinum copper tresses back into place. "I've called the secu-rity guard. He's on the way over to round up these darn ducks."

The summer heat flushed Flo's ruddy complexion, causing her granny glasses to slide down her nose. She pushed her glasses back into place and began fanning herself with the dish towel. "These quacks nearly scared the daylights out of me," she blustered.

No one dared snicker.

As if on cue, Walt magically appeared. "Sorry folks. I'll have these pests out of your hair in no time," he informed in a commanding voice.

Caroline looked at Aunt Flo. Her aunt's inquisitive chocolate-brown eyes stuck on Walt like glue. Sidling up next to Walt, Caro-line steered him in Aunt Flo's direction. "Meet my aunt from Atlanta, Florence Strickland," Caroline said, detecting a familiar twinkle in Walt's eyes. "She's spending the rest of the summer here with us."

Walt gave a slight bow. "How do you do, ma'am?"

The ducks began quacking and flapping their wings.

Walt shook his head. "I better get these ducks back across the road. We can't have them ruining the party." Walt's six-foot frame loomed over the ducks as he began to march them down the ramp, hopefully back to the lake.

"Way to go, Walt," everyone cheered.

"Nice to meet you," Aunt Flo shouted over the quacking ducks.

"That Walt is such a life-saver, isn't he Aunt Flo?" Caroline drawled, locking arms with her.

With a dreamy look in her eyes, Flo watched Walt waddle away with the ducks in tow. Nicknamed the Mother Superior of the Cloth, Flo had been the costume coordinator of the Atlanta Passion Play until its final season three years ago. Upon losing her husband a year later, the self-taught culinary artist developed a knack for catering parties. Everyone was excited to see what she had in store for the big event.

One catastrophe avoided, Caroline returned to the situation at hand. "What can I do to help you, Aunt Flo?" she asked as the two entered the beach pavilion's compact kitchen.

Flo's eyes darted around the kitchen taking a mental inventory. "The party trays are keeping cool in the fridge," she replied. "The lime sherbet and ice ring for the punch are in the freezer. I've also set up two metal tubs with ice, one for the canned sodas, and one for the bottled water."

Flo placed both fists on her curvy hips. "I wish I could have made the birthday cake," she sighed. "I wanted to surprise your mother, and I couldn't very well make the cake in her kitchen, could I?"

"We'll miss having one of your wonderful cakes at the party, Aunt Flo, but I know Mother appreciates all the work you've done for her big day."

"You're a sweet one, Caroline Celeste." Aunt Flo gave Caroline a wink. "That's why you're my favorite niece." She stacked the plates, cups, napkins, and eating utensils on the kitchen counter. "Speaking of family, it's a shame that Patrick, Tala, and the twins can't make it to the party."

Caroline nodded in agreement. Her brother, Patrick, was a successful advertising copywriter with a large video production company in Atlanta. "Patrick is overseeing the production of a TV commercial for a new client his agency finally landed."

Flo frowned. "Sis will miss not having both her children here on her special day, but your brother will come when he can." She continued organizing the kitchen like it was her very own. "Could you go check on the party girl for me?" she asked, glancing in Caroline's direction.

"Yes ma'am." Caroline stepped out of the kitchen and into party central. She surveyed her surroundings. Several guest tables had been set up in the center of the pavilion. A flameless candle encircled with yellow hibiscus and pink cottage roses graced the center of each table. She found Roseann supervising the table decorating. Her crew consisted of several youth from her teen mentoring program at the Seaside Community Center. A retired vocational education administrator, Roseann had a heart for her "kids" and they loved her right back.

In one corner of the pavilion, the local D.J., Music Man Dan, busied himself setting up sound equipment. His massive music collection contained enough beach music to last throughout the night. In the opposite corner, a red velvet birthday cake with white buttercream icing and pink and yellow flowers sat at one end of a long table. A crystal punch bowl sat at the other end. An assortment of nuts, mints, and cheese straws sat between the two. A gift table stood at the top of the stairs. Remembering the lace-covered guest book and quill pen she'd brought, Caroline retrieved them from her tote and placed them on the gift table.

As beach music began to stream through the speakers, Aunt Flo tromped out of the kitchen toting a huge box of leis. Spying Max, she made a beeline for him. "Max, I have a job for you, too," she instructed, not waiting for a response. "As each guest arrives, place a lei around their neck."

"That will take forever!" Max rolled his sky-blue eyes for dramatic effect. "I wanted to play volleyball with the other kids."

Caroline walked over to Max. "Would you like some cheese and crackers with that whine?"

"Oh, Mom," he sighed. "You think you are *so* funny." He shot her his special impish grin.

Caroline laughed. "I can't resist a good pun." She turned Max in the direction of the pavilion entrance. "Go help your Aunt, please."

Max took the box of leis from Flo and prepared for duty. Flo scurried back to the kitchen. At the same moment, Evan, and his friend, Dave Jenkins, blew past. Evan balanced a tray of hot dogs in one hand and a tray of hamburgers in the other. Dave followed behind with an assortment of buns and grilling utensils. Two commercial grills, fired up and ready to go, awaited them downstairs. Best buds for three years, Dave would be joining Evan at culinary school this fall.

"Thanks for your help tonight, Dave," Caroline called over her shoulder as the boys descended the stairs.

Flo reappeared with Jason following close behind. He carried several tiki torches in his arms. "Help!" he mouthed, giving Caroline a wide-eyed glare.

"Jason, you and Caroline Celeste take these tiki torches down to the beach and place them around the volleyball nets," Flo ordered. She shoved a lighter in Jason's pocket.

Tiki torches in hand, Caroline and Jason plodded down the beachside steps and traversed the long wooden walkway. The wooden planks creaked under their feet with every step. To the left and right, deep sand dunes, inhabited with tufts of sea oats, edged the length of the pavilion.

Arriving at the end of the walk, the two slipped off their sandals and sunk down into the sugar-white sand. Small quartz particles that originated in the Appalachian Mountain region of the country gave the sand its rich color and texture.

Reaching the volleyball nets, Caroline and Jason began setting up the tiki torches as instructed. After lighting each torch, they lingered at the water's edge, admiring the golden glow that reflected off the turquoise-green sea. A salty breeze bounced off the water and stuck to Caroline's skin, but she didn't mind. She'd always had the sea in her soul.

By the time they returned, the party was already underway. Hundreds of tiny white lights twinkled around the pavilion, emitting a romantic glow. A mound of colorful presents shimmered like shining jewels on the gift table, and a veritable feast awaited everyone's approval. Having completed their cooking assignment, Evan and Dave were now jamming with Music Man Dan. Jason grabbed the video camera and began recording the festivities.

Caroline spotted Max's sandy-blond head bobbing up and down

as he retrieved leis out of the box. Issuing a greeting of *Aloha*, he placed a lei around the neck of each guest.

Ever the social butterfly, Roseann flitted from guest to guest, basking in the warmth and love that radiated from them. Due to her magnetic personality, Roseann made friends easily and always made them feel like family. A gift that the family was thankful for as she battled breast cancer two years earlier. During her treatment, Roseann developed a special bond with her well-wishers. Now cancer-free, she understands the importance of giving back the love she receives from others.

The hickory-smoked aroma of chargrilled meat made Caroline's stomach rumble. She found Jason, hooked her finger through his belt loop, and guided him in the direction of the feast. They filled up plates and sat down at the seaside entrance of the pavilion to partake of Aunt Flo's delicious creations.

As Caroline watched the carefree interactions of the guests, overwhelming joy washed over her. She placed her hand over Jason's and gave it a squeeze. "It's humbling to have such wonderful friends and family," she said, wiping a tear from the corner of her eye.

She turned her attention to the vast expanse of the ocean. Mesmerized by the rise and fall of the waves rushing toward the shore, Caroline's brain drifted back to a time of lost love and unful-filled dreams. She turned toward Jason. "I thank God every day for his blessings, but do you think it's selfish to want more?"

Jason pulled his attention away from the festivities. "Trust God, Caroline. He's got you covered."

Distracted by a shadow in the distance, Caroline squinted, straining to see what it could be. On the far side of the volleyball nets, the tiki torches illuminated the silhouette of a man walking away from the pavilion. She tugged on Jason's sleeve. "Do you see that man on the beach?"

"What man?" He searched the shoreline.

Caroline pointed into the darkness, but the shadowy figure had vanished. "I think someone was on the beach watching the party."

In the next instant, Roseann blew in like a gentle breeze, grabbed Jason's arm, and the two descended upon the dance floor.

As Caroline watched her hubby twist and shout, she shrugged off the unsettling feeling that cloaked her. Pondering Jason's comment, she recalled the hopes and dreams that she'd long since hidden away. Could now be the time to let them see the light of day?

FOUR

Chandler's Cove Harbor

NATHAN SAT ALONE on the deck of the *C.C. Princess* with his feet propped up and a can of cold beer in his hand. An open bag of pretzels rested on the built-in deck table next to him. A pelican flew in to roost on a nearby dock piling, causing a camouflaged gecko to scurry away. The clang, clang, clang of a buoy echoed in the distance as it bobbed up and down in the water.

Nathan drew his attention to the expanse of emerald green sea. The setting sun painted a cloudless blue sky with hues of amber, periwinkle, and rose. The combination of colors provided the perfect backdrop for the Koke Island Lighthouse on the west side of Chandler's Cove Harbor.

Inhaling the clean sea air, Nathan massaged his aching hip and sighed. He recalled all the times he'd spent with his Uncle Bill, fishing, sailing, and building ships in a bottle. He smiled at the memory.

His parents had discouraged that relationship. Probably because his uncle had been a wanderer. Nathan also had that spirit of adventure flowing through his veins. For years he'd dreamed of buying a boat and sailing the seven seas. Now his dream was a reality.

Taking a swig of beer, Nathan recalled the grisly incident that had prompted him to come to Chandler's Cove six months prior. The hazy memory of the shooting in the Outer Banks still haunted him. Had the killer seen his face in the foggy darkness?

Nathan had been careful to keep a low profile around town thus far. That is, until last night. He knew he should have stayed away from Roseann's party, but he yearned to be near their daughter. He had taken a risk, and Caroline had almost seen him on the beach. Next time, he'd have to be more careful.

Shoving his hand in the pretzel bag, Nathan pulled out a salty stick, popped it in his mouth, and chewed. A streak of orange darted across his peripheral vision. Scanning the dock, Nathan spotted two golden eyes glowing in the semi-darkness. An orange and white tabby cat sat in the shadows, eyes unblinking.

"Hey there, pretty kitty," Nathan said. The cat continued to stare. Taking another pretzel from the bag, Nathan held it out for the cat. "Are you hungry?"

The fat cat moseyed over to the edge of the boat and jumped aboard. With a swish of its tail, the cat approached Nathan's chair, sniffed the pretzel, and retrieved it from his grasp. Once finished, the friendly feline gave his server another long look.

"Do you want one more?" Nathan asked, reaching for the pretzel bag. The cat meowed, turned around, and jumped back onto the dock. "See you later," Nathan called as the feline disappeared into the shadows.

Nathan polished off the last of his beer and tossed the can into the trash. As he did this, Roy Armstrong approached his boat. Captain Roy was the owner of *Roy's Toy*, a sleek 75-foot glass-bottom touring boat, and the self-appointed go-to man on the docks. He provided local dolphin tours and oversaw the Chandler's Cove Harbor Coalition. The coalition kept a record of all docked boats and scheduled boat tours and fishing trips. Upon arriving in Chandler's Cove, Captain Roy had helped Nathan find a duplex to rent just two short blocks from the docks.

Captain Roy boarded the *C.C. Princess*. He was a comical sight in his blue-banded Panama hat, Hawaiian-print shirt, long Bermuda shorts, and worn boat shoes. What he lacked in appearance, he more than made up for in personality. "Ahoy there, Nate. How are yeh this muggy Sunday evening?"

"I can't get used to the humidity down here," Nathan groaned. He wiped his sweaty forehead with a handkerchief, then reached into his portable cooler and pulled out a bottled water. "Help yourself to a cold one."

Captain Roy sat down next to Nathan and grabbed a soda out of the cooler. "It's a typical hot summer in Chandler's Cove, ta be sure." He popped the top on the soda can. "Takes some gettin' used to, but I'm thankful for another fine day."

The sea captains casually chatted as nightfall descended upon the harbor. Antique-style streetlamps switched on, casting pools of soft light onto the adjacent boardwalk. The after-dinner tourists would soon make their way down to the docks to browse in the gift shops and admire the huge array of sleek sailboats, party boats, and fishing boats.

The men's conversation ceased as Captain Mac Nelson from the *Destiny* scuttled in their direction. Captain Mac's boat was docked three slips down from Nathan's. Roy and Nathan gave a cordial wave. Mac, cell phone to his ear, strode right by the *Princess* without acknowledging his colleagues.

Nathan frowned. "Roy, how well do you know Captain Mac?"

Roy stroked his snowy beard. "I recollect that he got ta Chandler's Cove 'bout the same time yeh did. Seems nice enough, but there's somethin' fishy 'bout that fella." He watched Captain Mac head in the direction of the boardwalk. "Do yeh know him?"

"No—we've never met, but I think I've seen him somewhere before."

Roy eyeballed Nathan. "In another life maybe?"

"Déjà vu, I suppose." Nathan grinned.

"They say we're all connected somehow."

"You're a walking encyclopedia, buddy. What other pearls of wisdom do you have to offer?"

"How much time do yeh have?"

The sound of more footsteps on the docks interrupted the jaunty exchange, and Nathan's gaze wandered to the evening tourists as they strolled down the boardwalk. The urge to travel again entered his thoughts.

A kindred spirit, Captain Roy recognized the far-off gleam in Nathan's crystal-blue eyes. He finished his soda, threw it in the trash, and leaned forward in his chair. "I know what you're thinkin', brother. The allure of travelin' ta magical places is like a magnet pullin' old salty dogs like us out ta sea." Roy swept his palms outward in the direction of the ocean.

Nathan placed his water bottle on the deck table. It seemed as if his trusted friend could read his mind. "For too many years, I settled for the status quo, but it never really satisfied me. I always longed for something more."

"I'll admit the prospect of a new adventure has captivated me many a time, but I can honestly say there ain't a more peaceful place than Chandler's Cove."

Nathan removed his Greek fisherman's cap and ran agile fingers through his graying hair. He marveled at his chum's simplistic view of life. "What brought you to Chandler's Cove, Roy?"

"The wind blew me here, brother," Roy said with a chuckle. "At my age, yeh want ta slow down an' smell the sea air. Take things easy. Know what I mean?"

Nathan nodded in reply. He knew exactly what Roy meant. Eager to hear more about his new home, Nathan asked, "Do you know much about the history of the town?"

Captain Roy took off his hat, set it on the table, and rubbed his balding head. "Accordin' ta local history, fishin' vessels first explored this area of the gulf coast in the early 1800's. Fishermen found a warm climate, ample fishin', an' protection from the pirates who hunted in the local waters. They set up fish camps an' eventually established a settlement. Many of the first settlers were ship's chandlers who supplied provisions an' equipment ta travelin' fishermen. So, they nicknamed the village Chandler's Cove. The name stuck an' was never changed."

Nathan fixed his eyes on the hypnotic beam of light emanating from the nearby lighthouse, imagining how many ships it had steered to safety, wondering what it would say if its walls could talk. "Must have been a simpler time back then."

Captain Roy nodded. "I reckon the first settlers were lookin' for what can't be found in the world." He clasped his fingers together and rested his hands on his round belly. "An' maybe that's what you're lookin' for too."

Nathan continued to focus on the lighthouse's blinking Fresnel lens. "Maybe," he replied.

"Some things can only be found when we look on the inside. Think 'bout that, brother."

Nathan thought he understood what Captain Roy meant, but embarking on that kind of journey would have to wait. He grabbed his bottled water off the table, gulped down the rest, and disposed of it. "Thanks for your advice and your friendship, Roy."

"No problem, Nate." Roy grabbed his hat and placed it back on his head. He stretched his arms and stood up. "Well, I best be headin' home."

Nathan eased himself out of his chair and escorted Roy to the dock. "Have a good one," he said. "I enjoyed the company."

Roy rested a hand on Nathan's shoulder. "We do what we can an' let the universe take care of the rest." He stepped off the boat and lumbered down the dock, his bowlegs carrying him in the direction of the boardwalk.

As Nathan folded up the deck chairs, he contemplated the mysteries of the universe. Placing both chairs in their storage compartment, he entered the cabin. As fate would have it, the universe jogged his memory. Scanning the salon, Nathan spotted the recent edition of *The Village Times-Herald*. He snatched it up and shoved it in his back pocket. This keepsake would go with the others he'd collected.

Nathan turned off the galley light and exited the *Princess*. As he walked down the docks to his truck, he noticed a light coming from the shaded window of the harbor coalition office. "That's odd—Roy said he was heading home." He shrugged. Maybe his friend had remembered some last-minute paperwork that needed his attention.

Leaving the docks of the East End Marina, Nathan sensed that the universe was trying to tell him something. Although, this enigma intrigued him, he was presently too tired to think about it. Yawning, he headed home, hoping to get a good night's sleep for a change. He wanted to be ready to tackle whatever the universe had in store for him.

In the pre-dawn hours of the following morning, a nondescript boat turned off its running lights and eased into a slip at the far side of the Koke Island Lighthouse. Three men quietly disembarked and walked up the ramp, making their way to a waiting van at the water's edge. The first man slid into the back of the van, while the second man opened the passenger side door and climbed in. The third man went around to the driver's side door and spoke with someone through the open window. After a few minutes, man number three headed back down the ramp. He crept onto the boat and motored away from the marina, disappearing into the darkness.

FIVE

Monday Morning, Callahan Manor

THE BEDSIDE ALARM catapulted Caroline from dreamland to reality. She swatted the snooze bar and stretched the circulation back into her tired muscles. Her tummy rumbled as the aroma of fresh-brewed coffee and breakfast tickled her nose. Tumbling out of bed, she slid on her slippers and trudged down the stairs, plopping into a high-back chair at the oak claw-foot kitchen table.

The airy kitchen, decorated with accents of honey yellow and cornflower blue, sparkled as beams of sunlight peeked through the open bay window. A gentle breeze drifted in, causing the lace curtains to rhythmically rise and fall. A symphony of birdsong floated in on the breeze; the sweet melodic sound gently cradled Caroline's ears.

Potholder in hand, Evan removed a hot dish from the oven. "Just in time for a piece of my world-famous breakfast quiche," he boasted, beaming like a luminary.

"Evan, you're my hero," Caroline said, stifling a yawn. Standing, she shuffled across the tan tile floor to the coffee pot. "Shall I pour?"

"Be my guest," he announced with a bow.

She chuckled. "I feel just like Belle at the castle."

Evan brought two plates of quiche and sliced strawberries to the table as she placed two mugs of steaming hot coffee at their seats. Giving thanks, they wasted no time digging in.

Still half asleep, Max made his way into the kitchen. "What smells so good?" he asked, rubbing his sleepy eyes. The girls, two exuberant Welsh Corgis, trailed follow-the-leader style right behind him. Terra, a tricolor, and Windy, a red and white, sniffed the air, wagging their tailless rears in excitement.

Caroline pointed to the stove. "Evan made a breakfast quiche this morning. Feed Terra and Windy, then get yourself something."

Max poured kibble into two dog dishes and placed them on the floor. The dogs made a beeline for their bowls and dug in. He, then, plopped a heaping helping of quiche on a plate and sat down at the table, remembering to give thanks.

Shortly thereafter, Jason entered the kitchen. He poured himself a cup of coffee, cut a piece of quiche, and joined the others.

Caroline yawned. "Mother's big birthday bash wore me out. Are you as tired as I am?"

"More," Jason grumbled. "The things I do for the two of you."

"And I love you for it," Caroline replied. "How about a kiss until you're better paid?"

"I'll take what I can get," he teased.

Caroline pushed her empty plate aside, leaned over, and planted a big kiss on Jason's lips.

"Gross! Get a room you two," Max nagged.

"Mind your own business and eat your quiche," Evan chimed in.

Tuning out the boys' banter, Caroline grabbed the Monday edition of the newspaper, *The Village Times-Herald,* sitting in the center of the table. On the front page, she saw an article written by her friend and the editor of the paper, Zoe Castillo. Caroline taught dance classes to Zoe's daughter, Isabella, at her dancing school Leap of Faith Dance Academy.

An accomplished journalist, Zoe's credentials included an undergrad degree in English and a master's degree in Journalism, both from the University of Miami. Her extensive field experience, coupled with her impressive resume, landed her the position of editor at the *Herald*. While chasing down the latest newsworthy stories, Zoe met her husband, Sergio, on a flight to Rio de Janeiro. He was a flight attendant at the time. Now retired from Trans South Airlines, Sergio owns and operates a thriving real estate business in Chandler's Cove.

Caroline began reading Zoe's article about the oil spill that had recently taken place off the coast of Louisiana. The massive oil rig explosion had caused millions of gallons of oil to pour into the Gulf of Mexico. The gushing wellhead had been capped, thus stopping the leak, but the damage from the spill still plagued the coastal region.

Forty-five miles away in Pensacola, weathered oil continued to collect on the coastline, affecting the beaches and wetlands, trapping fish, birds, and other sea creatures in the gooey mess. To make matters worse, summer vacationers were hesitant to come to the gulf, thereby causing the local economy to suffer. Overwhelmed by complaints from local fishermen and businesses bemoaning their plight, the town mayor, Don Barfield, had resorted to locking his office door and hiding from the angry mobs.

The chatter of lively conversation interrupted Caroline's reading. She looked at Jason.

Jason pushed his empty breakfast plate aside and wiped his mouth with a napkin. He slid a yellow legal pad with a detailed drawing of the front of Callahan Manor in front of his wife. "Here's the preliminary sketch of the modifications I've planned for our front entrance."

He pointed to the page. "As you see here, I want to put in a circular drive and line it with Bismarck palms. I'd also like to replace the square porch supports with round columns."

Laying the newspaper on the table, Caroline leaned over to get a closer look at Jason's ideas.

"I also want to widen the steps leading up to the front porch and replace the wood with stone."

Caroline picked up the legal pad and studied the sketch. "How about angling the handrails outward and broadening the steps at the base? That way everyone can make a grand entrance," she said with a grin.

"Beautiful and witty," he replied, catching the pun she threw him. "I think I'll keep you."

"You better," she said in a playful tone. "Now getting back to your plans, I think emerald green arborvitae on either side of the steps would look nice." Caroline took the pencil from his hand and drew in a few shrubs. "Maybe some dwarf bottlebrush here, and over there," she directed, making x marks on the page where she thought the red flowering shrubs should go. She gave the legal pad back to Jason and he began considering her ideas.

Evan hopped up and started clearing plates off the table. He looked over Jason's shoulder, eyeing the sketch. "I vote for a pool," he exclaimed.

"Do I get a vote?" questioned Max as he devoured his second piece of quiche.

"Certainly," Jason affirmed.

"Then I want a tennis court, so I can practice anytime."

"*Only* a pool and a tennis court?" Jason queried, thumping his pencil on the legal pad. "I guess I better get to work. Someone's got to pay for all these additions."

"That's the spirit," Caroline said with a wink.

As she watched Jason revise his sketches, she was reminded of the chain of events that brought the family to Chandler's Cove. After an on-the-job hand injury, Jason had taken an early retirement package. During a trip to visit Roseann, they began toying with the idea of relocating.

Following weeks of searching the Internet for a new house, Jason came upon a grand older home in a remote area minutes north of the town square. Reminiscent of an eighteenth-century coastal plantation home, the dwelling sported an enormous front entrance with white wooden steps leading up to a full covered wrap-around porch of the same color. Atop the burnished copper metal roof, two evenly spaced dormer windows sat ready to keep watch over the pristine landscape.

The house was advertised as a handyman's special. "All it needs is a little TLC," the ad read. Jason knew what that meant, but he was not deterred. So, when the boys were out of school for Spring Break, the family traveled back to Chandler's Cove to see for themselves.

The fixer-upper was in desperate need of repairs. The wooden board and batten siding was faded and worn, the old single pane windows were drafty, and the interior cosmetic upgrades were too numerous to count. On the plus side, the house came with a separate cottage, storage barn, eight wooded acres, and a small lake. Underneath all the hard work, Caroline and Jason envisioned a secluded vacation retreat. Taking a leap of faith, the family made the move to Chandler's Cove.

Equipped with a contractor's license, exceptional carpentry skills, and a truckload of power tools, Jason began the renovations. His first task had been to convert the 16x30 wooden storage barn into a workshop. He also replaced the old wooden siding with coral-colored maintenance-free vinyl and installed cost-efficient double pane windows. Year two, he installed new flooring downstairs and plush mocha-colored carpeting upstairs. Last winter, the renovation efforts included upgrades to the electrical wiring, along with new light fixtures and kitchen appliances.

More recently, Jason had enclosed part of the sunroom beyond the kitchen to use as an office. Both spaces now provided a relaxing view of a covered patio surrounded by a lovely flower garden. With good reason, Jason had nicknamed Callahan Manor the money pit, but Caroline, on the other hand, liked to refer to it as her diamond in the rough.

The clatter of plates and glasses roused Caroline from her daydream. She looked up to see Evan standing at the sink, washing the breakfast dishes. "Do you have anything planned for today?" she asked him.

He gave her a peripheral glance. "I thought I'd do some yard work, if that's okay?"

"You must be running low on funds," Caroline alleged with a smirk.

"Maybe, maybe not," he quipped.

"Far be it from me to look a gift horse in the mouth," she confessed. "I'll green-light that project."

"Great! I'll do it now before it gets too hot. I'm meeting Dave later to go to the comic book shop…" Evan's voice trailed off as he swept up the stairs, leaving the dirty dishes to fend for themselves.

Caroline addressed Max. "Put the girls in their play yard and give them some water. Don't forget, Nana's coming to take you to your tennis lesson, then to the pool afterwards." She checked the time. "She'll be here in thirty minutes."

Max gave an excited, "Oh, boy!" as he rushed the dogs out the door and into the backyard.

Jason sat back in his chair and rubbed a hand over his scruffy beard. "Do you think I need to shave this morning?"

"Looks good to me." Gray or no gray, Caroline thought Jason always looked good. "What's your plan for the day?" she asked.

Jason thumbed through his pocket calendar. "I'm going over to Barry Chapman's house. He's considering enclosing his garage and he wants an estimate."

Caroline cocked her head to one side. "Do I know him?"

"I don't think so. He moved to town about six months ago."

"Where does he live?" she asked.

"He has a 1,200 square foot bungalow on Orange Blossom Avenue, near the center of town."

"What does he do for a living?"

Jason raised an eyebrow. "What's with all the questions, darling? Could it be that you don't trust me?"

She shrugged. "Just curious, I guess."

Jason laughed. "To answer your last question, I believe he's in logistics management. All I know is that he travels a lot."

Caroline patted Jason's hand. "Just looking out for your safety, honey."

"And I appreciate that," Jason said, giving her hand a squeeze. "Enough about Barry Chapman. What are *you* doing today?"

"I thought about sitting around the house all day eating bonbons," she answered with a mischievous grin. "But I guess I'll go to the dance studio instead. I've got some cleaning to do, and I want to rearrange a few things before the open house this Saturday."

Caroline stood up, leaned over Jason's chair, and stole a quick kiss.

"What's your hurry?" He pulled her onto his lap and gave her a smoldering smooch.

"Yes—that's much better," she admitted, coming up for air.

Jason lifted Caroline out of the chair and steadied her feet on the floor. "I hate to kiss and run," he said, "but I need to go to Builder's Barn before I meet with Barry." He headed out the door, and she headed to the sink.

As Caroline washed the remaining breakfast dishes, she received a text from Zoe inviting her to partake in an early lunch and some desperately needed girl talk. They agreed to meet at The Well, a popular restaurant on the downtown square. The restaurant's name had been inspired by the biblical story of Jesus and the woman at the well. Jesus had come seeking a drink and had left having made a new friend.

Dishes done, Caroline dashed upstairs. An hour later, she dashed back downstairs, donned in a white Dotted Swiss blouse, chartreuse Capri pants, and practical, but dressy white slip-on sneakers. The house was quiet except for the muffled sounds of the lawnmower somewhere in the yard. She let the dogs in and placed them in their crates, grabbed her keys and butterfly print purse, and rushed out the door.

SIX

CAROLINE APPROACHED THE DOWNTOWN SQUARE, rounded the corner, and pulled into a parking space in front of Leap of Faith Dance Academy. She checked her watch, noting that she had five minutes to get to the restaurant. She applied a hint of mocha freeze lipstick and fluffed her hair into place with her fingers. Grabbing her purse, she exited her trusty SUV.

Locking her door, Caroline surveyed the multitude of dings and scratches that resembled honored battle scars. The fifteen-year-old vehicle had seen better days. For months now, Jason had been pestering her to buy a newer model. Truth be told, she had her eye on a tangerine pearl Crosstrek that sat on the sales lot of the Subaru dealership in Fort Watson. Faithful to her number one motto, however, she remained debt-free and happy.

Caroline joined the activity on the square and power-walked in the direction of the restaurant. The streets were busy with pedestrians, either taking care of business, doing a little shopping, or enjoying a bit of lunch. With the midmorning temperature on the rise, it appeared that Chandler's Cove was in for another scorcher of a day.

Caroline breezed past The Jiffy Java, noticing the Opening Soon sign in the window. Moving along, she glanced at the plethora of notions from the past in the shop front of Granny's Antiques. Next in line was the Best Ever Bakery. She inhaled the sweet smell of baked goods as she sprinted by, then halted at the corner in front of Cove Office Supplies.

As Caroline waited for the light to change, she shot a glance toward the center of the square. The recently renovated courthouse complex was teeming with activity. The bright morning sun bounced off the Old Courthouse's new gray stone and stucco façade. The broken antique clock, atop the rectangular clock tower, had been replaced with a new one that chimed on the hour. A flowing fountain, complete with a family of playful dolphins, graced the center of the front courtyard.

On a tree-shaded bench by the side entrance, Caroline spotted an older gentleman in a Greek fisherman's cap and dark sunglasses reading a newspaper. A student of human nature, she began observing the man. The interesting character appeared to be the only one on the square who wasn't in a hurry. *Is he a fisherman?*

As the light changed, Caroline crossed the street and continued walking in the direction of The Well. Her mind drifted to Saturday's open house and the mountain of preparations she still had to tackle. The harsh blast of a car horn broke her concentration. She spun in the direction of the noise. The courthouse bench was now empty, the older gentleman no longer in sight.

In the next instant, Caroline was bumped from behind by a determined woman carrying an armload of packages. Her purse slid off her shoulder and landed on the sidewalk. As she bent down to pick it up, she came face-to-face with the man in the Greek fisherman's cap. He scooped up the purse and offered it to her with a slight smile. Caroline attempted to thank the man, but he made a hasty retreat, vanishing as quickly as he had appeared.

Shaking her head, Caroline clipped past *The Village Times-Herald*, the bookstore, and the florist, finally arriving at The Well. She entered the restaurant and scanned the room. Colorful travel posters peppered the sepia-toned walls, the idyllic locales sparking the urge to travel to exotic lands.

Spotting her best friend sitting at a table for two, Caroline walked in her direction. Zoe looked up and waved. Dressed in a smart lace-yoke sheath dress with matching Christian Dior open-toe high heels, her classy friend looked like she'd just stepped off a fashion runway. The stylish beige ensemble complemented her olive skin tone and highlighted deep brown hair. Zoe's cherished possession, her grandmother's sterling and turquoise eagle *notch-kah*, hung around her neck.

"That was odd," Caroline said, joining Zoe at the table.

"What's odd?" Zoe asked.

"I'm not sure," Caroline replied, somewhat perplexed. She told Zoe about the man in the Greek fisherman's cap. "Something about him felt familiar." She took a quick breath and continued. "Of course, it could just be my imagination."

"Could be something, could be nothing," Zoe said. She picked up two menus and handed Caroline one. They began reading the lunch specials.

"That makes me feel *so* much better," Caroline said with a chuckle. "On the other hand," she added, wagging an index finger at Zoe, "I *have* had an uneasy feeling in my gut lately." She told her friend about the shadowy figure on the beach at Roseann's party.

Zoe placed her menu on the table and looked at Caroline. "My maternal grandmother was one-half Seminole Indian, and she used to have those same 'gut' feelings. *Wykas-chay*—be still—she would always say." Smiling, Zoe fingered her silver necklace. "I remember Grandane wanted to name me Echo—Seminole for fawn—but my *very* Greek paternal grandmother insisted on naming me Zoe. The rest, as they say, is history."

Caroline set her menu aside. "Both names are beautiful," she affirmed. "Who knows? Maybe Echo can be your *nom de plume* when you become a famous author."

Zoe huffed. "Maybe when I'm old and haven't lost all my brain cells to this crazy newspaper." Her brown eyes rested on her friend. "But seriously, go with your gut, Caroline. It won't fail you."

"You know me so well," Caroline laughed, hoping to lighten the mood. She was glad that Zoe understood her 'gut' feelings, but she hoped she didn't sound too mental.

Zoe gave Caroline's hand a squeeze. "Just be careful," she advised, her reporter senses compelling her to err on the side of caution. "And let me know if you see him again, okay?"

Caroline didn't want to worry her. "I promise—scout's honor," she said, holding up three fingers.

A waitress appeared at the table, and they ordered the daily special, the grilled chicken wrap with a side of fresh fruit and sweet tea to drink. Moments later, the waitress returned with their drinks, then quickly disappeared.

As they waited for their lunch, Caroline told Zoe how much she appreciated the lovely birthday announcement she'd placed in the paper for Roseann. Zoe had extolled Roseann's virtues, bragged about her accomplishments within the community, and had mentioned Caroline's business in the article, as well.

A few minutes later, the waitress brought their lunch, and the two hungrily dug in. Between bites, the friends filled each other in on the latest happenings in their busy lives.

After they'd finished lunch, Zoe pulled a notepad from her purse. "Remember when you told me how you regret not pursuing your graduate degree in counseling?"

Giving a nod of affirmation, Caroline took two Dove Dark Chocolate Promises from her purse. She handed one to Zoe and popped the other in her mouth, savoring the candy's bittersweet goodness.

Zoe slid the notepad in front of Caroline. "I got a story from Coastal University this morning. I think you might find it interesting."

Picking up the notepad, Caroline began reading Zoe's notes. As she gleaned the information, she was reminded of her original career plans. She had been researching grad schools when she'd first met Jason. While working as a patient advocate at a South Atlanta hospital, daredevil Jason's curvy road had crossed her straight path. He was bruised and contused from head to toe following a motorcycle accident. Caroline liked to say that their first date took place at the hospital ER.

After six whirlwind months of dating, Caroline and Jason entered the mysterious world of matrimony and began a family shortly thereafter. Caroline quit her full-time social work job and began teaching dance part-time. Thus, her life took a turn in a totally different direction. That's not to say that she didn't cherish that direction. On the contrary, she'd never regretted her decision to stay home and raise her children. For Caroline, family always came first.

As she pondered that thought, a vision of Caroline's smart and talented niece and nephew appeared in her mind's eye. Their autism diagnosis at the age of two had spawned a desire in her to develop a therapeutic movement program for special needs youth. She'd often wondered what life would be like if she'd pursued her dream to become a counselor.

Zoe interrupted Caroline's thoughts. "The newspaper is going to run a full-page ad announcing the college's new hybrid master's degree programs," she informed her. "The ad states that on-campus classes will be held one night a week. All other coursework can be completed online. What do you think about that?" She drummed her long, sculptured nails on the table waiting for Caroline to respond.

Caroline set the notepad down on the table and began tapping her index finger on her bottom lip. "Twenty years is a long time to be away from the world of academia," she mused, "but it does sound intriguing. I'm not sure that I could handle the college environment after all this time."

Zoe stilled her fingers, allowing Caroline time to think.

Caroline frowned as she contemplated the added responsibility of going back to school. "I'd have to get a new laptop. And, when would I find the time to study? Between family, dance classes, and church, my days are packed." She looked at Zoe, seeing that she had taken the wind out of her friend's sails.

"That's true," Zoe admitted. Her thick, wavy hair caressed her shoulders as she shrugged them in response. "It's a lot to think about." Intelligent eyes displayed a sense of introspection as she considered Caroline's dilemma. "But in the words of William Faulkner, 'You cannot swim for new horizons until you have courage to lose sight of the shore.'"

Caroline took a moment and offered up a silent thank-you for her dear friend. "You're right," she confessed. "I need to stop dwelling on the negatives. Nothing productive will come from it."

Zoe picked up her notepad and turned the page. "Let's make a pros and cons list."

Since the cons had already been mentioned, they took a few minutes to write a list of pros. Caroline could pursue her goal of getting a master's degree. She could become licensed and receive her credentials. With that, she could better serve the special needs community. Not only would she be able to help others, but she would also be helping herself in the process. It sounded like a win-win situation to Caroline. But what would her family think about this major life change?

Returning to the real world, they paid the lunch bill and stepped outside into the bright sunshine. Zoe's purse buzzed. She pulled out her cell phone and checked the text message.

"Sorry to eat and run, but duty calls," she said, slipping her phone back into her purse. "Sergio was supposed to pick up Isabella from her girlfriend's house this afternoon, but he has to show a house in Fort Watson." She glanced at her watch and sighed. "I need to leave in thirty to go get her. That means I'll have to work late again tonight."

The twosome strutted back in the direction of the *Herald*. In her three-inch heels and long legs that looked good in a skirt, Zoe stood head and shoulders above her friend. Caroline felt dwarfed by comparison. *Maybe I should get me a pair of those three-inch bad boys,* she thought, then visualized herself tumbling out of her shoes and twisting an ankle. Not a good thing for a dance teacher to do at her age. She immediately nixed the silly notion.

They reached Zoe's destination, and Caroline waved good-bye as her friend hastened through the door of the newspaper. Continuing her walk to the dance studio, Caroline reflected on the blessing of friendships. With a spring in her step, she entered Leap of Faith and plopped down in her cushy desk chair. Grabbing a notepad, she began a to-do list of activities she needed to accomplish before Saturday. Across the middle of the page, she wrote in big, bold letters CLEAN EVERYTHING.

Oh, boy! She had her work cut out for her.

SEVEN

Friday Afternoon, Leap of Faith

"T.G.I.F.," Caroline sighed as she plopped down in her office chair. With the help of family and friends, Leap of Faith was finally ready for tomorrow's open house. What began as a few simple tasks had morphed into a major overhaul. She could only surmise that her mother's recent redecorating efforts had motivated her into action.

Breathing in the clean smell of fresh paint, Caroline mentally reviewed the fruits of her family's week-long labor. Jason had buffed the hardwood floors and re-taped the performance vinyl in the ballet room. Evan, Max, and Roseann's community outreach group had painted the interior a nice shade of pink. Posters of dancers leaping, turning, and performing barre exercises hung on the rosy-hued walls.

Tan resin chairs with burgundy cushions now circled the perimeter of the front sitting room. A wooden plaque inscribed with Psalm 149:3 hung by the front door displaying the school's mission statement. It read, "Let them praise His name with dancing."

As she sat, Caroline surveyed her clutter-free office. Photos of her great-grandparents and a 1927 Vaudeville booking agreement sat on the shelf over her desk. In the first photo, her grandfather's parents, Nora and Charles, smiled down at her. The couple had toured the country on the Vaudeville circuit with their unique song and dance act. It was unique because Charles performed with a wooden leg. The second frame held a photo of her grandmother's parents, Emma and Cornelius. They hadn't been professionally trained, but they still loved to kick up their heels at local social events. Caroline guessed the gift of dance hadn't fallen far from the generational tree.

Hearing the familiar tinkle of her door chime, Caroline peered through the office wall opening and saw Roseann and Aunt Flo walking through the front door, flashing bright smiles. From their appearance, one would never guess that they are from the same gene pool. Two years Roseann's junior, Flo is tall, with a buxom build, and likes to wear comfortable clothing and sensible shoes. Roseann, on the other hand, has a short, petite frame and wouldn't dare leave the house without her chic color-coordinated outfits and accessories. Regardless of their outward appearance, the two sisters have always shared similar dreams and ambitions.

"Hey, y'all," Caroline greeted as she walked from her office into the sitting room. She gave each a big hug. "Have you come to feast your eyes on the new décor?"

"The place looks great!" Roseann acknowledged with glee. Aunt Flo's head bobbed up and down in agreement. "Is everything ready for the open house tomorrow?" Roseann asked.

"Just about," Caroline replied. "I haven't finished decorating yet. I'd appreciate your expert advice Aunt Flo, if you have the time."

"Sure thing, sweetie," Flo said, beaming. "Sis and I can help with that. Just lead the way."

Caroline motioned for Roseann and Flo to follow her. They stepped out of the sitting room, headed down the narrow hallway, and stopped at the second door on the right. Caroline turned on the light, and they entered the large dance room. Round tables and folding chairs were arranged in the center of the room. Two rectangular tables were positioned near the mirrored wall. "I'm going to have the reception in here," she told them.

Flo scanned the room, then began making mental notes. "We'll decorate the tables with white tablecloths and pink floral center-pieces." She looked at Roseann. "How about draping some decorations on the mirrors?"

Roseann nodded. "Party Town has some cute ballerina party accessories."

"We can get some matching plates, cups, and napkins for the refreshment table," Flo added.

Caroline walked toward the mirrored walls. "We should keep the barres on the back wall free, in case the dancers want to stretch out or work on technique."

"What about the refreshments?" Flo asked.

"I was going to pick up some cupcakes, chips, and dips from the store on my way home today," Caroline said.

Flo poo-pooed the idea. "We'll take care of the food, too."

Caroline frowned. "Are y'all sure you want to do all of that work?"

"Of course, dear," Roseann cooed. "Now don't think another thing about it. Flonnie and I will handle the details. You'll have a lovely open house tomorrow."

Caroline gave Roseann and Flo big hugs. "You two are the greatest."

"What about the advertising?" Roseann reminded.

"Zoe will be here tomorrow. She's going to cover the event for the *Herald*."

The wind chime jingled again. Caroline headed to the front, while Roseann and Flo continued making plans. She found Jason and Max standing in the sitting room.

"We're here to take you out to dinner," Jason informed. "Evan is meeting us at Ryan's Irish Pub."

"You're not cooking tonight, Mom," Max chimed in.

"That's music to my ears *and* my feet," Caroline joked, dancing a little jig.

"Mom—don't embarrass yourself," Max deadpanned, scrunching up his face for dramatic effect.

"Done and done," she agreed, ruffling Max's hair. "Let's get out of here, ladies," Caroline shouted down the hall.

Roseann and Flo sauntered back to the sitting room. Caroline turned off the lights, and everyone exited the dancing school.

"Don't forget to be at the studio by noon tomorrow," Caroline reiterated as she walked the sisters to Flo's car.

"Will do," Aunt Flo promised as she and Roseann slid into Flo's white and woodgrain Buick Roadmaster wagon.

Flo pulled away from the curb as Roseann blew kisses out the window. Caroline waved good-bye until the car was out of sight. She linked arms with Jason and Max and they walked across the square to the Irish pub.

EIGHT

Monday Morning, Callahan Manor

AFTER A SUCCESSFUL OPEN house at the dance studio on Saturday and a super-charged Sunday worship service at the Seaside Community Church, Monday morning dawned bright and sunny. Outside her bedroom window, a chorus of blue jays, northern cardinals, and a tufted titmouse or two, roused Caroline from a restless slumber. Glancing at the bedside clock, she realized that she'd overslept. Rolling over, she stretched her tired muscles.

Max popped into the room. "Oh good, you're finally up," he broadcasted, jumping onto the bed.

"And good morning to you, too," Caroline replied, rubbing the sleep from her eyes.

Max grabbed Jason's pillow and began tossing it in the air. "I found a new boat set for my LEGO City collection. How much money have I earned?"

"Your allowance is marked on the calendar downstairs," Caroline reminded him as she caught the pillow and placed it back on

Jason's side of the bed. "Don't forget that five dollars goes to the children's mission in Guatemala."

Caroline inched out of bed and plodded to the bathroom to brush her teeth. Minutes later, she returned to find Max sitting in the middle of the bed with a perplexed expression on his face.

"I *want* to help the mission, Mom, but what if I don't have enough money to buy my LEGO set?" The little guy appeared torn between two decisions.

Caroline sat down next to Max. "It might help to remember what the Bible says about reaping and sowing. If you sow a blessing into someone else's life, you'll reap a blessing in return."

"Which one comes first, reaping or sowing?" Max asked, clearly confused.

"Well—let's say you plant a pumpkin seed. That's sowing. After some time, you grow a pumpkin. That's reaping. In other words, by sowing a blessing, you set the blessing in motion. First you sow, then you reap. Does that make more sense?"

Max scratched his head. "I think so, but I'm gonna pray about it." A strategic plan in hand, Max bolted off the bed. "Thanks, Mom," he hollered as he whooshed out the door.

"Love you," Caroline called after him.

Knowing that she'd be stiff without her morning stretch, Caroline slid off the king-sized bed and began a series of stretches, then headed to the bathroom to freshen up. As she showered, her mind drifted to her fall dance schedule. Saturday's open house had surpassed her expectations. The student roster now topped 125 students. Since she was currently the only dance instructor on the payroll, this might prove to be a problem.

Thirty minutes later, fresh, but frustrated, Caroline descended the stairs and headed straight for the caffeine. She poured a mug of coffee, added a splash of creamer, and took a sip of the steaming liquid. A batch of butterscotch biscones sat next to the coffee pot. She stuck her nose over the plate and breathed in the gooey goodness. The aroma brought back cherished memories of baking butterscotch cookies with Granny Fi in her cheery kitchen. Oh, how she loved sleeping in her grandmother's big feather bed and resting in her comforting arms during times of turmoil. Granny Fi had been her refuge back then, her port in the storm.

Pushing the bittersweet memories aside, Caroline grabbed a biscone and dragged herself to the sunroom to enjoy the gorgeous Florida morning. Two white wicker armchairs with floral print cushions occupied the center of the room. A matching loveseat sat across from the chairs, and a glass-topped wicker coffee table rested in between. The perimeter of the sunroom sported a bountiful assortment of indoor greenery and house plants, creating the illusion of a jungle.

Jason lounged in one of the chairs reading the *Herald*. A neglected biscone and a half-empty mug of coffee sat on the table in front of him. Caroline placed her plate and mug next to his and took a seat in the other chair. "Why did you let me sleep so late?" she sighed.

Jason looked up from the paper. "You tossed and turned all night. Plus, you were sleepwalking again. I thought you needed the rest."

Caroline furrowed her brow. "What did I do this time?"

"You were sitting in the dark, reading from your dance notebook, and mumbling something about having too many students. I tried to take the notebook from you, but you told me to mind my own business." His bare foot reached over to play with hers.

Caroline rubbed her foot on top of his. "Don't take it personally. I guess my subconscious is trying to tell me something."

"That you don't like your husband very much?"

She sent him an air kiss. "More like, I need to do something about my abundant student enrollment."

"It'll work itself out. Have a little faith."

"It's just that classes start soon, and you know I'm not a very patient person."

Jason slid his sensuous hazel eyes in her direction. "That I do, darling, but I still love you."

"Good to know," Caroline replied, picking up her biscone. "I see that Evan's been rummaging through my recipe box again." She took a bite of the semisweet biscuit. "Um…this is good."

"Not bad," Jason commented. "I'm not a fan of scones, but I *do* like biscuits." He patted his belly.

Caroline swallowed her bite and took a sip of coffee. "Where is Evan anyway?"

"He and Dave are meeting the gang at the beach for the day." Jason returned his attention to the newspaper.

"Any *good* news in the paper this morning?"

"As a matter of fact, I was just reading an advertisement for Coastal University. Did you know that they're offering online graduate degree programs for adult learners?" Jason turned the paper around, so that Caroline could read the advertisement. The ad read: "Ride the Wave to a New Career at Coastal University."

"Zoe told me about that the other day," Caroline stated. "She seems to think that I should enroll."

Jason quirked an eyebrow. "That might not be a bad idea. You've always wanted to get your master's degree. Maybe you should think about it."

As Jason resumed reading and eating, Caroline peered out the sunroom window into the backyard. In the garden, the sun bounced off the lavender hibiscus, yellow lantana, and red blanket flowers, producing a rainbow of color. Several gulf fritillary butterflies flitting from flower to flower. Their bright orange color glowed in the sunshine. Amid the flowers, two bird feeders hung from a bronze Shepherd's hook. A pair of indigo buntings took turns gathering seeds from one feeder, while a ruby-throated hummingbird played hide-and-seek at the other. A brilliant red summer tanager splashed in the birdbath at the center of the garden.

Caroline caught sight of the Corgis attempting to catch a dragonfly. The tiny winged creature, just out of reach, randomly swooped down as if to attack. As she watched the pair frolicking in the yard, she began thinking about what Jason had said and what she and Zoe had discussed the previous week. Was God speaking to her through her husband and her best friend?

After several minutes, Jason rose from his chair and stood behind Caroline. He began massaging her shoulders. "What are you pondering?"

Caroline rolled her head from side to side, absorbing the full effect of the massage. "It *might* be doable."

Her husband's skillful fingers worked their way up her neck. "You mean returning to college?"

"Uh-huh," she uttered, making a mental pros and cons list. "I'd only have class one night a week, but I'd have to get a new laptop—and you know I'm electronically challenged." Caroline tilted her head back and looked up at Jason to gauge his reaction.

"No worries," he assured her. "It's definitely doable."

Caroline grimaced. "How much do you think all this will cost?"

Jason kissed the top of her head. "We'll manage. And besides, I have faith in you."

"From your mouth to God's ears," she avowed, "but do you think that I could ride that wave without wiping out?"

Jason gave Caroline's shoulders a squeeze. "You'll never know if you don't try."

Going back to college after all these years might be difficult, but she had to admit the idea intrigued her. Changing the subject, Caroline asked, "Are you leaving soon?"

Jason sat back down and slipped on his steel-toed boots. "Yes, I'm off to Builder's Barn for supplies, then to Barry Chapman's to work on his garage enclosure. I'll be there most of the day."

"How's the project coming along?"

Jason grunted. "My work is on schedule, but Barry is not. Time management isn't one of his strengths." He drained his mug and set it on top of his empty plate. "He's been late to every one of our meetings."

"Where do you think he's spending all of his time?"

"Apparently, he's been spending a lot of time at the docks. Something about buying a fishing boat, I think. He's rather vague on the subject." Jason stood up, dishes in hand. "As long as I'm paid on time, I don't care what he does."

Caroline stretched out her arms and began circle rotations with her hands. "A paycheck in the hand is worth two in the bush, I always say."

Jason smiled. "If we had as many paychecks as we do birds, we'd be millionaires."

Caroline winked at her handsome hubby. "Speak it into existence, honey."

Jason shot his eyes heavenward, then back to his wife. "In the meantime, why don't you pull up the Coastal University website and get some more info on their master's degree programs?" He strode to the kitchen with his dishes.

"I guess it couldn't hurt to inquire," she mused, taking another bite of her biscone.

Hearing the side door shut, Caroline turned her attention back to the colorful butterflies playing chase in the garden, their graceful dance reminding her of their transformation from caterpillar to new creation. *Therefore, if anyone is in Christ, he is a new creation; the old has gone, the new has come!* She considered the implication of God's uplifting words. Like the butterfly emerging from its cocoon, she, too, began a new life the day she had accepted Jesus Christ as her Lord and Savior.

The sound of heavy footfalls on the stairs interrupted Caroline's thoughts. Max bounced into the room and plopped down beside her. Summer vacation was almost over for the two of them. In a couple of weeks, he'd be back in school and she'd be back at work. "What shall we do today?" she asked him.

Max's face brightened. "Can we go swimming at Nana's?"

"That sounds like a plan."

Max sprinted to the phone and called Roseann. Getting the go-ahead, he rushed upstairs to change into his swimsuit. Caroline followed him up and slipped on the new floral print baby doll swimsuit she'd recently purchased from her favorite shop, The Sporty Lady. Gathering the sunscreen and beach towels, she placed them in her beach bag and began tidying up the bedroom.

Ten minutes later, Max bounded back into her bedroom carrying a canvas tote full of pool toys. The two headed downstairs, and Caroline secured Terra and Windy in their crates.

Entering Jason's office, Caroline strode to his desk to turn off the light. Her outdated laptop sat by the antique brass lamp taunting her. On an impulse, she grabbed it up and stuffed it in her beach bag. Jumping into the Subaru, she and Max headed to Roseann's for a carefree afternoon of fun in the sun.

NINE

AFTER A QUICK STOP at the Grab-N-Go for bottled water and healthy snacks, Caroline and Max arrived at Sandpiper Shore. They drove to the rear of the complex and parked the SUV in front of Roseann's four-unit building. Situated on the east end of Chandler's Cove Harbor, Sandpiper Shore offered guests and residents private beach access, a yacht club and marina, five pools, lighted tennis courts, and a 9-hole par 3 golf course. Roseann's condo sat near the yacht club and overlooked the East End Marina.

"Knock-knock," Caroline announced as she and Max entered the front door.

"I'm out on the deck, dears," Roseann answered.

Caroline entered the kitchen and put the water and snacks in the fridge, then she and Max joined Roseann on her covered deck. Her mother had decorated the deck with two wicker chairs and a matching round wicker table. Seafoam green accent cushions enhanced the aesthetic and comfort value of the chairs. A ceiling fan with round woven blades rotated overhead, providing a gentle breeze.

Max ambushed his Nana with hugs and kisses, then began unloading his swim gear from his canvas tote.

"Slow down, partner," Caroline ordered. "You have to put on sunscreen first."

"Darn! I hate that gunky stuff," Max complained.

"It's better than a sunburn, isn't it?" she asked.

"Yeah—I hate sunburns worse than I hate gunky sunscreen."

Giving Roseann a hug, Caroline retrieved the sunscreen and her laptop from her beach bag and placed them on the table. Max grabbed the sunscreen off the table and began smearing on the creamy protection.

Caroline sat down next to Roseann and surveyed the surrounding landscape. Majestic Palms swayed in the breeze as patrons lunched on the yacht club's waterside patio. The Koke Island Lighthouse stood sentinel on the far side of the harbor. Shifting her focus to the pool, she spotted Roseann's summer neighbors. "Look, Max. Your friend, Zack, is swimming today."

Max yelled, "Hey Zack," and gave a big wave.

Zack saw Max and waved back. Zack's mother, Sheila, looked up and waved. She rose from her lounge chair and sashayed to the deck. Caroline noticed that she filled out her teeny bikini quite nicely.

"Hi ladies," Sheila greeted. "Caroline, I can watch Max if you want to chat with your mother for a while."

"That would be great, Sheila. I didn't want to get much sun today anyway." Caroline took the bottle of sunscreen from Max and spread some on his back. "Max, you go swim with Zack. Nana and I will watch from over here."

"I'll be out to swim with you shortly," Roseann promised.

Max grabbed his beach towel, pool toys, and goggles. "Awesome," he shouted as he skipped down the steps. "I'll see you in a little while, Nana."

"See you later, alligator," Roseann threw back.

"Thanks, Sheila," Caroline said, placing the bottle of sunscreen next to her laptop. "I promise to watch the boys next time."

Sheila smiled. "No problem. What are neighbors for?"

Sheila Downing and her husband, Rick, lived in Birmingham and owned Unit 1013 next door. The family spent a month at the beach every summer. As Sheila walked back to the pool, her blonde hair and tanned skin glistened in the sunlight.

Roseann picked up the bottle of sunscreen and began slathering lotion on her arms. "Your brother called yesterday," she said. "He wanted to wish me a happy birthday and to say that the family is hoping to come for a visit this fall."

"That's nice, Mother. I hope Patrick will be able to get away. How are Tala and the twins?"

Roseann's pretty face darkened. "About the same, unfortunately. Mean girls and bullies at school who don't understand the twins' unique learning differences."

Caroline blew out a sigh. "I wish Patrick would reconsider taking that job transfer to Tallahassee. We'd be able to see the twins more often. They're growing up so fast."

"Yes…" Roseann got that far-off look in her eyes. She finished applying her sunscreen and set the bottle back onto the table. "What's the laptop for, dear?" she asked.

Caroline propped her feet up on the porch railing. "Zoe and Jason have ganged up on me," she groused.

Roseann frowned in puzzlement. "How so?"

"Before I catch you up on the latest news, let me get us something to drink. What would you like?"

"A bottle of spring water would be nice," Roseann said, shifting her gaze toward the pool.

Caroline stood up as Roseann's landline began ringing. "I'll get it." She stepped back into the condo and picked up the wireless handset. "Roseann's residence," she answered. "Yes, it's nice to speak to you, too…The whole family is looking forward to the seafood festival...Yes, Mother will definitely be there...Hold one moment and I'll check."

Caroline muted the phone. "Mother, Mayor Barfield wants to talk to you." She handed the phone to Roseann. "It's on mute."

Roseann wiped her hands on her beach towel and grimaced. "What does that old windbag want?"

Caroline shrugged. "I'm not quite sure."

Roseann cleared her throat and un-muted the phone. "Hello, Don. How are you today? So nice of you to call." The sweet sounds of Southern gentility gushed from Roseann's pouty lips.

Caroline rolled her eyes and headed to the kitchen, nearly bumping into Aunt Flo as she strutted out of the guest bedroom dressed to the nines. "You're all dolled up today," she commented. "Are you going someplace special?"

"I've got a date," Flo boasted. She twirled around to show off her new floral print dress and red pumps. "How do you like my manicure?" She held out both hands to show Caroline her cherry red nails.

"It's beautiful and so are you." Caroline was surprised to see her aunt so dressed up. To be sure, Roseann had prompted such a glorious transformation. "Who's the lucky guy?" she inquired.

"Walt Gaston, the security guard," Flo crooned, her brown eyes twinkling like stars.

Caroline smiled from ear to ear. "I know Walt. He's a great guy. I hope the two of you have a wonderful time."

Flo walked over to the wall mirror to check her appearance. Her coppery tresses were twisted into a bun at the nape of her neck. Soft ringlet curls framed her round face, and a red silk flower balanced on top of her bun.

Roseann strolled into the den and hung up the phone. "Don't you look as pretty as a picture, Flonnie," she purred, placing her seal of approval on her sister's ensemble. She popped into the bathroom and came back with a small tube in her hand. "Here—use some of my passion pink lip intensifier. It will make your lips pop."

As Flo applied the shimmery pink lipstick, the doorbell rang. "That's Walt," she sputtered. She was as giddy as a school girl going to her first prom.

"Don't worry. You'll have a great time," Roseann encouraged. "Just be yourself and don't be nervous."

Flo took in a deep breath and blew out the tension that engulfed her. "You're right," she said, taking one final look at herself in the mirror.

Caroline zipped to the door and returned with Walt. When he saw Flo all dressed up, his eyes grew as big as saucers. "Aren't you a sight for sore eyes," he declared.

"Most definitely," Caroline concurred.

Flo's cheeks turned the color of her lips. She and Walt stood gazing at each other. Hoping to break the ice, Roseann asked, "Where are you two headed this afternoon?"

"To the senior center in Fort Watson," Flo replied, steadying her voice. "A special agent from the FBI is coming to speak about protecting our financial assets from scam artists."

"That sounds beneficial," Caroline stated.

"Now you two go and have a wonderful day," Roseann instructed, nudging them to the door.

"We definitely will," Walt boomed. He held out his hand. "Are you ready to go, Florence?" Flo placed her hand in Walt's, and the two walked to the door.

"I'll be back to cook dinner, Sis," Flo called over her shoulder as the couple made their exit.

Caroline guessed that Aunt Flo and Walt hadn't dated much since losing their spouses, and she hoped that they'd have a good time.

Roseann heaved a heavy sigh, breaking the silence. "I love my sister and I think the world of Walt. I just hope that this date doesn't turn out to be a disaster for either of them."

"O, ye of little faith," Caroline teased. "Those two deserve some happiness after losing their spouses." She immediately recognized her verbal faux pas. "I'm sorry, Mother. I know it's hard on you, too."

"Yes dear," Roseann conceded. "It does get lonely at times."

Caroline gave Roseann a one-armed hug. "I'll get those bottles of water and meet you on the deck." Stopping in the kitchen, she grabbed the water and headed back outside. "By the way, what did Mayor Barfield want?" she asked, handing Roseann a bottle.

"He wants me to have dinner with him before the fireworks show at the Seafood Festival Saturday night. I told him that I already have plans." Roseann took a sip of water. "That man is a hound dog! He won't leave me alone."

Caroline eased into the cushiony chair and opened her bottled water. "How many times has he asked you out?"

She huffed. "Too many, as far as I'm concerned."

"He's nothing if not persistent," Caroline admitted. "When are you going to ease his suffering and go out with him?"

Roseann's cheeks flushed. "When Hell freezes over."

"That's sounds definite," Caroline said, studying her mother's face.

"Let's not talk about it." Roseann looked back toward the pool. "Let's just enjoy the day."

"Whatever you say, Mother." Caroline sipped her water and pondered Roseann's sudden shift in demeanor. Something was up, but she couldn't put her finger on it.

The two continued to chat as they watched Max play in the pool. Caroline decided to share the visions of grad school that had been dancing in Jason and Zoe's heads.

"I know that you talked of getting your master's degree in counseling before you met Jason." Roseann's voice resonated concern, not criticism. "But after all these years, I thought you'd given up on that dream."

"I thought so too, but the opportunity has presented itself and I feel compelled to, at least, check into it." Caroline opened her laptop. "I thought I'd browse the Coastal University website to see what options are available."

"My fitness instructor says that you can't turn back the clock, but you can wind it up again." Roseann patted Caroline's hand. "I believe the sentiment applies here as well."

Caroline began singing one of her favorite songs about turning back time.

Roseann leaned over and kissed her daughter's cheek. "You go on singing, dear, and I'll go swim with Max." She slipped on her sandals and grabbed her towel and bottle of water. "I'm off to brave the waves," she joked as she made her way poolside.

Roseann entered the pool gate and removed her tan cover-up, revealing a cute one-piece leopard print swimsuit that accentuated her petite, curvy figure. With her compact, muscular frame, Caroline often wondered if she had inherited her biological father's bone structure. When she tried to talk to Roseann about him, her mother avoided the topic like the plague. It frustrated Caroline to have more questions than answers, but Roseann remained tight-lipped.

Returning to the task at hand, Caroline pulled up Coastal University's home page and began half-heartedly surfing the site. As she browsed, she pondered the hidden anger and resentment she'd harbored for the man who had abandoned her all those years ago. From time to time, she considered letting go of the unhealthy emotions, but her stony heart remained steadfast in its convictions.

Unable to concentrate, Caroline shut the laptop and sighed. Did she seriously think that she could become a counselor? She couldn't even face her own demons!

TEN

Tuesday Morning, Nathan's Duplex

NATHAN SAT at the bar that separated his kitchen from his den, downing his morning coffee and pondering his perpetual state of aloneness. As a child, the only time he hadn't felt alone was when he was with his uncle. Staring off into space, he daydreamed about the day he could be happy again. What would that day look like? Nothing other than reuniting with Caroline would give him the elusive happiness he yearned for.

Nathan's eyes wandered into the den. An ornate wooden shelving unit spanned the far wall. Hand carved lighthouses and ships of all sizes lined the shelves. The final project he and his uncle had built together, his cherished ship in a bottle, sat front and center. Nathan recalled the time with mixed emotions. A few short months after that day, he lost the most important person in his life to cancer.

After his uncle's death, Nathan turned to woodworking as a way of coping with his loneliness. For some unknown reason, he felt more grounded when he could take a piece of raw wood and carve out a new creation.

Tabling his thoughts, Nathan slid off his barstool and carried his mug and plate to the sink. As he washed the breakfast dishes, he peered out the window, checking the weather. Dark clouds threatened to rain at any moment. Not wanting to waste a trip to the docks, Nathan decided to take his truck in for an oil change and maintenance check-up instead.

Placing the last dish in the rack, he threw the dish towel over the drying dishes and walked to the door. He donned his Greek fisherman's cap, grabbed his keys, and exited the duplex. Jumping into the F-150, he started the engine, turned the air conditioning on high, and eased down the short drive.

Ten minutes later, Nathan arrived at One-Stop Auto Repair. He handed his keys to the service manager and was told to come back in a couple of hours. Stepping outside, he put on his sunglasses and surveyed his surroundings.

Noticing the Chandler's Cove Library next door, he decided to go in and peruse the local authors section. Once inside, he began browsing the library's bookshelves, discovering two books on Chandler's Cove maritime history. He got a library card, checked out the books and exited the library, spotting The Well across the street.

Nathan made his way to the restaurant as the first drops of rain began to fall. He briefly hesitated, remembering that Caroline and her friend often met there for lunch. Had his daughter recognized him the other day? It didn't seem so, but maybe he should play it safe and go somewhere else. As he considered his options, gusty wind began to blow heavy rain in all directions. Holding the library books close, he rushed to The Well and shot under the restaurant awning.

Walking inside, he searched the seating area for any sign of a familiar face. Not seeing any, he hustled to an empty seat at the bar. No—the bar was too close to the front door. He asked the hostess for a seat in an unoccupied area, and she escorted him to a table in the back of the restaurant. He slid into the booth, making sure he had a good view of the front door and the other tables.

Not particularly hungry, Nathan eyed the menu, deciding on a roast beef sandwich and glass of sweet tea. As he waited for his food, he opened one of the library books and propped it up on the table in front of him, hoping to avoid making eye contact with anyone.

After a short wait, the waitress brought his order. Nathan took a swig of tea, then began to eat his sandwich. As he took the first bite, the sound of familiar laughter attacked his ears.

Panicking, he slid to the back corner of the booth and bent down to conceal himself from view. At the same moment, Roseann and her sister appeared at the hostess stand. Holding his breath, Nathan waited. The hostess grabbed two menus and walked in the opposite direction. She sat them in the dining room on the other side of the restaurant.

Phew. Nathan exhaled. That was too close for comfort. He flagged down his waitress, got the check, and placed a twenty-dollar bill on the table. He scooped up the library books and strode to the front door, leaving the uneaten sandwich on his plate.

Outside, the sun peeked through the waning cloud cover. Nathan scanned the parking spaces across the square, looking for Caroline's Outback. No red Subaru in sight. Relief and disappointment collided in his chest. He knew his daughter wasn't teaching this summer, but his heart always felt a little lighter whenever he saw her.

Nathan checked his watch. His truck wouldn't be ready for another thirty minutes, so he made his way to his favorite tree-shaded bench at the Old Courthouse to sit and wait. From this vantage point, Nathan had a perfect view of the businesses on the square. He would be able to spot Caroline coming to the dance studio or Roseann leaving the restaurant.

Nathan smiled to himself as he thought about his enterprising ex-wife. It appeared that she had done all right for herself. No surprise there. Roseann had always been confident and head-strong, even to the extent that it had driven a wedge between the two of them. Well—water under the bridge as they say, but it still didn't hurt any less.

Nathan opened the book, *Chandler's Cove Maritime History*, and began reading the first page, thankful that he didn't need reading glasses. His eyesight had always been excellent. He wished it hadn't been so good that dreadful October night.

The visions were bad, but the nightmares were worse. The same images night after night; cold, dark eyes piercing through the fog; a lifeless body covered in blood. Many nights, he woke up drenched in sweat, his heart pounding in his chest.

Nathan wondered if the incident would haunt him for the rest of his life. The traumatic event had affected his work, his relation-ships, and his sanity. He just didn't know if he dared talk about it. He knew that he could trust Captain Roy to keep his secret, but fear kept him silent.

Taking a deep breath and slowly exhaling, Nathan looked up from his book. Out of the corner of his eye, he saw Caroline's red Subaru pulling into a parking space in front of her dance studio.

Holy mackerel. I better get out of here before she sees me again.

Snatching up the library books, Nathan snuck around the corner of the Old Courthouse, just out of sight of Leap of Faith. A pain shot through his bad hip. Shifting his weight onto his good leg, he quietly watched as Caroline got out of her SUV and entered the dance studio. *Good. It didn't appear that she'd seen him.*

Nathan heaved a sigh. How much longer would he have to wait before he could talk to his daughter again? So much time had passed. Would she even want to talk to him after all these years? Fear weighed Nathan down like an anchor. The thought of her rejection was more than he could bear.

And what about Roseann? She wouldn't be any help. She'd promised to skin him alive if she ever saw him again. Maybe he should give Captain Roy another shot at straightening out his psyche. His friend sure couldn't make it any worse. Or could he?

After a few more minutes, Nathan decided it was safe to go back to the repair shop to retrieve his truck. He slinked in the direction of One-Stop Auto Repair, unaware that a man in a ball cap and dark shades watched him from across the square. Leaving the repair shop, Nathan headed home, not realizing that he was being followed. As he pulled into his duplex's single carport, the man that had been following him drove away.

Several minutes later, the man in the ball cap and shades pulled into the back lot of the Koke Island Lighthouse and parked in the shadows. He looked at his watch. Right on time. He lit a cigarette and waited.

Five minutes passed. He finished the cigarette and threw the butt onto the gravel. He waited ten more minutes. His contact was late again. Yeah—the guy was undependable, but he'd have to wait if he expected to get his money.

As he waited, the man remembered the fated October night that changed his life forever. He recalled the chain of events that had thrust him into his no-way-out situation. He had killed an innocent man. Albeit regrettable, he now lived with the consequences of those actions. They were a constant reminder of his past mistakes.

After he'd moved the operation to the gulf coast to keep an eye on Nathan Beall, the powers-that-be made it abundantly clear that any foul-up in the plans would be on his head. Too much money was at stake. Not to mention all the people that would be sent to prison if their elaborate scheme was exposed.

The man lit another cigarette and mentally reviewed the details of the upcoming Saturday night delivery. The boat would dock on the far side of the lighthouse at midnight. The docks and the boardwalk would be cleared out by then. Finishing his second cigarette, the man checked his watch again. He hoped he didn't have to wait much longer. He needed to be back on the clock in half an hour, and he didn't want to be late.

ELEVEN

Wednesday Afternoon, Leap of Faith

FRUSTRATED AND RUNNING low on patience, Caroline removed her pink reading glasses and rubbed her tired eyes. After spending most of the day attempting to finalize the schedule for the upcoming dance year, her notes looked like a combination of ancient hieroglyphics and chicken scratch. "Not to worry," she reminded herself. "It's only a temporary inconvenience." Still not convinced, she took a mental health break.

Switching on her mini sound machine, Caroline closed her eyes and leaned back in her cushioned desk chair, meditating to the soothing sounds of the gentle ocean waves. After several minutes, she spun her chair around and forced herself back to reality.

Standing, Caroline slipped off her sandals and walked into the ballet room. She did a visual 360. Visions of special memories, forever friendships, and rewarding achievements passed before her eyes. In her youth, the world of dance had been a place where she could dream great dreams and be the person she wanted to be. Today, it was still a place where dreams and talents thrived.

She walked to the dance barre and ran her feet over the smooth vinyl flooring. Warming up her body, she did several knee bends and toe rises, what dancers call *plies* and *releves*. She continued with a series of *tendues*, pointing her toes front, side, back, and side four times on each foot. Leaving the barre, she glided to the center of the room and performed a graceful ensemble of *arabesques, jetes*, and *pique* turns. Winded, but exhilarated, Caroline walked back to her office and looked—once more—at the papers on her desk, pondering the reason for her procrastination.

Monday, while investigating the Coastal University website, she'd discovered that a master's level hybrid counseling program was being offered. An informational meeting was set for the following day, so she and Jason had attended. At the meeting, Caroline had discovered that the next start date would be in October. The opportunity to return to college had officially presented itself, but what should she do about it?

Taking the plunge would require her to be on campus every Monday night from 6:00 to 10:00 p.m., with an additional two-day weekly internship thrown in for good measure. Jason had suggested that she strike while the iron was hot, but the more she thought about it, the more she feared she would surely get burned. When all was said and done, God, family, and Leap of Faith took precedence over any notion of academic achievement.

Caroline swept the spider webs of doubt out of her head and returned to her scheduling woes. Grabbing her yellow legal pad, she drew several columns on the page, penciling in her preschool classes for Monday afternoon. Her beginner classes would fill up Tuesday, and her intermediate classes could go on Thursday. She penciled those in, as well, added her company classes to the Saturday morning time slot. That left only Wednesday and Friday in which to schedule any potential internship hours.

As Caroline stared at the tentative outline, her mind went numb. The projected calendar did not lie. There wasn't an inch of breathing room in the schedule anywhere. The increased student enrollment was proving to be both a blessing and a curse.

She shook her head in disbelief. "I need to stop tap dancing around the problem and face the music," she complained to the universe. Her words echoed through the silence. "Heavens to Betsy," she moaned. "I'm talking to myself in clichés. I must be losing it."

As Caroline sat feeling sorry for herself, she sought out some words of wisdom. She opened her Bible, and the pages fell upon Philippians 4:13. She read the highlighted verse out loud. "I can do everything through Him who gives me strength."

As her ears absorbed God's Words, her outlook changed. She meditated on the powerful meaning. As she did so, her thinking cleared. "I obviously need an assistant to help me teach the dance classes," she told herself. "And I need one fast."

Caroline picked up the phone and called Zoe at the newspaper. Her friend promptly answered.

"Help!" Caroline roared.

"Caroline. Are you okay?"

"I just realized that I can't teach all of my dance classes and go to school, too." The pitch of Caroline's voice rose with every word. "I need to hire an assistant ASAP."

"Take a deep breath and relax," Zoe stated in a calm tone. "Now, you are going to get up from your desk and forget about that horrid schedule. Are you listening?"

"I don't know what's wrong with me," Caroline whined. "Maybe I'm having a midlife crisis."

"No, you're not," her friend confirmed. "Your brain's overloaded with thoughts of Caroline. You need to get your mind off yourself." Zoe paused to gauge her distraught friend's response then continued. "Novelist James M. Barrie said that those who bring sunshine to the lives of others cannot keep it from themselves."

"True words," Caroline admitted. "I could give it a try. Maybe a little sunshine will help me see things more clearly."

"That's the spirit," Zoe cheered her on. "It's almost time to pick up Isabella and Max from acting camp. I'll go get them, while you take a few minutes to find your happy place. Then, we can meet for a snack and work up a plan to get you some help at the dance studio."

"It's a start," Caroline dithered, "but let's not forget that the person I hire will undoubtedly want to get paid."

"Details, details. It'll work out just fine. You'll see."

"Where shall we meet?" Caroline asked.

"Why don't we try that new place next to you—The Jiffy Java," Zoe replied. "Did you get the ad flyer?"

"I believe it's on my desk here somewhere." Caroline rifled through the stacks of miscellaneous papers, dance magazines, bills, and solicitations. "Here it is," she said. "The Jiffy Java is having its pre-opening all this week. Sounds like fun."

"So, it's settled then. The kids and I will meet you at The Jiffy Java at four o'clock. Bring your thinking cap and be prepared to be dazzled."

Ending the call, Caroline organized the dressing room and vacuumed the carpet. Taking a can of air freshener off the shelf, she began spritzing every room with fragrant peach blossoms.

A few minutes to four, she returned to her office, collected her yellow legal pad and her imaginary thinking cap, and secured the studio. As the chimes of the Old Courthouse clock tower signaled the four o'clock hour, she stepped out into the sweltering afternoon heat and proceeded next door to The Jiffy Java.

Upon her arrival, Caroline noticed a **HELP WANTED** sign posted in the storefront window. She made a mental note of it as she entered the establishment. A welcoming blast of cool air and a juke box playing fifties music greeted her.

She took a quick look around. The Jiffy Java resembled an old-fashioned soda shop. Retro movie posters and large framed photos of legendary actors decorated the walls. Chrome and white bistro tables with red covered barstools occupied the central floor space, and red-cushioned booths lined the left and right sides of the room.

A service bar and cash register were positioned on the back wall, and to the right of that, she caught a glimpse of what she guessed to be the entrance to the kitchen.

Caroline found Zoe, her daughter, Isabella, and Max already seated at one of the bistro tables. Isabella and Max were running lines in preparation for their September production of *Seussical, the Musical.* Isabella would be playing one of the melodious Bird Girls, and Max had the role of Judge Yertle, the Turtle. Zoe saw Caroline and waved.

Caroline crossed the black and white tile floor and joined them at the table, giving each kid a one-armed hug. "Hey y'all. How'd rehearsal go?"

"Great!" Max responded.

"Superb!" Isabella chimed in.

Caroline hopped up on a barstool and grabbed a menu, marveling at the long list of specialty coffees, teas, smoothies, and milk shakes. The food items consisted of sandwiches, burgers, salads, and decadent desserts.

Zoe looked up from her menu. "I was thinking about trying a coconut smoothie. Are you having your usual latte?"

As Caroline tapped her bottom lip trying to decide, a thirty-something woman of medium height and build bounced toward the table. She wore a white button-down blouse and blue Capri jeans that accentuated her full curvy figure. Her raven-colored hair was pulled back at the nape of her neck with a lacy red ribbon, and a ponytail of tight curls rested on her square shoulders. Her clear, smooth skin mimicked the color of rich mocha.

She walked up to the table. "Hi. My name is Lucy Ledbetter," she announced, flashing a friendly smile that plumped her rosy brown cheeks. "I'm the manager of The Jiffy Java."

Zoe shook hands with Lucy. "Hi, Lucy. My name is Zoe Castillo, and I'm the editor of *The Village Times Herald.*" She placed a hand on Isabella's shoulder. "This is my daughter, Isabella."

Isabella flashed a bright smile. Her brown eyes, the color of espresso, displayed a combination of innocence and maturity. With her straight black hair and flawless tawny complexion, Isabella was a striking Latina version of her mother. "Pleased to make your acquaintance," Isabella replied in a grown-up voice.

"My name's Caroline Callahan," Caroline added with a handshake, "and I own Leap of Faith Dance Academy next door." She tousled Max's hair. "This is my younger son, Max."

Max jumped off his barstool. "How do you do, fine lady?" He offered Lucy a grand bow, then jumped back onto the barstool.

Isabella and Max puppy-dog grinned at each other, then burst out laughing. Two years Max's senior, Isabella hadn't yet decided that it was uncool to hang out with him. They both shared a love for musical theater, and the two budding thespians never missed an opportunity to make "all the world their stage."

"Nice to meet everyone," Lucy stated with a laugh.

"What do you think of our actors-in-training, Lucy?" Zoe asked.

"They're two fine specimens, indeed." Lucy's cocoa-brown eyes twinkled with merriment. "My son and I are new to the area. Is there an acting school in town?"

"Yes. It's off the square at the Seaside Community Center," Caroline explained. "How old is your son?"

"Sam is nine years old and quite a character. I want to get him involved in an activity, so that he can meet other kids his age. Maybe he could try a class or two?"

"Sam is the right age for Max and Bella's acting class," Zoe told Lucy. "Have him come to class with them. They can introduce him to the other students."

"That would be great!" Lucy said. "Sam and I very much appreciate the offer."

"How is Sam keeping himself busy this summer, Lucy?" Caroline asked.

"He's been attending some camps during the day, and my neighbor's teenage daughter watches him when I have to work late." Lucy shrugged. "I hate to be away from him so much, but I really need to make The Jiffy Java a hit in Chandler's Cove."

Understanding the complexities of living and working in a new town, Caroline wondered if Lucy and Sam were alone here. If that were the case, she hoped her group could help mother and son make a smooth transition. Remembering the Help Wanted sign in the front window, Caroline asked Lucy what jobs she still needed to fill.

"I'm looking for someone to bus tables, wash dishes, and assist with the prep work," Lucy responded, her mood beginning to brighten. "It's a part-time position. Do you know of anyone who would be interested?"

"Actually, I do," Caroline remarked. "My older son, Evan, is entering culinary school in the fall, and he's looking for something part-time. This job would be a great opportunity for him."

"Your son sounds like the perfect candidate," Lucy informed. "Have him come by and talk to me. I'd like to fill the position as soon as possible."

"I'll tell Evan about the job tonight," Caroline assured her.

Lucy retrieved an order pad and pen from her shirt pocket. "Are you guys ready to order?"

Max snapped to attention. "Order, order, order, order in the court," he boomed, practicing one of his lines from the musical.

Isabella punched Max on the arm. "Show-off," she teased. This produced a round of laughter.

Bringing their attention back to the menu, the group gave Lucy their order, and she headed back to the kitchen. Isabella and Max returned to their script, and Caroline and Zoe began making adjustments to the dance schedule. Within a few minutes, Lucy returned with a coconut smoothie for Zoe, a caramel latte for Caroline, and vanilla milkshakes for the kids. They enjoyed the delicious beverages while continuing to work. After more brainstorming, Caroline and Zoe fine-tuned the schedule and wrote a job posting for the assistant dance instructor position.

"I'll place this ad in the Friday Help Wanted section of the *Herald*," Zoe promised.

"And I'll call some of my dance contacts in the area to see if a teacher is available." Caroline breathed a semi-confident sigh of relief. "Thanks for the help, Zoe. Two heads are definitely better than one."

Caroline, Zoe, and the kids conversed for a while longer, and at five o'clock, the friends gathered their belongings. Lucy came back to their table with the check and promised to bring Sam to Isabella and Max's next acting class. They paid their bill and made their way to the door. Stepping outside, throngs of people milled about, either shopping or grabbing an early dinner.

Zoe and Isabella waved good-bye and headed in the direction of the newspaper. With a spring in her step, Caroline ushered Max to the SUV. It felt good to be making some headway with her dilemma. Whether she had an actual dilemma or not was irrelevant. As a social worker, she knew that her perception of reality, for all intents and purposes, *was* her reality.

Caroline considered her next step. She understood that she might have to give up something to gain something. Consequently, if she stayed rooted in the present, she could not step into the future. During the drive home, she pondered that bittersweet revelation. Even though the unknown was a scary place, she had set the wheels of progress in motion and wasn't about to turn back now.

TWELVE

IT WAS JUST about dinnertime when Caroline and Max returned
to Callahan Manor. Max shot upstairs to work on his LEGO City
creation, while Caroline followed the savory aroma of peppers and
onions into the kitchen. Evan greeted her with a wave of his spatula.
Terra and Windy sat at his feet, ready to inhale any fallen morsels of
food.

Caroline's stomach rumbled. "Something smells good. What
is it?"

"Chicken and vegetable stir-fry," Evan said. "My new wok is
great—the perfect size for cooking at home."

"I'm glad you like it—and thanks for making dinner. I'm not in
the mood to cook tonight."

"What's up?" he questioned.

"Just some scheduling problems I'm trying to iron out." Caroline
didn't want Evan sensing her doubts about returning to college,
since he was about to embark on the same journey.

She remembered Lucy's offer to consider Evan for the part-time
position at The Jiffy Java. "By the way, I have some good news for
you."

"That's the only kind of news to have. What is it?"

"You know The Jiffy Java—the new business located next to the dancing school?" Evan acknowledged that he did. "The manager, Lucy Ledbetter, has one more part-time position to fill. I told her that you will be starting culinary school soon, and that you might be interested."

A smile lit up his face. "That sounds great! What kind of job is it?"

"I guess you would be an apprentice of sorts," Caroline speculated. "The job involves bussing tables, washing dishes, and helping out in the kitchen."

Evan thought for a moment. "So, I'd be learning and getting paid at the same time. Sounds like a sweet deal to me."

Striding to the stove, Caroline snatched a succulent orange pepper from the wok, blew on it, and popped it in her mouth.

Evan continued to stir the ingredients. "Hey Mom—can you do me a solid?"

"A solid?"

"You know, a favor," he clarified.

"Is that the expression *du jour*?"

"Something like that."

"I guess it depends on the favor," Caroline teased. "What do you need?"

Evan pasted a manipulative grin on his face. "Could you create a resume for me to take to The Jiffy Java tomorrow, please?"

Caroline pretended to contemplate the request. "It *is* for a worthy cause. And you *are* cooking dinner tonight. *So*...okay."

Evan grinned. "Thanks for having my back, Mom."

"Sure thing, Chef." Caroline zipped to the fridge, took out a fresh-brewed pitcher of sweet tea, and set it on the counter. "Speaking of jobs, has your friend, Dave, found one yet?"

Evan retrieved a bag of Asian slaw mix from the fridge and poured it into the wok. "He's working at the Laughing Gull on the harbor."

She nodded. "I'm glad Dave found a job. I know he needs the money for culinary school."

"As do I," Evan voiced.

Caroline snagged two dog biscuits from the treat tin on the counter, coaxed the corgis outside for some exercise, and re-entered the kitchen. "Where's your dad?" she asked.

Evan pointed with his spatula. "He's in his office—and dinner will be ready shortly."

Stepping through the French doors into the sunroom, Caroline crossed the tile floor and entered Jason's office. He sat at his antique mahogany desk pouring over the plans for Barry Chapman's garage enclosure. She tiptoed up behind him and gave him a kiss on the neck.

Jason reached behind her and pulled her close. "Hi, stranger," he whispered in her ear. "Do you still live here?"

"I think so, but I'm not sure," Caroline stated. "I haven't been home much lately, have I?"

Jason spun his red leather chair around and pulled his wife onto his lap. "Let's not waste time talking." He planted a steamy kiss on her lips.

At that moment, Evan popped his head into the office and cleared his throat. "There's no time for that lovey-dovey stuff," he chided. "Dinner is served." He strutted to the foyer and stopped at the foot of the stairs. "Dinner's ready," he called up to Max before returning to the kitchen.

Caroline and Jason snickered at the role reversal.

"I can't believe how responsible Evan is becoming," Caroline whispered.

"I thought the day would never come," Jason confided with a hint of relief in his voice.

"We better go eat, or Evan will come in here and drag us to the kitchen," Caroline said, attempting to stand.

Jason held on tight. "Don't forget where we left off," he teased.

She answered with a quick kiss.

Jason loosened his hold, and Caroline wiggled out of his grasp. He stood up and wrapped his strong arms around her waist. Lifting her feet off the floor, he set her back in the chair. "Race you," he challenged as he sprinted out of the room.

"No fair," Caroline complained as she entered the kitchen. "You cheated."

"All's fair in love and foot races, darling," he crowed, patting her on the behind.

The couple's playful banter was cut short by Max's footfalls on the stairs. He ran down the hall and into the kitchen. "What smells so good?"

"One of your favorites. Chicken stir-fry," Evan said, attempting to swat Max with a dish towel. Used to such trickery from his brother, Max skillfully dodged the towel.

Placing the towel on the counter, Evan waved his hand, presenting the dinner. "*Bon appétit,*" he annunciated in a French accent, revealing his inner Julia Child.

"Yum," Max exclaimed as he grabbed a plate and began heaping food onto it. He carried his plate and drink to the table, sat down, and scooped up a spoonful of the delicious creation.

"Don't start eating until we've said the blessing, Max," Jason reminded him.

Max's spoon stopped in front of his mouth. He lowered it down and set it on his plate, waiting for everyone to join him at the table. Joining Max, Jason asked him to give thanks. The family bowed their heads and Max prayed, "Thank-you for the world so sweet. Thank-you for the food we eat. Thank-you for the birds that sing. Thank-you, God, for everything."

As the family finished dinner, they heard a knock at the front door. Max jumped up to see who was there. "It's Nana and Aunt Flo," he announced, ushering them into the kitchen.

"Good evening everyone," Roseann descanted. "We're not inter-rupting dinner, are we?

"No. We're just finishing up," Caroline told them.

"What smells so delicious?" Flo asked, taking a whiff of the food-scented air.

"It *was* chicken and vegetable stir-fry." Evan beamed. "I'd let you try some, but there's none left."

"Evan made dinner tonight," Caroline pointed out. "The meal was excellent."

"How wonderful, Evan," Roseann cooed. She glided over to her first-born grandson and gave him a kiss on the cheek.

Aunt Flo reached over and gave Evan a high-five. "Let's do some cooking together soon," she proposed. "We can swap recipes."

Evan's face brightened. "That sounds great, Aunt Flo. You're the best cook I know." He stood up and began removing the dinner dishes off the table. "Don't worry about cleaning up the kitchen, Mom. I'll do that."

"Thanks Evan." Caroline grinned. "Cooking *and* cleaning. It's my lucky day."

Max began shuffling his feet under the table. "May I be excused?"

"Yes, you may," Caroline assented, "but say good-night to Nana and Aunt Flo first."

Max jumped up from the table and gave Roseann and Flo squishy hugs.

"Call me when you're ready for bed," Caroline instructed.

"Okeydokey. See you in the funny papers," Max hollered as he rushed upstairs.

Jason glanced at the clock on the wall, then stood. "Have a seat, ladies." He indicated the vacated chairs. "I hate to eat and run, but duty calls." With a slight bow, he exited to his office.

The sweltering heat of the day had turned into a warm and muggy evening. Roseann pulled a lace fan from her pink purse and began fanning herself.

"Would y'all like some sweet tea?" Caroline queried.

"That would be nice, dear. I'm parched from the heat." Roseann continued fanning.

Caroline retrieved three tall glasses from the cabinet, added ice and tea to each, and garnished them with a lemon wedge. Placing the glasses on a tray, she ushered the matriarchs into the sunroom and set the tray on the coffee table. Roseann and Flo sat down on the love seat, and Caroline handed each one a cool glass. Sitting down across from them, she inquired about Aunt Flo's date with Walt.

A big grin formed on Flo's face. "We had a very good time," she purred like a kitten with a bowl of warm milk. "Truth be told, I think Walt fancies me."

"How do you feel about that, Flonnie?" Roseann asked.

"Honestly, I'm not sure how I feel." Flo shook her head in bewilderment. "When I see Walt, I get butterflies in my stomach. I'm excited and nervous—all at the same time."

"There's no doubt that Walt is a great guy," Roseann said, shifting her gaze to the greenery on the far wall, "but you'll be going back to Atlanta at the end of the summer."

Flo huffed a sigh. "Yes…"

Roseann looked back in Caroline's direction, quickly changing the subject. "Incidentally, how is the dance schedule coming?" she asked her.

Realizing that they were now talking about her, Caroline took in a deep breath and let it out. "Zoe saved me from a meltdown today," she confessed. "To save my sanity, I've decided to hire a teaching assistant."

Roseann cut her eyes at her sister, then looked back at her daughter. "That's a fabulous idea, dear. You don't want to be stressed all year, do you?"

Caroline frowned, exasperation beginning to show on her face. "You're right Mother, but I don't have a clue who to get."

Aunt Flo eyed Roseann like a cat with a canary in its mouth. "What about one of the girls at the community outreach, Sis?"

"Let me think," Roseann mused. She took another sip of her sweet tea. The ice cubes clinked in her glass as she placed it back on the table. "Caroline, you remember that I teach a weekly Bible study class at the Angel's Wings group home for girls."

Caroline nodded.

"Well, the home provides food, clothing, and shelter to the residents for an eighteen-month period, while they recover from their addictions and learn a job skill."

Caroline saw where this conversation was headed.

"One of my favorite girls, Olivia Styles, will be graduating from the program soon. Of course, she will need a job and someone to oversee her transition into a new working environment. Since her mother lives in Pensacola and her father lives in Apalachicola, she'll also need a place to live."

Skeptical, but curious about what her mother was saying, Caroline asked Roseann to give her the scoop on Olivia. Roseann sat back and began her story.

"At sixteen, Olivia was caught in the middle of a bitter divorce and custody battle. After her parents separated, she spent every other weekend with her father in Apalachicola. She was unsupervised most of the time and fell in with the wrong crowd. Over the period of a year, drugs were a major part of Olivia's life. She became increasingly dependent upon them until she was totally addicted." Roseann realized that she had a captive audience, so she kept going.

"Olivia had become so out of control that her mother could no longer take care of her. At age seventeen, she hit rock bottom. That's when Olivia and her mother decided to let the counselors at Angel's Wings help her become a whole person again." Roseann paused to take a breath. "I've known Olivia for a year, and in the past several months, she's made a remarkable recovery. Through the ministry at Angel's Wings, Olivia is beginning to heal from her brokenness."

Caroline had to admit that she was impressed with Olivia's story. Beginning to wonder why her mother was telling her this, she delved deeper. "Did Olivia train to be a dance teacher at Angel's Wings?"

"No dear," Roseann admitted. "She was an accomplished dancer and assistant teacher before she succumbed to her drug addiction, so I thought she might be able to teach for you."

Love resonated from Roseann's voice as she spoke about Olivia. It seemed to Caroline that Roseann had confidence in her mentee's capabilities, but she sensed that her mother was not telling the whole story. Caroline opened her mouth to question her further, but she was interrupted by Max calling for her to come upstairs.

Caroline stood up. "I need to say bedtime prayers with Max. Why don't you two take a look at Jason's current plans for Callahan Manor? I'll be back shortly, then we can talk more about Olivia Styles." She headed up to check on Max.

Several minutes later, she came back downstairs and headed toward the sound of female voices. Roseann stood on one side of Jason and Flo stood on the other. All three had their heads together studying something on Jason's desk.

Caroline entered the office. "What's this—a meeting of the minds?"

The trio turned to face her. "We're going over plans to remodel your cottage," Roseann said matter-of-factly.

Caroline's eyes widened. "I thought those plans were on hold for the time being?"

"I thought so too," Jason responded in an even tone, "but your mother and aunt have very strong powers of persuasion."

Typical Roseann, Caroline thought. She shut the office door. "What's the urgency with the cottage renovations?" she questioned.

"It seems that your new assistant dance teacher, Olivia Styles, will need a place to live in a month," Jason said, attempting to explain. "Roseann and Florence thought it would be a good idea for her to live in the cottage." He gauged his wife's level of irritation. "Congratulations on your decision to hire her, by the way."

"My decision?" Caroline eyeballed Roseann and Flo. "It looks like the decision has already been made for me."

Aunt Flo shot Roseann a look of warning. "I told you to tread lightly, Sis."

"You have this all planned out, don't you Mother?" Caroline declared, struggling to keep her voice calm.

"I've thought for a while that Olivia would be a good fit for you at the dancing school. And, when it looked as though you would be needing an assistant…" Roseann's voice trailed off. "I just wanted the time to be right before I approached you with my idea. I hope you can see that my intentions are honorable." Roseann's big doe eyes searched her daughter's.

Staring daggers at the three of them, Caroline mentally counted to ten. She wasn't about to admit that Roseann could be right. "Even if I *do* hire Olivia, and that's a big if, we can't afford renovations to the cottage right now. Besides, Jason is busy working on Barry Chapman's garage enclosure."

Roseann perked up. "Jason and I have discussed that. The good news is that the ministry that supports Angel's Wings will be able to provide the supplies for the renovations. Also, they have a couple of guys who can help Jason with the labor."

Caroline thought that sounded too good to be true. "They're willing to do that for Olivia?"

"As I understand, it's all part of the transition process." Roseann looked at her daughter in earnest. "Furthermore, Olivia has been training to be a seamstress. She's been working part-time for the alteration shop off the square. That leaves her afternoons and evenings free to teach for you. And the best part is that she'll be able to pay you rent and take care of her utilities as well."

"Olivia and I can make the drapes for the cottage, Caroline Celeste," Flo offered, smiling broadly. "It sounds like a win-win situation to me."

Caroline's arm felt like a pretzel being twisted into a painful knot. "Well Mother, I guess there's only one question left to ask. What does Olivia think about the plans you've made for her?"

"I broached the subject with Olivia, after you told me that you might be returning to college. I told her that it was only a possibility, but she was very receptive to the idea." Roseann turned her palms upward. "Olivia believes that her story could be a blessing to others who struggle with similar problems and temptations. So, you see—"

Caroline cut Roseann off at the pass. "It appears your visit here tonight was a ruse to convince me to hire Olivia."

Jason proceeded with caution. "Your mother presents a good argument, Caroline."

Oh no! He did not just say that. Caroline crossed her arms in front of her. "It seems as though the three of you are convinced that this is a good idea. That's all well and good, but I'm still going to run some ads and make a few phone calls. I'll meet with Olivia, but I have two weeks before I need to make a decision."

"Fair enough," Roseann conceded. "I'm sure that Olivia will be delighted to talk with you."

"If I do decide to hire Olivia and have her live in the cottage, I'm not going to take on this responsibility all by myself. We are all in this together." Caroline pointed her index finger at each one of them. "I hope that we're not biting off more than we can chew."

Flo pointed her index finger upward. "And don't forget our fifth partner."

"Heavens no," Roseann pledged, placing her hands over her heart. "Without our most important partner, none of this will be possible."

Roseann and Flo began their good-byes. Jason resumed making the necessary adjustments to the remodeling plans, while Caroline walked the two Nosy Nellies to the door. She kissed them both on the cheek and wished them a safe journey home. Closing the front door, she entered the library and sat down in her thinking chair, an antique rocker given to her by her Granny Fi.

Closing her eyes, Caroline pondered Roseann's proposal. Olivia deserved a second chance, but would the added responsibility and job stress cause her to fall back into her old ways of coping? The girls at Leap of Faith would be accepting of Olivia, but would their parents be as understanding? More importantly, would she be causing herself a bigger problem if she hired her?

Suddenly, the roller-coaster emotions of the day caught up with her, depleting her energy reserves. Temples throbbing and a headache forming at the sides of her eyes, Caroline realized that she'd been clenching her jaw. Returning to the kitchen, she put the corgis to bed, then trudged upstairs. She looked in on Evan, promising to work on his resume the first thing in the morning.

Entering her bedroom, Caroline put on her nightshirt and jumped into bed. As her head hit the pillow, she wondered why she was so mad at her mother. After all, Roseann was only trying to help. Yawning, she pulled the covers over her head. Like Scarlett, she'd have to think about that tomorrow.

THIRTEEN

Thursday Morning, Callahan Manor

HEAVY RAIN POURED down on Caroline as she trudged up the hill on her bicycle. Why had she picked today of all days to ride her bike to work? She was going to be late for sure. From somewhere far away, she could hear music playing and a faint female voice singing something about it being a good morning. Instantly, the bicycle was gone.

Bright sun filtered through the wooden slats of Caroline's bedroom blinds. She was having that darn bicycle dream again. Rolling over, she hid her face under the covers. *What's so good about it?* She thought.

The singing ceased, and a muffled voice told Caroline that the high today would be 98 degrees, but the heat index would make it feel like 108. Would this infernal heat and humidity ever end?

Caroline reached one hand out from under the covers and slammed it down in the direction of the noise. Blissful silence resumed. Ten more minutes of sleep. That's all she needed.

The sound of running water and gleeful whistling roused her. *Drat! No rest for the weary.*

Caroline felt around in the bed until she found the TV remote. Aiming it in the direction of the TV, she pressed the power button and peeked out from under the covers. Hoda Kotb and her new co-host were showing her how to accessorize for less. As tempting as it was to remain in bed watching morning talk shows, she needed to get a move on. She'd promised Evan that she would create his resume today.

Caroline placed the TV on mute and noticed that the water and whistling had stopped. Throwing the covers back, she dangled her feet off the raised bed and did a few foot exercises. A series of neck and shoulder stretches along with some deep breathing exercises followed. As she stretched and breathed, Jason sauntered into the room smelling of crisp cologne.

"Good morning, Sleeping Beauty," he crooned with way too much enthusiasm.

Choosing to ignore his obvious attempt to get on her good side, Caroline continued her deep breathing. Jason came around to her side of the bed. "You're not still mad, are you?"

"And why not?"

"Well…I thought since you had the chance to…"

Caroline stopped him before he could irritate her any further. "Jason, you know how I feel about my mother's meddling! Why in the world would you agree with her?" She continued her tirade. "I've worked so hard to get on an equal footing with her, and now she's gotten the upper hand." Her face began to burn.

"Whoa! Simmer down, Hot Stuff. You know I've always got your back." Jason sat down on the bed next to his wife and gave her a bear hug, his touch dissipating her steamy mood.

Caroline grimaced. "You don't have to squeeze me so tight. I won't hit you."

Jason released his hold and kissed the top of her head. "That's my girl," he said. "Let it go. You know she's never going to change."

Caroline took in a deep breath and blew the frustration over her lips. "That's true, and I don't think that I would want her to, even if she could." She shook her head. "It's just that Mother really knows how to push my buttons."

"You're not the only one." Jason stood up and walked over to his dresser. "You just seem to be her favorite."

Caroline began dropping her head to the right and left. "Why do you always have to be the voice of reason?"

Jason grabbed his watch from the valet tray and placed it on his wrist. "One of us has to be, and frankly darling, it's not in your nature."

Caroline slid off the bed and walked over to the treadmill. Exercise had always been her answer to stress. "If you're lucky, I *may* think about doing better," she countered, "but don't hold your breath."

Jason walked over to the treadmill and lowered the walking deck. "No need. I love you just the way you are." He gave her derriere a pat.

"I remember when you used to play that song on your guitar," she said, stepping onto the treadmill. The motor began to hum as she started her warm-up.

Jason headed back to his dresser. "That was a long time ago." He clipped his cell phone onto his belt. "Evan is the musician in the family now."

Caroline looked at Jason. "I'm just saying that maybe you should dust off that poor, neglected instrument and start serenading me again."

"The twelfth of never might be a good day for that," he stated, retrieving his wallet.

"Well, at least you've set a date."

Jason shoved his wallet into his back pocket. "My hand doesn't work as well as it did before the injury, but stranger things have happened." He walked back over to the treadmill. "Changing the subject—now that you've had time to sleep on it, are you any more agreeable to the idea of Olivia Styles coming to work for you?"

Caroline increased her speed a notch. "I'd prefer to procrastinate, but I'm running out of time. I have to make a decision soon."

He pressed on. "Why don't you call Roseann and get Olivia's number?"

She huffed. "I don't want to talk to my mother today."

Jason pulled out the desk chair next to the treadmill and sat down. "Caroline, you're the relationship expert. You've got to be the bigger person here."

"My head comprehends, but my heart doesn't want to cooperate," Caroline admitted, adding a slight incline to her walk.

"I seem to recall the preacher talking about relationship building last Sunday. Didn't he read from Hebrews?" Jason stretched out his long legs and waited for her to respond.

Pretending to ignore his comment, Caroline cranked up the speed a little more and kept walking.

After a long pause, Jason continued needling. "*Yes*, he did." He grabbed his cell phone, pulled up his Bible app, and searched for the Scripture. "Here it is. Let me refresh your memory. Hebrews 12:14. 'Make every effort to live in peace with all men and to be holy; without holiness no one will see the Lord.' Does that ring a bell?" He put his phone back on his belt and grinned at her.

Caroline knew that she'd lost this round. Feigning contempt, she quipped, "You better wipe that smug grin off your face, or I'll jump off this treadmill and do it for you."

Jason shrugged. "*C'est la vie*, as they say in France."

Caroline arched an eyebrow. "Wow—wise *and* worldly. When did you visit France?"

"It's on my bucket list."

"*Le mien aussi*," she agreed. "Mine, too."

"Practicing you're French again, I see."

"*Oui*—I'm a tad rusty. It's been a long time since I spent that semester in Paris."

Jason's attention shifted to the TV as tall, pencil-thin blondes and brunettes modeled the latest swimsuit styles.

"I bet there's plenty of gorgeous models in France," Caroline drawled. "I'd better watch out, or one day some sweet young thing will try to steal you away from me."

"That's what I keep telling you," he said with the confidence of someone who is adept at fighting off pretty women.

She gave Jason the evil eye. "Well, I'm not worried about Barry Chapman, but if you know what's good for you, you'll stay away from his wife."

"Jealousy becomes you," Jason teased, "but you're safe for now. Barry doesn't have a wife."

Caroline bristled. "Why do you think I'm killing myself on this blasted treadmill? I haven't reached my target weight loss goal yet."

"No worries," he replied. "You'll be down to your fighting weight in no time."

Caroline decreased her incline and continued walking at a leisurely pace. "I'm not worried. I can fight at any weight."

"You don't have to tell me, darling." Jason stood up and pushed in the desk chair. "But all joking aside, you need to call your mother."

"Roger that," Caroline conceded. The increased oxygen to her brain had apparently brightened her mood.

"Go get 'um Tiger," he instructed, heading to the door. "Time is of the essence."

"*Au revoir*," she called over her shoulder. "*Je t'aime.*"

Caroline un-muted the TV. Hoda was making fresh hummus with Chef Pierre. The recipe looked scrumptious. She made a mental note to look it up for Evan. *Oh, boy.* Time was of the essence with his resume, too.

She recalled Jason's remark about her relationship training. The prudent thing to do would be to talk to Olivia Styles. But would she be loosening her boundaries if she gave in to Roseann?

After pondering her conundrum for several more minutes, Caroline decreased the treadmill's speed and began her cool-down. For a fleeting moment, she considered eating crow and giving her mother a call. She knew Roseann would be thrilled, but the verdict was still out on her feelings. Reluctantly, Caroline added Call Mother to her to-do list. But first she had to get to work on Evan's resume.

FOURTEEN

Leap of Faith

THE SQUARE WAS BUSTLING with activity Friday afternoon as Caroline pulled up in front of Leap of Faith. She spotted a familiar copper Scion parked two spaces down. It was Evan's first day on the job at The Jiffy Java. After Labor Day, he would begin culinary school. Caroline told herself that she should be happy he was following his passion. Truth be told, she wasn't sure how she felt.

Gathering up her purse and dance bag, Caroline locked the car door and rushed into the dance studio. She flipped on the office light and placed both bags beside her desk. Plopping down in her desk chair, she stared at the mound of papers needing her attention. She retrieved her yellow legal pad from under a stack of costume catalogues and jotted down a few back-to-school details that she'd neglected.

One glaring detail was that she had not yet hired a teaching assistant. To her dismay, the ads that she and Zoe had placed in the newspaper and on the Jobseeker website hadn't produced one single applicant. Was it a sign? Caroline wondered.

On second thought, it could be because she'd waited so late to run the ads. Dance classes would begin soon, and she was desperate to get the problem resolved. Still harboring concerns about Olivia Styles' ability to do the job, Caroline had scheduled a job interview with the young girl today.

The door chime on the studio door jingled. Caroline looked up from her desk to see a tall, slender girl with well-developed leg muscles and excellent posture, glide into the sitting room. The girl exuded self-confidence as she entered. She wore a modest white sundress dotted with tiny violets that complemented her tanned skin and adorable figure. Her long, straight hair, the color of honey, was pulled up in a ponytail. It flipped back and forth as she walked. Bright lavender-blue eyes peeked out from under long, wispy bangs.

Caroline rose from her chair and walked into the sitting room. "Olivia Styles?" she asked, holding out her hand.

"Yes ma'am," the girl replied, shaking Caroline's hand. "And you must be Mrs. Callahan. Your mother talks about you all the time." Her eyes sparkled like amethysts as she spoke.

"Call me Caroline. We don't stand on formality here." Caroline ushered Olivia into her office. "Please, have a seat." She offered Olivia the resin chair beside her desk, and they both sat down.

Olivia placed her hands in her lap and looked at Caroline. "I appreciate you taking the time to meet with me today, Miss Caroline."

"I'm glad you could come," Caroline said with a smile. "Let me begin by telling you a little bit about my dance background." She moved the distracting stack of papers to the other end of the desk. "I have over twenty years of teaching experience in all sorts of environments. I'm classically trained in the Cecchetti ballet method and teach that method here."

Caroline observed a blank expression on Olivia's face. "I hate to say it, but I'm not sure what ballet method I've been taught," she admitted.

"Don't worry." Caroline laughed. "Most students have no idea either. We can schedule a time to run a typical ballet class. I'm sure you'll pick up the technique quickly."

Olivia heaved a sigh of relief. "Thanks. That would be great."

"Are you familiar with the Al Gilbert graded tap technique?"

"Yes! I love it," she exclaimed.

"Great. That's what I use. However, the most important thing to remember is that, at Leap of Faith, I have a higher philosophy about dance." Caroline shifted in her chair and continued. "From the time the students enter until the time they leave, I strive to provide an atmosphere of love and trust. I want Leap of Faith to be a safe-haven where everyone feels comfortable discussing their cares and concerns."

"Almost like dance therapy," Olivia mused, "and definitely very different from many dancing schools today. Most focus on making lots of money or winning trophies at dance competitions. These schools have lost their heart," she added with a sad expression on her face.

"I remember those days well." Caroline crossed her legs and got comfortable in her seat. "It sounds as if you're speaking from personal experience, too."

Olivia made eye contact. "Yes, unfortunately I am, but I'm pleased to hear that your school has a different outlook."

"Leap of Faith is a joint venture between me and God," Caroline pointed out. "A few years ago, I embarked on a study of Christianity's Hebraic roots. As I studied, I learned about the special way that King David worshipped the Lord. He sang, played musical instruments, and danced. David was not afraid to physically express his profound love and reverence for his Heavenly Father. I was moved by David's dedication to the Lord and, from that day forward, I began to see my gift of dance in a different light."

As Caroline spoke, Olivia's countenance began to change. The girl appeared to be taking in the concept of total worship. A peaceful expression spread over her face.

Caroline uncrossed her legs and leaned forward. "This new

insight began stirring within me, and I knew that I had to make a decision. Was I going to continue to dance for man, or was I going to dance for my Maker? At first, it was a struggle. Then I remembered that I am *in* the world, but not *of* it. After that, the answer became clear." She gauged Olivia's responsiveness to this information.

"Have you ever regretted your decision?" Olivia asked.

"Not for a moment, but I must confess, it's been hard at times. I've lost students whose parents prefer a more competitive environment."

"Your story is a breath of fresh air." Olivia beamed with excitement. "I would be honored to be a part of the Leap of Faith family, if you'll have me."

"Obviously, Leap of Faith is near and dear to my heart," Caroline confided. "As a teacher, I strive to discern the unique talent hidden within each student. I work to develop and nurture that talent, so that every child has the opportunity to reach their full potential."

She opened the portable office fridge behind her desk and pulled out two bottles of water. She offered one to Olivia. They removed the caps, and both took a sip.

"That's an awesome perspective," Olivia affirmed.

"In order to be an effective teacher, I know that I must lead with a servant's heart." Caroline set her water bottle on the desk. "Gerald Brooks made a profound statement about leaders. He stated that, 'when you become a leader, you lose the right to think about yourself.' Putting my students first is what it's all about for me." She finished her loquacious speech and leaned back in her chair.

Olivia gave a nod. "It sounds like you're talking about servant leadership. That concept is not always embraced, is it?"

Caroline smiled. "Not always, but my goal is to please God and to help others."

"I'm sure that you must have questions about the past seventeen months of my life," Olivia said, averting her gaze. "I'll admit that when I entered the eighteen-month discipleship program at Angel's Wings, I was at my lowest. I let the problems between my parents affect me, and I was bitter about their breakup."

Olivia heaved a sigh and looked in Caroline's direction. "I started doing drugs to punish them, but it backfired on me. Before I knew it, I couldn't live without the drugs, and I didn't know what to do about it. I know that I became out of control, but I don't remember much about my actions during that time."

Caroline sat quietly listening to Olivia's story. It surprised her that Olivia was being so candid about her addiction, but she was careful not to let it show on her face.

Olivia took another sip of water and continued. "The first month at Angel's Wings was almost unbearable for me, but everyone there kept telling me that I could make it, and that God loved me. I thought that I was being brainwashed at first." She gave a little giggle.

Passion lit up Olivia's face as she explained her story of recovery. "Eventually, I gave in. I kept repeating over and over, 'I know that I'm a sinner saved by grace.' Those simple words got me through a very dark time in my life. After a few months, my mental outlook began to improve."

"The counselors and helpers at Angel's Wings are a remarkable bunch of people," Caroline commented. "I know that they have a genuine love for those in need."

Olivia nodded in agreement. "During my stay at Angel's Wings, I've been able to break my addiction to drugs and begin to heal physically and emotionally. I've also learned healthy ways to cope with stress, but, most importantly, I've learned that it's not a sign of weakness to depend on others from time to time." She shrugged her shoulders. "All in all, it's been a very positive experience. One that I will not soon forget."

Caroline felt compassion stirring in her heart for the child who had grown up much too fast. "Thank you for sharing your story with me, Olivia. I know how much courage it takes to be honest, and I'm humbled by what you've been able to accomplish in your life."

Beginning to see Olivia from a different perspective, Caroline took a moment to mentally apologize for not wanting to hire a recovering addict. Her problems seemed small in comparison. All her obstacles suddenly became like pieces of a complex puzzle. As she picked up each piece, she easily found where it fit. A bigger picture was taking shape right before her eyes. The fog was beginning to dissipate, and she was starting to see a little more clearly.

Caroline and Olivia spent the next thirty minutes talking about her teaching experience, her knowledge of tap and ballet technique, and her salary requirements. They also perused the schedule to see what classes she felt comfortable teaching. To put Olivia's mind at ease, Caroline told her that she would be at the studio the entire month of September. She wanted Olivia to get acclimated to her new surroundings. She also wanted to be available if she needed any help. After taking care of dance business, they came to the topic of housing.

"I know that Miss Roseann talked with you about my coming to live in the cottage at Callahan Manor," Olivia confessed, "but I know that it's a lot to ask of you. I don't want to inconvenience you and your husband." Olivia touched her palms together and placed them over her heart. "Please don't feel obligated to fix up the cottage on my account. I need to be responsible for myself."

"I want you to know that my husband, my mother, my aunt, and I have discussed your situation, and we want to help you."

Tears welled up in Olivia's big blue eyes.

"We know it's not right to hold onto our gifts, and we believe that God brought you to us for a reason."

Olivia jumped up and gave Caroline a big hug. "I don't know what to say but thank you—and thank God for your generosity."

"Welcome to the family," Caroline whispered with a crack in her voice. She was beginning to tear up too. "I know that you have a mother and a father who love you and care about you, but since they aren't local, think of us as your surrogate family."

"Thank you, Caroline. Your family's generosity makes me believe that a new beginning *is* possible for me."

Caroline grabbed two tissues and gave one to Olivia. They dabbed their eyes. Olivia gave Caroline a big contagious smile, and she had no choice but to smile along with her.

"Now, tell me who I need to contact at Angel's Wings to get the ball rolling. With a little luck and a lot of help from above," Caroline pointed heavenward, "we can have the cottage renovations finished by the time you graduate from the program."

She and Olivia spent thirty more minutes ironing out the details of Olivia's new living arrangements. They scheduled to meet again the following week to work on lesson plans.

After Olivia left, Caroline thought about their conversation. She recalled that Olivia had spoken of God but had neglected to mention having a relationship with her Heavenly Father. Regardless of that fact, Caroline felt a divine connection forming between the two of them, and God's irony was crystal clear. By helping each other, they would be helping themselves. But without each other's help, their plans would not succeed.

Maybe that's what Zoe had meant when she'd suggested that Caroline step out of her world and into someone else's. Her wise friend's paradoxical advice had produced a magical transformation within her. Her mind was now clearer, and her heart felt lighter. She had to admit that God's plan surpassed her own. She was even beginning to think that she should be thankful for Roseann's interference. But for now, that would be her little secret.

FIFTEEN

Chandler's Cove Harbor

TO CELEBRATE Caroline's decision to hire Olivia Styles, the Callahan Clan was meeting at the Laughing Gull, the harbor's latest place to see and be seen. Saturday evening, just after 6 p.m., Jason drove into the packed parking lot adjacent to the harbor docks. Spotting an opening at the far end of the lot, he maneuvered the Subaru into a narrow parking space. Not the best spot on the lot, but they were happy to get it.

Wearing the latest in Florida summer fashion, the trio exited the vehicle and trekked to the restaurant. The muggy evening air clung to them like Spanish moss on a bald cypress.

Entering the restaurant, Jason gave the hostess his name and the headcount for dinner, while Caroline did a visual inspection of the restaurant's interior design. Nautical-themed pictures covered the wood-planked walls, and fishing paraphernalia hung from the ceiling. The lighting was dim.

Scanning the crowded lobby, Caroline spotted Roseann, Flo, and Walt coming through the door. Walt saw her and waved. The threesome weaved through the jammed sitting area and joined the others.

Still somewhat miffed with Roseann, Caroline had promised herself that she would be on her best behavior for her mother's benefit. Be that as it may, the over-analytical part of her couldn't decipher the reason for her mother-centered negativity. She knew that, sooner or later, the two of them needed to clear the air.

"Hi, everyone," Roseann greeted as the group gathered together to wait for a table.

"Evening, ladies," Jason responded. "Good to see you, Walt." The two men shook hands.

"Is Evan joining us for dinner?" Roseann questioned.

"Evan's having a jam session with his buddies," Caroline replied, "but he promised to meet us at the boardwalk later."

Aunt Flo gave the group the once over. "Look at all your Florida tans. Everyone's tanned but me," she said, pouting. "I look like the Pillsbury dough girl. What should I do about it, Walt?"

"I'm off work tomorrow," Walt said. "How about I take you to the beach?"

"I'd like that, but Sis and I are going fabric shopping tomorrow." Flo looked like someone had popped her favorite balloon.

Walt frowned. "I understand if you're busy. We can do it another time."

Roseann intervened. "Flonnie, we can do that on Monday. You should get to the beach before the summer's gone."

Flo opened her mouth to object, but Roseann held up her hand. "I don't want to hear another word about it. You two go have fun tomorrow."

"So, it's a date then, Florence?" Walt asked.

"You talked me into it," Flo said, blushing.

At that moment, "Callahan—party of six" reverberated from the overhead speaker. The group followed the hostess to their table and took their seats, taking a moment to admire the glorious sunset over Chandler's Cove Harbor. Picking up their menus, they began scanning the selections.

A waitress appeared with two loaves of brown bread, while a second server filled the water glasses. After hearing the chef's specials, the hungry group chose one of the many variations of fresh gulf shrimp. Within minutes, the waitress brought the salads, and Jason sliced bread for everyone. The group thanked God for the food and dug in.

After a sufficient wait, the waitress reappeared with their food, and the group enjoyed lively conversation as they ate. When they'd finished the entrees, the waitress strolled back to the table pushing the dessert cart. They decided to share a few pieces of homemade Key lime pie.

Upon paying the check, the group left the restaurant and strolled down to the boardwalk. The Chandler's Cove Seafood Festival was in full force, and the crowd was as thick as the fog that had begun to roll in. The Beach Channel had forecasted rain for tonight or early tomorrow morning. Regardless, everyone decided to take their chances and brave the elements.

Roseann, Flo, and Walt found three empty seats near the exit. They hurried over and sat down to wait for the fireworks display to begin. As she looked for seats, Caroline spied a clown sculpting objects out of balloons. Further down, a jester entertained the crowd by juggling balls of bouncing light. Food and souvenir carts were selling popcorn, cotton candy, snow-cones, and glow sticks. Max pointed to a neon glowing stand and pulled Jason in the direction of the shiny gadgets.

Caroline recognized a familiar fisherman setting up a podium down by the fishing boats. The captain of *Roy's Toy* was no stranger to the Callahan Clan. The family had taken one of Captain Roy's dolphin cruises after moving to Chandler's Cove. Since the captain headed up the harbor coalition, he oversaw the seafood festival's annual charity fundraiser.

The flamboyant mariner was a comical character, but he always organized a successful fundraiser. This year, he'd chosen a pirate theme. The gift shops on the boardwalk had donated items for the evening treasure chest raffle. The coalition had been selling gold doubloons all week, and each numbered coin sold for twenty dollars. Pirates, dressed in their finest regalia, were currently wandering through the crowd selling the last of the raffle coins. Before the fireworks display, the treasure chests would be awarded to three lucky winners.

Caroline had scheduled to meet Zoe, Sergio, and Isabella on the boardwalk, so that their families could view the fireworks together. Caroline scanned her surroundings looking for any sign of her three amigos. Spotting Sergio's muscular six-foot frame, she waved her arms in the air, hoping to attract his attention. Sergio caught sight of her through the masses and pointed to a just-vacated bench a few feet away. He dashed over to the bench and sat down, followed by Zoe and Isabella.

Caroline bumped her way through the crowd and sat down next to Zoe, greeting her friend with a hug. Calypso music played over the loudspeakers making it hard to hear. "Hey, y'all," she yelled over the din.

Sergio stood up and strode over to Caroline's seat. "*Buenas noches,* Carolina," he said, kissing the back of Caroline's hand. "How nice to see you again." He flashed an infectious smile that showed off his straight white teeth.

A first generation Latino American, Sergio's father grew up in Mexico and his mother came from Spain. With blue-black hair, smoldering brown eyes, and bronze skin, Sergio was the epitome of tall, dark, and handsome.

After a few minutes, Max appeared, his arms laden with goodies and a balloon animal on his head. He sat down next to Isabella and handed her a glow stick and a bag of popcorn, keeping a glow stick and a bag of cotton candy for himself.

Jason popped up from behind a family of six and greeted Sergio.

Sergio removed his new Canon EOS camera from its case and began discussing its features with Jason.

"That's a fine camera you have there, Sergio. Very nice indeed," Jason said, sounding somewhat envious.

"I thought I'd take some shots of the festivities," Sergio explained. "Perhaps a couple will be good enough for the newspaper."

"With that camera, you can't miss," Jason assured him.

The pre-firework activities were due to start, and Caroline had yet to find Evan and Dave. She searched the crowd and found them down by the fishing boats talking to Captain Roy. All three stood near the podium that had been set up for the evening's announcements. Three gigantic beach-themed treasure chests sat on a table next to the podium.

Evan looked up, saw his mother in the crowd, and waved. As Caroline waved back, she spied activity on the docks behind the podium. Two fishermen conversed with a third man who stood on the aft deck of one of the fishing boats. The dim lighting on the docks hid the man's face in the shadows. As he stepped off the boat onto the dock, Caroline noticed a Greek fisherman's cap on his head. She attempted to point the man out to Zoe, but before she could get the chance, he was gone.

Was that the same man from the square? Caroline couldn't be sure. Curiosity crept into her imagination. Since she didn't believe in coincidences, she thought it might be interesting to check out the name of the boat after the fireworks.

"Looks like the show is about to begin," Zoe stated, rousing Caroline from her thoughts.

Mayor Barfield approached the podium strutting like a political peacock in a red-banded straw hat, a polo shirt with a big American flag on it, and navy-blue leisure slacks. Patriotism oozed from his pores.

"Good evening, and welcome to the tenth annual Chandler's Cove Seafood Festival Fireworks Spectacular," Don Barfield's authoritative voice boomed over the loud speaker. "Before the light show begins, I would like to report that the Chandler's Cove Harbor Coalition sold a total of 300 coins for this year's fundraising event. The money raised tonight will help support the local food pantry and homeless shelter."

As the audience clapped and cheered in response to the mayor's announcement, Caroline thought it odd that an affluent beach town would have a need for such things. The sad fact of the matter was poverty knew no boundaries.

The mayor continued his speech. "Now, I would like to announce the three winning numbers for the treasure chest give-away."

Captain Roy handed the drawing box to Mayor Barfield, and he began shaking up the numbers. Plunging his hand down into the box, he pulled out the first number. He cleared his throat and announced, "The first winner is number fifty-seven." Caroline looked at her coin. She had number two hundred.

A middle-aged man in a Dale Earnhardt, Jr. T-shirt and baseball cap shouted, "That's my number." He ran up to the podium waving his gold coin in the air. Captain Roy verified the first winner's number, handed him a treasure chest, and instructed him to stand in front of the gift table.

The mayor, then, pulled out the next number. "The second winner is number two hundred one."

"Darn—so close," Caroline repined.

"Close only counts in horseshoes, darling," Jason kidded.

"Don't rub it in," she grumbled.

"I won" echoed through the crowd as a petite girl with spiky fluorescent pink hair made her way to the podium. She flashed her coin, grabbed her treasure chest, and took her place next to winner number one.

"Only one winning number remains," announced the mayor with a grin. He reached into the box and pulled out the third number. "If your coin has the number eight on it, you're the third and final winner this evening." The crowd quieted down, and everyone looked around to see who possessed the winning number. "Number eight," Mayor Barfield repeated.

"I've got it! I'm number eight," a familiar voice squealed. Caroline's eyes searched the crowd as Aunt Flo jumped up from her seat. She displayed her winning coin for all to see, then sashayed to the podium, her brightly-colored muumuu glowing in the darkening night. Captain Roy handed out the last chest, and Flo joined the other two winners.

"Ladies and gentlemen," Mayor Barfield broadcasted. "Let us give a round of applause to tonight's winners of the treasure chest give-away."

Always ready for an opportunity to show off his town, the mayor positioned the three winners in front of the podium for a photo shoot. This spot on the docks sported a perfect view of the Koke Island Lighthouse in the distance. As flashbulbs began snapping on and off like fireflies, Sergio made his way to the winning trio and began taking photos of Mayor Barfield and the winners with their chests full of pirate booty.

"There's Barry Chapman down by the docks," Jason said, pointing in the direction of the fishing boats. "We need to discuss the status of the electrical permit. I'll go see if I can catch him." He took off before Caroline could respond.

Eager to congratulate her aunt, Caroline made her way to Flo's seat. She and Walt began discussing whether the rain would come in tonight or hold off until the morning, while Roseann chatted with her summer neighbor, Sheila Downing. After several minutes, Flo returned toting her treasure chest and wearing a big smile. Caroline stood up to let her aunt sit down.

Flo plopped down and began fingering through her chest of beach essentials. "Look at all this stuff," she raved, her face beaming. "It'll come in handy at the beach."

Walt leaned his head in toward Flo's. "Now there's no excuse for that pasty complexion, Cupcake." He chuckled. "You can start working on your tan tomorrow."

A rosy hue spread over Flo's cheeks in response to Walt's affectionate term of endearment.

Caroline slid up behind Flo and rested her hands on her aunt's shoulders. "Congratulations," she spoke in her ear. "You got lucky number eight."

Flo gave her niece a questioning look. "Isn't it the number seven that's supposed to be lucky?"

"In the Bible, the number eight represents a new beginning," Caroline told her, "and it's no coincidence that you received that number tonight." She squeezed her aunt's shoulders. "A new beginning is definitely in your future."

Flo cast a searching gaze into the darkness. "Who would have thought that a new beginning would be possible at my age?"

Walt patted Flo's knee. "You're never too old to start something new."

"Well, if I'm going to begin again, I'm going to do it with a bang," Flo avowed. As she spoke those words, a big explosion of color lit the night sky. It appeared that the "powers that be" agreed with her.

Caroline hurried back to her seat and scooted up next to Jason as the fireworks showcase commenced over the harbor. For the next twenty minutes, non-stop flashes of blue, white, purple, green, red, and gold twinkling lights cascaded down from above. Oohs and aahs echoed from the docks, adding to the excitement. As the light show ended, dozens of rockets simultaneously burst in a blaze of brilliance.

Watching the last of the bright lights fading into the night, the crowd began cheering in appreciation. The fireworks display was always a huge hit, and the town never tired of its beauty and grandeur. This honored tradition reminded everyone that summer would soon end, and that fall was right around the corner.

Caroline placed her hand in Jason's. "Did you speak with Barry Chapman?"

Jason pressed his lips to her ear, sending a tingling sensation down her neck. "I lost him in the crowd. I'll try to catch him in the morning."

The crowd began to thin out, nudging the lovebirds back to reality. Caroline's cell phone vibrated in her pocket, and she pulled it out to read the text message. Evan would be home after dropping off Dave. Sergio promised Caroline that he would send her the photos he'd taken of Flo and the festivities. Saying good-bye to their friends, the group parted ways.

Over by the exit, Caroline spotted Roseann, Flo, and Walt among the throng of people attempting to leave. She guided Jason and Max to the other exit at the far end of the boardwalk, omitting her real reason for wanting to traverse the docks. A streak of lightning lit up the sky, swiftly followed by a crack of thunder. They picked up their pace.

Reaching their destination, the trio hustled down the dock ramp and turned left. Charter fishing boats sat side by side, resting in their slips. The fifth boat on the right was Caroline's objective.

As they approached the boat, a faint glow emanated from its cabin. Drawing closer, Caroline squinted her eyes to read the name scrawled on the stern—*C.C. Princess. Interesting.* Those were her initials. She filed the name away and made a mental note to research the boat later.

Passing the *C.C. Princess*, Caroline glimpsed a shadow moving about in the cabin. Could it be the man that had piqued her curiosity? Another flash of lightning and peel of thunder caused them to increase their speed. Caroline took one last look at the boat. The cabin was now dark, but no one exited. She thought it odd that someone would want to remain on board with a summer storm brewing.

The threesome made their way through the crowd and arrived at the SUV as the first drops of rain began to fall. They jumped in and braved the bumper-to-bumper traffic filing out of the parking lot. On the drive home, Caroline shut her eyes and thought about the week ahead. A few more days of freedom before returning to school days and dance classes. She also had to train a new teaching assistant and figure out if returning to college was in her best interest. So why was she thinking about the man in the Greek fisherman's cap?

SIXTEEN

Sunday Morning, Chandler's Cove Harbor

DODGING puddles of muddy water and broken tree branches, Nathan maneuvered his F-150 down the slippery streets and made his way to the docks. The overnight storm had departed, but the evidence of its ferociousness still lingered. Peering through the windshield, he watched the morning sunrise play hide and seek with fluffy nimbus clouds, wondering if the rain would soon return. Finally arriving at the docks, Nathan reversed the truck's long bed into its allotted parking space. Shutting off the engine, he removed his keys and opened the heavy door. He eased his left foot onto the gravel pavement, feeling a twinge in his hip. Hobbling down the dock ramp, he passed the harbor coalition office, noticing movement by the window. *Roy must have been up before the roosters this morning*, he thought.

As he approached the *Princess,* Nathan was relieved to see that she hadn't sustained any damage from the heavy wind and rain. He stepped onto the slick deck and headed to the door. His feline friend sat guarding the entrance.

Nathan bent down and scratched the elusive tabby's head. "Good morning, kitty cat. What have you been up to?" The cat meowed. Nathan unlocked the cabin door, opened it, and stepped over the threshold. The tabby rushed inside and pranced to the galley. "What's your hurry?" he asked the tiny tiger. The cat did not reply.

Shutting the door behind them, Nathan hung his Greek fisherman's cap on a nearby peg and placed his keys on the small triangular coffee table by the couch. He strode to the galley and flipped on the light. The cat sat by the fridge looking up at him.

Nathan grinned. "Hungry again, I see." He opened the compact fridge and took out a bottle of iced coffee for himself and a can of tuna for his guest. He popped the top off the tuna can, scooped the contents onto a paper plate, and placed it on the floor. The cat dug in.

Nathan slid into the bench seat at the built-in dinette table and took a gulp of the iced coffee. What had he been thinking last night? He shouldn't have let Roy talk him into staying for the fireworks. Out of the hundreds of people on the boardwalk, what were the odds that he'd have a near-miss with Caroline?

The fat cat finished the tuna and licked its lips. It sauntered over to Nathan, jumped into his lap, and began licking his hand. "You're welcome," Nathan said, stroking the cat's smooth fur.

Hearing a knock on the door, he looked up to see Roy's face in the window. The tabby jumped down and pussyfooted across the cabin. Nathan ambled to the door and opened it. The cat rushed out and brushed up against Roy's leg.

Roy looked down at the friendly feline. "Have yeh been botherin' Nate?"

The tabby meowed and jumped onto the dock, swishing its tail as it strutted away.

Roy entered the salon sporting rainbow-colored Bermuda shorts and a purple T-shirt with the message "What happens on the boat, stays on the boat" written across the front. "Top of the mornin' ta yeh," he greeted. "Tiger's harmless, by the way."

Nathan smiled. "I think I've made a new furry friend."

"That yeh have, my boy," Roy boomed, slapping Nathan on the back.

"You sure are chipper this morning," Nathan noted. "I saw a light on in the coalition office. After your busy night, I didn't expect to see you up so early."

"What can I say?" Roy crowed. "I *do* love the sunrise."

"Come in and have a seat." Nathan walked back to the galley. "Can I get you something to drink?"

"I'll have what you're havin'."

Nathan grabbed another iced coffee from the fridge and retrieved his from the table. He handed a bottle to Roy and joined him on the L-shaped couch.

"Yeh goin' out on the water today?" Roy asked.

"Probably not. I just came to check on the *Princess*. A couple of my usual fishing spots are closed today."

"This bein' the peak of the tourist season, business should be boomin'." Roy heaved a sigh. "But with the bad publicity from the oil rig fiasco, it's a wonder that anyone is comin' ta the gulf coast this summer."

"My friend, Jim Pritchett, is coming down next weekend for the fishing rodeo," Nathan informed. "I hope the turnout is good this year."

"Me too. Maybe then we can recoup our losses." Roy took a swig of his coffee. "Wish they'd tell us more 'bout the oil spill though. I reckon we'll know somethin' soon."

"I'm keeping my fingers crossed," Nathan stated, crossing his fingers. "I need a bit of luck from this lucky little fishing village."

"We make our own luck, brother," Roy clarified. He leaned back and looked skyward. "It's all a state of mind, yeh know."

The two men sat pondering that thought for a moment. Indeed, the old-timer was full of surprises, and Nathan never knew what his friend would say next.

Nathan rubbed his bloodshot eyes and yawned.

Roy studied Nathan's worn countenance. "Why didn't yeh sleep in this mornin'? Yeh look plum tuckered out."

Nathan rubbed his stubbly chin. "Truthfully, I haven't been sleeping well lately."

"Why's that?"

"I keep having this crazy dream. I can't figure out what it means." Nathan took another sip of the cold beverage.

"Yeah—I know what yeh mean. I sometimes dream that I'm the ringmaster at a three-ring circus. A bunch of circus clowns drive a tiny car into the ring. They pile out and start runnin' all over the place. An' here I am, chasin' 'em with my whip. Darndest thing."

Nathan visualized Roy chasing clowns. "That's easy to figure out," he said with a grin. "We fishermen are the clowns, and it's your job to make us toe the line." Nathan didn't know much about Captain Roy, but he *did* know one thing. His friend had a big heart and a genuine love for the wayward bunch of seafaring vagabonds who called Chandler's Cove home.

Roy stroked his beard. "Yeh might be right," he said with conviction, "but I love every minute of it. Now what's your dream about?"

"Nothing funny, that's for sure." Nathan's expression became grim. "In my dream, I'm wandering in the night, lost in a fog. I come upon a deep, dark pit in the ground. There's a gooey red substance oozing out from its center. It heads straight for me and covers my feet like glue. A sudden thunderous boom throws me off balance, and I begin to fall in the pit. That's when I wake up."

Captain Roy's sea-green eyes sparkled. "Boy, that's a deep one," he razzed.

Nathan gave a big belly laugh. "One thing's for certain, Roy. A man can't feel sorry for himself when you're around."

"So true, so true." Roy laughed along with his mate. "Seriously though. Yeh know that dreams are the windows ta the soul." He furrowed his brow. "Yeh need ta look in that window an' see what it all means."

"Maybe one day, Roy, but for now, I need to keep from falling in that hole."

"Speak it to the universe," Roy instructed. "Can't happen otherwise."

Nathan gave Roy a muzzy stare. Changing the subject, he asked, "So, how did you make out with the fundraiser?"

"Quite the success, indeed," Roy boasted. "We raised six thousand dollars for the food pantry an' homeless shelter."

"Congratulations, buddy. I'm impressed." Nathan gave a smile. "Do you always fare so well?"

"Pretty much. The harbor coalition sponsors the food pantry every year, but this is the first time sponsorin' the homeless shelter." Roy shrugged. "I'm a good salesman, if I do say so myself."

"Nothing wrong with tooting your own horn, partner." Nathan chuckled. "If you got it, you got it."

Sadness registered in Roy's kind eyes. "I've been ta that shelter, Nate." He slowly shook his head. "Frightened women with bruises an' broken bones totin' two or three little ones no higher than your knee. It's a dangerous world, brother."

Nathan was touched by the old sailor's compassion. "It's a scary prospect, that's for sure. But you're doing a great thing. You brought the community together for a worthwhile cause." He drank the last of his coffee and placed the empty bottle on the coffee table.

"I wish it coulda been more," Roy admitted. "Six thousand dollars don't go as far as it used ta."

"It's a great start, but you need to find a way to keep the momentum going." Nathan had never been much of a motivational speaker, but he hoped that Captain Roy understood his intent.

"Spoken like a true humanitarian." Roy gave Nathan a questioning look. "Don't suppose yeh'd consider headin' up the next fundraiser, now would yeh?"

Nathan backpedaled. "Well—I don't know about that. You're the cock of the roost around town, Roy. I don't have the connections you do, not to mention the charisma."

Roy leaned forward in his seat and looked Nathan straight in the eyes. "Yeh would if yeh'd put yourself out there a little more. Don't yeh think it's high time yeh stopped hidin' on your boat an' started makin' a few more friends?"

Tension tightened Nathan's face. He touched his fingertips together and looked down at the floor. Both men were silent for what seemed like an eternity. Finally, Nathan cleared his throat and spoke. "You don't know how much I would love to do that, Roy, but the situation is complicated." He rested his head on the couch and closed his eyes.

Giving Nathan time to process his feelings, Roy rose and picked up the empty coffee bottles. He went to the galley and threw them in the trash, then re-joined Nathan on the couch.

Nathan lifted his head and looked at his friend. "There have been so many times that I wanted to tell you the real reason I came to Chandler's Cove, but I was afraid." His face began to soften. "This place is the best thing that's happened to me in a very long time. I hope that, one day soon, I'll be able to share my story with you. But for now, it must remain a secret."

Nathan expected his friend to argue the point, but that did not happen. Captain Roy placed his hand on Nathan's shoulder and spoke, "All in due time, brother. Yeh can count on me ta have your back—no questions asked."

Nathan couldn't believe his ears. No relationship had been unconditional since his uncle died. People always wanted something from him. Be a good boy. Make good grades. Get a stable job. Be conventional. Settle down. Never once had anyone said, "be yourself."

At that moment, the heavy weight that had been hanging around

Nathan's heart began to lighten. He yearned to blurt out the whole awful mess so that Roy would finally understand, but he knew that the safety of his family depended on his keeping silent for a while longer. Before confessions were in order, Nathan had to know for sure that the Outer Banks incident had been resolved. What he needed now was answers. He wished that his cop friend, Stan, would call with an update.

After a long pause, Nathan spoke. "Your friendship means the world to me, Roy. I hope I never take advantage of it."

"Not possible, Nate. I see yeh for who yeh want ta be, an' I don't believe you'll disappoint me."

Nathan wished he had as much faith in himself as the wise sea captain had in him. In a short time, Roy had become a trusted friend. This thought made Nathan think of his friend, Jim, and the happy reunion he hoped they would share this weekend.

The sudden onset of flashing lights and screaming sirens bombarded the boardwalk, interrupting the men's conversation.

"What's going on out there," Nathan said, as he craned his neck to see outside.

Roy cocked his head. "Can't be good."

Both men made a beeline for the aft deck, hoping to get a better look. The lights and sirens drew closer, distracting boat captains and crew members from their morning duties. Amid the commotion, Nathan spotted Captain Mac from the *Destiny* running down the dock ramp.

"What's going on, Mac?" Nathan yelled.

"There's a dead body on the docks," Mac shouted back, averting his gaze. "The police have taped off the area. I got to find my crew." He took off in the direction of his boat.

Panic registered on Nathan's face. It can't be. Not another dead body?

Noticing his friend's distress, Captain Roy placed his hand on Nathan's shoulder. "No need ta panic. It's probably an accident. Bein' near the water and all—it's an occupational hazard."

Nathan took in a deep breath and exhaled. A familiar cloud of doom overtook him. His face turned pale, and his right eyelid began to twitch.

Roy turned Nathan around. "Looks like yeh need somethin' stronger than coffee. Let's go back inside." He led Nathan into the cabin. "Let's see what yeh have."

The room spun. Weak-kneed, Nathan plopped down on the couch and lowered his head. Roy rummaged through the cabinets until he found a bottle of brandy. He poured Nathan a small glass of the amber liquid and placed it in his friend's shaky hands.

"Here—drink this. It'll calm your nerves."

Nathan obeyed, sipping the brandy. Roy sat down beside his friend, instructing him to take slow, deep breaths.

Get a hold of yourself, man. You're not in the Outer Banks—you're in Chandler's Cove...

Nathan kept running this mantra through his head until his pulse slowed down, and his heart stopped twisting inside his chest. After a few minutes, he relaxed.

Captain Roy scuttled to the door and opened it a crack. "I reckon I should go see what the ruckus is all about. Are yeh goin' ta be okay without me?"

Nathan wasn't sure, but he knew he wasn't going anywhere near the boardwalk. "You go ahead. I'll be okay." A sense of déjà vu enveloped him. "The police might want to question you about the festival activities last night."

Roy gave Nathan a wary look. "No need ta worry 'bout that right now."

Nathan couldn't seem to think straight. His thoughts were jumbled up in his brain. He attempted to stand, but his legs felt like two columns of molten lead.

"Sit and drink your brandy—an' don't leave the boat till I get back." Roy's tone was commanding. "Shan't be too long. I'll bring back news."

News of the incident was the last thing Nathan wanted to hear right now. "Aye, Aye, Captain," Nathan conceded.

Roy left the boat and breezed down the docks.

Nathan staggered to the door, locked it, and fell back on the couch. "What am I going to do now?" he moaned. The terror was starting again, and he felt powerless to control it.

SEVENTEEN

NATHAN PACED the cabin floor anxiously awaiting Captain Roy's return. At his wits end, he plodded to the galley and poured himself another brandy. A pain shot through his hip as he sat at the dinette table.

Deciding, instead, to head downstairs, Nathan hobbled down the short steps to the staterooms. Passing two stacked bunks on the right and the guest stateroom on the left, he entered the master stateroom, placed his drink on the built-in nightstand, and turned on the wall lamp. Picking up the TV remote, he eased his tall frame onto the double bed, attempting to get comfortable. He shifted onto his good hip and began massaging the bad one.

Beginning to feel some relief from the pain, Nathan turned on the wall-mounted TV and scanned the channels in search of the local news. He stopped as he recognized Brenda King from WCOV standing to the right of a long strip of yellow and black crime scene tape. She held a wireless mic in one hand, while brushing long platinum blonde hair from her face with the other. Her cameraman panned out to give the viewers a visual of the area. Nathan caught sight of familiar surroundings and turned up the volume to hear what the field reporter had to say.

"We are waiting to hear from the detective in charge of the investigation," Brenda King said in a smooth, throaty voice. "What we know, so far, is that local police and rescue units were dispatched to the East End Marina at Chandler's Cove Harbor just before 7:30 this morning. There is some indication of foul play, but we have yet to determine the exact reason for the 9-1-1 call. Excuse me, sir—"

The cameraman shifted his focus to the right as a bow-legged man dressed in loud Bermuda shorts and a purple T-shirt drew near. The image of Captain Roy appeared on the TV screen.

Brenda King sidled up next to Roy. "Could you tell us your name, sir?"

Roy stared at the camera. "My name's Roy Armstrong. I'm captain of *Roy's Toy* an' head of the Chandler's Cove Harbor Coalition."

"Is your boat docked at the East End Marina, Mr. Armstrong?"

"Yes ma'am. On the far side over there." Captain Roy indicated the location of his boat. "Can't get ta it though."

"Could you estimate how many boats are docked at the marina?" the reporter asked, displaying curiosity.

"The fishin' fleet averages around fifty, and there's ten sightseein' party boats. That's on the east side. The West End Marina is over by the lighthouse. It's mainly transient slips, so the number varies there."

Still fishing for information, Ms. King inquired, "Captain, do you know what happened on the docks?"

Captain Roy looked upward and frowned. He began stroking his beard. "Can't rightly say. I was chattin' with my pal this mornin' when we heard the sirens." He pointed to Nathan's boat. "We came out ta look an' saw boat captains an' crews runnin' all over the place. Bein' head of the harbor coalition, I thought it best ta see what all the commotion's about."

A worried look spread over the reporter's pretty face. "I imagine you and your friend have cause for concern. Is he also a boat owner?"

"Yes ma'am. He owns a charter fishin' boat. The *C.C. Princess*."

Distracted, Brenda King looked over Captain Roy's shoulder. "It appears that a police official may be ready to give a statement. Thank-you for your time Mr. Armstrong." The determined reporter turned her focus back to the crime scene, and Captain Roy stepped away from the camera.

"Confound it, Roy!" Nathan shouted at the TV. "Now the reporters will be knocking at my door." He sat up in bed and took a swig of his brandy. With shaking hands, he attempted to set the glass back down, but it fell off the edge of the nightstand and crashed onto the floor.

Nathan swore as he slid off the bed and began picking up pieces of broken glass. Stepping into the head, he threw the sharp objects in the waste can and grabbed a towel off the rack. He wiped up the spilled liquid and any residual glass fragments and tossed the towel into the trash, as well.

Limping back into the bedroom, Nathan sat on the end of the bed. He closed his tired eyes, wondering if the situation could get any worse. Brenda King's sultry voice brought his attention back to the TV.

A lanky man wearing faded jeans, a green polo, and a handgun on his hip crossed over the crime scene tape and strode in the direction of the news crew. His shoulder-length pale blond hair was pulled back in a ponytail, and he sported a soul patch on his chin. As he attempted to pass, Brenda King blocked his path. Ponytail's piercing eyes shot daggers at the diligent reporter, but she was not deterred.

She shoved the mic in Ponytail's face. "Brenda King with the WCOV news team. Could you give us an update regarding the incident on the docks?"

Noticing the camera, Ponytail pasted a fake smile on his face.

"The chief of police will be issuing a statement soon," he tersely replied.

"And your name is?" she pressed.

"I'm Detective Ronald Lobo."

The reporter gave Lobo the once-over. "Do you work with the CCPD, Detective?"

"No. I work in Pensacola. I'm on temporary assignment with the Chandler's Cove Special Crimes Unit."

She nodded. "What is the Special Crimes Unit? Can you describe it for our viewers?"

Glancing toward the crime scene, Lobo responded. "The SCU is a newly formed unit that works in tandem with the Chandler's Cove Police Department. It investigates drug and gang-related crimes, as well as, murders and kidnappings."

"I see," Brenda King acknowledged. Like a dog with a bone, she continued her interrogation of the busy detective. "So why was the SCU called in on this case?"

"I'm not at liberty to say, but the chief of police may be able to answer that question shortly." A man with golden-brown skin, wavy, jet black hair, deep-set brown eyes, and a Roman nose approached Lobo. He was stylishly clad in a vibrant blue polo that emphasized his bulging biceps and tight-fitting tan chinos. His service weapon was also holstered on his hip.

Brenda King's eyes lit up, enjoying the view. She gave Mr. GQ a seductive smile and shoved the mic in his face. "Do you have any news for us—um…Detective?"

The cop clenched his square jaw and hesitated before answering. "We're still investigating the scene, ma'am."

Brenda batted her eyelashes a time or two. "And your name is?"

"I'm Detective Kale Kalani with the Special Crimes Unit." Shifting his gaze toward Lobo, he addressed the senior detective. "You're needed at the crime scene, sir." The two men did an about-face and headed back to work.

Nathan put the TV on mute. Confusing thoughts twirled around in his head like acrobats on a trapeze. *No news is good news*, he thought. But in his gut, Nathan knew that, once again, bad news had reared its ugly head. Panic-stricken, the overwhelming urge to flee returned. But where would he go?

Nathan liked his new life in Chandler's Cove. He had a good friend that he could depend on, and no way was he going to leave Caroline again. Nathan didn't want to run from happiness anymore. Not when he was so close to getting his family back.

Positive thoughts of Caroline began to push their way up from the massive mound of negativity in Nathan's brain. His daughter sure had looked pretty in her polka-dotted sundress last night. No matter what happened in the future, Nathan was determined to keep that image of innocence in his mind. As he relaxed, he heard a rapping at the door.

Nathan stood up and turned off the TV, carefully putting a little weight on his arthritic leg. The pain had lessened—most likely due to the alcohol. He lumbered up the steps and crossed the cabin floor. To his relief, Captain Roy stood at the door. Nathan unlocked the door, let Roy in, and locked it back again. He sat down on the couch and stretched out his throbbing hip. "What did you find out, Roy?"

Roy joined Nathan on the couch. "It's a mad house out there, sure as shootin'," he groused. "Yeh can't get near the crime scene, an' the cops ain't sayin' zip."

"I know—I saw you on the TV just now." Nathan grinned through gritted teeth. "You're a regular celebrity."

Roy looked across the room at the blank TV. "Why'd yeh turn it off?"

"I was watching the TV in my sleeping berth." He reached for the TV remote on the coffee table and winced. "Needed to lie down for a bit."

"What's ailin' yeh?"

"My bad hip's flaring up again." Nathan turned on the TV, and both men resumed watching the action unfold.

Don Barfield stood next to Brenda King with a professional look on his face. Ms. King addressed the mayor. "Mayor Barfield, the word on the docks is that there has been an unconfirmed shooting on the boardwalk. Can you comment on that?"

Mayor Barfield leaned into the mic. "As you well know, Brenda, Chandler's Cove prides itself as a safe place to live, work, and play." The mayor cleared his throat. "I can assure you that this recent incident is an isolated event. The SCU is on the case, and a suspect will be apprehended posthaste." The mayor rocked back on his heels, puffing out his chest.

"Mayor, when will the police chief be giving a statement?"

"Chief Mitchell is still gathering information, but he should be able to give a brief statement within the hour."

"Thank you for the update, Mayor." Brenda King looked back into the camera. Her expression was nonplussed. "For those of you who are just joining us, I am live with the mayor of Chandler's Cove, Don Barfield. We are on the scene of an apparent overnight shooting at the East End Marina. Police and rescue units were dispatched to the docks this morning and have been on the scene for the past hour and a half. Local police, along with the state Special Crimes Unit, are investigating. We are standing by for an official statement from the chief of police."

Nathan looked at Captain Roy with raised eyebrows. "A shooting?"

"Well, I'll be darned. Thought for sure it was an accident." Roy scratched his head. "Can't remember the last time such a thing's happened here."

A knot began to form in the pit of Nathan's stomach. *So much for being positive,* he thought. He rubbed his jaw. "The police will be wanting to question all the boat owners, I suppose."

The words and sounds from the TV began mixing together. Nathan tuned out the babble and tried to recall what time he'd left the docks. It had to have been after 10 p.m. He remembered waiting a good thirty minutes after he saw Caroline pass by the *Princess*. As shocked as he was at their near run-in, he had been even more surprised when he saw her taking a close look at the boat. He wondered what *that* was all about.

"Earth ta Nathan," Captain Roy echoed.

Nathan snapped out of his daydream. "Sorry, Roy."

"Yeh been actin' mighty strange lately."

Muting the TV, Nathan replied, "I was thinking about what time I left the docks last night. My best guess is that it was close to 10:15. How about you?"

"T'was pretty near eleven o'clock when I got the podium an' tables put away an' the boardwalk tidied up a bit. Yeh woulda passed me on your way out. Funny thing though. Don't remember seein' yeh leave." Captain Roy leveled a keen eye on Nathan.

"You don't think that *I* had anything to do with the shooting, do you?" A look of astonishment shown on Nathan's face. "Man, I don't even own a gun."

"Enough with the negative waves, Nate. I ain't accusin' yeh of anything. Just concerned, that's all."

"I'm sorry for jumping down your throat, buddy. I'm a little on edge." Nathan's expression softened, and he drew quiet for a moment.

Captain Roy shrugged. "Well—it's neither here nor there till we find out what time the shootin' took place."

"And *where* the shooting occurred," Nathan added. "I wish that police chief would hurry up and tell us something."

Captain Roy looked back at the TV. A commotion appeared on the screen and he pointed to it. "Look, there's the police chief now. Let's hear what he has ta say."

Nathan un-muted the TV. The WCOV cameraman zoomed in for a close-up of the podium that had been set up on the boardwalk. Both men watched as Chief Beau Mitchell stepped up to the microphone. Nathan recognized the ponytailed detective standing behind the chief, to his right.

Chief Mitchell introduced himself and began his statement. "At

7:25 a.m. this morning, a 9-1-1 call came in reporting a lifeless body floating in the water next to a dock piling at the East End Marina. The call was placed by a fisherman from the docks. Police and rescue units were dispatched, and they arrived just after 7:30."

The chief looked at his notes. "The body is that of a dark-skinned male with dark brown hair. He is of medium height and build and appears to have been in his mid to late 20's. The decedent was wearing blue jeans and a white T-shirt when he was discovered. No identification was found on his person. A preliminary examination of the victim revealed a gunshot wound to the chest. The body is presently being transported to the Koke County morgue for a full autopsy."

Detective Ponytail stepped forward and spoke in Chief Mitchell's ear. The chief continued. "If anyone has information regarding a missing person fitting this description or any information relevant to this case, please contact Detective Ronald Lobo with the Special Crimes Unit. He can be reached at the Chandler's Cove Police Department. Most importantly, the taped off area is an active crime scene and the CSI's are still collecting evidence, so please do not cross it. Thank you and have a safe day."

Chief Mitchell stepped down from the podium and walked in the direction of the crime scene, skillfully avoiding any questions from the media. The WCOV cameraman got a shot of a covered stretcher being wheeled up to a waiting ambulance. Nathan placed the TV back on mute and looked away.

"Blast it all!" Captain Roy exclaimed. "Bad mojo's swarmin' like bees. Not a good sign." He looked wide-eyed. "What yeh think's gonna happen next?"

Nathan sat up and began rubbing the back of his neck. "God only knows, Roy. I wonder if this is an isolated incident like the mayor says. Or if this is the beginning of something bigger?"

"Time will tell." Roy nodded. "Time will tell."

Nathan's face looked grim. "I guess they won't know time of death until they finish the autopsy."

Captain Roy gave Nathan a shrewd look. "Sounds like you're talkin' from experience."

Roy's sixth sense was coming too close for comfort. Nathan hated to deceive his friend, but now was not the time for such a conversation. He forced himself to make eye contact.

"I must be watching too many crime shows on TV," Nathan countered, trying not to sound too guilty. "Sooner or later the cops will be asking everyone what time they left the docks. I can't imagine that I was here when the shooting went down. If so, I think I would have seen or heard *something*."

Roy stroked his beard. "It coulda happened durin' the fireworks an' no one woulda heard it," he considered. "Don't think it was before eleven o'clock though, so it seems like we're in the clear, as they say."

Nathan's hip began to throb again. He shifted into a more comfortable position. "Do you think the detective with the Special Crimes Unit is in charge of the investigation?"

"Could be. What was the fella's name?"

"Lobo, I believe. Should we find him and tell him what time we left the docks last night?" *Please say no.*

Captain Roy shook his head. "Don't want ta borrow trouble. Maybe we should wait an' go ta the police station tomorrow mornin'. Got a dolphin tour this afternoon. Hope I don't have ta cancel it." He stood up to leave.

Nathan pushed himself up from the couch. "The last thing we need is for this fiasco to scare off what tourists we *do* have. I've got a group from Macon scheduled for Tuesday morning. I hope they don't back out."

Roy strode to the door. "Don't fret, Nate. Things have a way of workin' out. You'll see." He gave a wink.

Nathan followed his friend. "Thanks for the pep talk today, buddy. One of these days I'm going to repay the kindness."

"Ain't keepin' score, brother." Roy slapped Nathan on the back and stepped outside. "Call yeh *manana*," he boomed over his shoulder. "We'll go ta the station together."

Nathan locked the door behind Roy and shuffled down to the sleeping berth. He turned off the bedside light and forced himself back up the stairs. With each step, Nathan's legs seemed to be slowly sinking into a mire of fear and confusion. As he reached the top landing, the small cabin began to spin, and white orbs appeared before his eyes. A tornado of deadly images began swirling around Nathan's head, sucking the air from his lungs and knocking him off-kilter. Struggling to breathe, he tottered to the dinette table and fell into the bench seat. His head dropped into his folded arms as the room descended into blackness.

EIGHTEEN

BANG, bang, bang. Nathan stirred in his seat. *Oh, no—the shooter's back!* *Bang, bang, bang.* Louder this time. *Is someone shooting at the boat?*

His arms shielding his face, Nathan raised his head and glanced toward the door. Brenda King stood outside banging on the small glass window. Relieved, Nathan exhaled and rose from the bench. *What am I going to say to her?*

Still somewhat dizzy and stiff from pain, Nathan limped to the door and opened it a crack. Before he could respond, the tenacious reporter placed a pointed-toe stiletto in the opening. "Excuse me sir, do you have a moment for a few questions?"

Nathan shot her a drop-dead look. "I don't have anything to say. You need to leave."

Brenda King did not budge. Over her shoulder, Nathan noticed the cameraman's handheld camcorder trained on him.

Nathan placed a bent arm over his face. "Shut that camera off now," he shouted, "and no recordings. I'll give you one minute, and then you need to get off my boat."

Brenda King passed a well-manicured index finger across her

throat, and the cameraman lowered the camcorder. Nathan opened the door a little wider, but did not let her in.

"Thank you, Captain—?"

Nathan did not offer his name.

Unaffected, Ms. King pressed on. "Captain Roy Armstrong said that you were here this morning when the body was found on the docks. Have the police interviewed you about the incident?"

"I haven't talked to the police, and I don't know anything about what happened on the docks. That's all I have to say." Nathan began to shut the door.

The seasoned reporter was not about to leave without a tidbit of information for her viewers. "Sir, surely the horrendous incident on the docks has you concerned for your safety and the safety of your guests. What do you and the other boat owners plan to do about this recent turn of events?"

"That's not for me to decide. I'm sure the police will handle it." Nathan kept inching the door closed.

"One more question, please." Brenda King shook bleached blonde bangs out of her eyes. "How do you think this will affect the present sluggish economy in Chandler's Cove?"

Nathan heard footsteps on the dock and looked up to see Captain Roy several feet away frantically waving his arms in the air. The reporter looked over her shoulder. Detective Lobo and his stylish sidekick, Detective Kalani, were making their way toward the *Princess*. The cameraman aimed the camcorder in their direction.

"Ms. King, you'll have to leave now," Lobo advised. "This is police business, and we can't have you hindering our investigation."

Detective Kalani stepped in front of the cameraman and pushed the camera down.

Deciding to go after bigger fish, the reporter addressed Lobo. "Have there been any new developments regarding the shooting on the docks, Detective?"

"Chief Mitchell will be issuing a news release tomorrow," Lobo informed. "You're welcome to go to the station in the morning for the briefing. Until further notice, please refrain from interviewing potential witnesses."

Brenda King motioned for the cameraman to follow her as she sashayed off the boat, seeking other prey.

Captain Roy hovered at the edge of the boat. Nathan waved for him to come aboard.

The detectives approached Nathan and flashed their gold shields. "Are you Captain Nathan Beall?" Lobo asked, flashing a smile that did not reach his eyes.

"Yes, I am," Nathan warily replied.

"Sir, my name is Detective Ronald Lobo," he announced, clearing his throat. "I'm with the Special Crimes Unit, and this is Detective Kale Kalani." He glanced in Kalani's direction. "May we come in and ask you a few questions?"

"I guess that would be okay, but I want Captain Armstrong to be present in case you have any questions related to harbor coalition procedures."

"I suppose so," Lobo huffed.

Nathan opened the door, and the three men entered the salon. Detective Kalani stood slightly shorter than Nathan and Roy's six-foot height, while Detective Lobo was a head taller than the trio.

Nathan strode to the couch, and Captain Roy joined him. They glued their eyes on the detectives. "Have a seat, gentlemen," Nathan offered.

Lobo and Kalani slid onto the tan leather cushions of the dinette table's bench seat. Lobo reached into his back pants pocket and pulled out a pack of gum. He took out a stick, unwrapped it, and popped it in his mouth. He wadded up the paper and shoved it in his pocket. "Would anyone like a piece of gum?" he asked, holding out the pack.

Everyone declined. Lobo replaced the pack of gum. "Some men can't help their habits," he said with a mischievous grin. Something about the senior detective's demeanor rubbed Nathan the wrong way, but he couldn't put his finger on it.

Kalani retrieved his notepad, and Lobo began the questioning. "Captain Beall, we understand that you were here on the docks last night and again this morning. Is this information correct?"

Nathan glanced at his friend, then looked back at Lobo. *Thanks, Roy.*

"Yes, that's correct," Nathan affirmed. "I returned from a charter trip around 5:30 and stayed at the docks to watch the fireworks."

Kalani sat taking notes, while Lobo threw Nathan another question. "I understand that the fireworks were spectacular. Is this your first time enjoying the festivities in Chandler's Cove?"

"No. I was here for the 4th of July fireworks, as well."

"So, your boat has been docked at the East End Marina since July of this year?"

Lobo's stone-faced stare was beginning to worry Nathan. Nervousness crept into his voice. "No. I've been in Chandler's Cove since February. Captain Armstrong can verify that."

"Yeh bet I can vouch for Captain Beall, Detectives," Roy interjected, aware of the tension in the room. "Nathan's a respected member of the harbor coalition. No complaints from anyone. Got an A-number-1 reputation. Yessiree."

Kalani tapped his pen on the notepad. "Thank-you, Captain Armstrong. Captain Beall's reputation is not in question here. We're just trying to determine how long he has been residing in Chandler's Cove."

"Got the paperwork in the office. I can show yeh. No trouble a' tall." Captain Roy attempted to rise.

"That won't be necessary at present," Lobo told him, not taking his eyes off Nathan. "So, we have clarified that you were on the docks Saturday night. What time did you leave?"

Nathan tried to clear his dry throat. "I believe it was just after 10 p.m. I waited for the crowds to thin out before trying to leave. Probably about thirty minutes after the fireworks ended."

Kalani addressed Nathan. "I see. Did you notice any strange activity on the docks when you left?"

"Captain Armstrong and I were discussing this earlier. It had been a long day and I was tired. I locked up the boat and headed to my truck. I didn't see anyone on the docks, but there were a few families still milling around on the boardwalk."

"Of course. Getting to this morning," Lobo cut in, "what time did you arrive on the docks?" His expression did not waver.

Nathan's palms were beginning to sweat. He wiped them on his jeans. "It must have been around 7 a.m. Just after sunrise."

Roy sensed Nathan's discomfort. "Yep—that's right. I came ta talk ta Nate right after he got here this mornin'."

Kalani looked up from his notetaking and leveled his gaze on Nathan. "Did you see anything out of the ordinary when you arrived?"

Nathan thought for a moment. "No…there weren't many people here yet. I believe last night's storm delayed most boat owners. The roads were pretty hard to travel." Nathan's eyebrows shot up. "I *did* notice Captain Mac Nelson running down the docks after the police cars arrived. He's the owner of the *Destiny* a few slips down."

"Was Captain Nelson on the docks the night of the seafood festival?" Lobo queried.

Nathan shook his head in the negative. "I don't know, but I did notice a light on in his cabin."

"Can't rightly say," Captain Roy inserted. "Didn't see him, but I was busy handin' out treasure chests."

Lobo and Kalani gave the two men a puzzled look.

Nathan grinned. "Captain Armstrong was in charge of the seafood festival raffle and activities."

"I know about the raffle," Lobo returned impatiently.

"I see," said Kalani, shaking his head. "How well do either of you know Captain Nelson?"

"Not very well," Nathan answered.

"Chap keeps ta himself mostly," Captain Roy added.

"We'll be speaking with the other boat owners in the next few days," Lobo said, standing.

Kalani closed his notepad and joined Lobo. "Thank-you for your cooperation Captain Beall."

Lobo shot Nathan a swift icy glare, then smiled broadly. "Let's hope we don't have to trouble you again."

Nathan involuntarily shuttered as if he had been hit with a cold blast. Confused, he rose from the couch.

Roy stood up with Nathan. "I'm headed back ta the office," he stated. "Do yeh need ta see any documents?"

"We got all the information we needed when we questioned you earlier," Lobo remarked. "We'll contact you if we have any further questions." Both detectives marched to the door and abruptly left.

Captain Roy shrugged. "Well—I guess we don't have ta go ta the station now." He looked at Nathan. "Are yeh okay? Yeh look like somethin' Tiger dragged in."

Nathan knew that he couldn't hold out on his friend any longer. "You got some time later today?"

"I got time now. My dolphin cruise got cancelled by the CCPD. *Roy's Toy* is behind the yellow tape." Roy went to the galley and pulled two bottles of water out of the fridge.

"This is a nightmare," Nathan moaned. He sat back down on the couch and propped his foot on the coffee table. Boy, his hip hurt.

Roy re-joined Nathan on the couch and handed him a bottle of water.

"Thanks, man. I hope you're not in a hurry." Nathan opened the bottle and chugged the cool beverage. "Because after you hear my story, you're bound to have questions."

Roy's eyes grew big. "Bad news, brother?"

"I'm afraid it's worse than bad. I think it might be downright dangerous."

NINETEEN

Monday, Callahan Manor

IT WAS A BRIGHT, sunny morning, and all was quiet on the home front. Jason had risen early to meet with a contractor to discuss the cottage renovations before heading to Barry Chapman's. Evan was working at The Jiffy Java, and Max was spending the day with Lucy Ledbetter's son, Sam. Lucy and the boys were venturing to the LEGO store in Fort Watson for an afternoon of brick building.

Still in lounging pajamas and slippers, Caroline scuffed to the kitchen and popped a Dunkin Donuts K-cup in the Keurig. Sliding a mug under the spout, she added a heaping spoonful of caramel creamer and pressed the brew button. As the coffee brewed, she peeked into the backyard and spied Terra and Windy sitting by the door. Grabbing two chew bones from the pantry, she let the dogs in. The precious pair snagged their treats and headed to the sunroom. They plopped down on their rugs and started chewing.

Caroline palmed her steaming mug of coffee and followed the dogs into the sunroom. Placing the mug on the coffee table, she sat down at one end of the love seat and propped her feet up on the other. Her ancient laptop sat on the table taunting her. She picked it up, connected to the Internet, and googled Chandler's Cove deep-sea fishing charters. The harbor coalition website popped up. She opened it.

Colorful images of sleek boats gliding across crystal waves filled the screen. Caroline scanned the website's headings, finding links to the West End and East End Marinas. She clicked on East End Marina and scrolled down the page.

After gleaning through several images, a sleek, white vessel caught her eye. There it was—the *C. C. Princess*. Caroline clicked on the image, reading the boat's specifications, but the captain's name was not there. "Who is the captain of the *C. C. Princess*?" she spoke into the silence.

Terra and Windy stopped chewing their bones and cocked their pointy-eared heads at their master.

"I'm talking to myself again, girls. Chew your bones."

They concurred and resumed with their treat feast.

Continuing her search, Caroline googled *C. C. Princess,* but no other web addresses appeared. The man in the Greek fisherman's cap remained a mystery.

No problem. Caroline had grown up with some of the best sleuths in the business: Nancy Drew, Sherlock Holmes, and Miss Jane Marple. If her literary friends could solve a mystery, then so could she. But right now, she had more pressing issues to attend to, like getting the dance classes ready to start next week.

Caroline powered down the laptop and placed it on the coffee table, glancing at the bird clock on the wall. She and Olivia Styles were due to meet at Leap of Faith in an hour, and she didn't want to keep her new employee waiting.

Jumping up from the love seat, Caroline bent down and scratched the corgis on the head, leaving them to their own devices. Her well-trained girls would finish their bones and then take a nap in their crates.

Rushing up the stairs, Caroline took a quick shower, towel dried her hair, and styled it with a dollop of mousse. Then, she slipped on a pair of black jazz pants and a dance T-shirt, checking her reflection in the mirror. Sun-kissed rosy cheeks looked back at her. No makeup needed. She brushed her teeth and applied shimmering pink lip gloss to her lips, then checked the time on the bedside clock. Right on schedule.

Caroline rushed back down the stairs and hustled to the mudroom. Securing the corgis in their crates, she went to the kitchen, grabbed her keys, cell phone, and purse, and rushed out the door. Since Callahan Manor was located on the outskirts of town, the drive to the square would take roughly fifteen minutes. She zipped to the dancing school, remembering to slow down at the speed trap right outside the town limits.

Not finding an empty space in front of Leap of Faith, Caroline parked in front of the Best Ever Bakery. Sliding out of the SUV, the aroma of vanilla and sugar surrounded her. *Yum.* She glanced at the list of daily cupcake specials hanging in the store window. They'd baked her favorite—Black Forest. She made a mental note to swing by and pick up a box of four to take home. Glancing across the square, she spied Olivia parking her canary yellow VW Beetle.

Caroline entered Leap of Faith, turned on the lights, and sat down in her comfy desk chair. She dug into her basket of dance shoes and pulled out her low-heeled black and white taps and a pair of stretchy socks. She slipped off her Crocs and began putting on her socks. The door chime jingled, and a bright ray of sunshine bounced into the office wearing a big smile on its bonny face.

"Hi," Olivia said, plopping down in the middle of the office floor.

"Hey, bright eyes. How are you today?" Caroline answered, tying her tap shoes.

Olivia opened her Capezio dance bag and looked inside. "I'm doing a little better every day. Thanks for asking." She pulled out a pair of tan taps with two-inch heels, along with a notepad and a pen for note-taking. "My tap technique's a little rusty." She began strapping on her shoes. "It's been a while, you know."

Caroline smiled. "No problem. It's like riding a bike. Once you learn, you never forget."

Gathering their necessities, they marched down the hall and entered the smaller of the two dance rooms. This room had a raised wooden floor, perfect for executing steps and differentiating tap sounds.

Olivia meandered to the back of the room, scanning her surroundings. She viewed the various pictures of dancers that hung over a long dance barre mounted on the wall. Her eyes rested on a poster of a rain-drenched Gene Kelly swinging on a street lamppost. The caption at the bottom read: "Life is not about waiting for the storm to pass, it's about learning to dance in the rain."

A far-off expression spread over Olivia's face. "I feel like I've done a lot of dancing in the rain lately." She sighed. "It's been worth it, but sometimes I don't recognize the *new* me."

Caroline came up beside Olivia. "Much of life is about working hard and overcoming adversity, but God has promised to always be with us." She fell silent, leaving Olivia to reflect on that thought. After a few moments, Caroline spoke. "Well—I don't know about the *old* Olivia, but I think the new and improved version is great."

Olivia's smile returned, illuminating the room. "Thanks, Miss Caroline. I appreciate your encouragement. You've offered me a new beginning, and I hope that I don't let you down."

"When I'm in doubt, I remember what God promised his people in Jeremiah twenty-nine: eleven. 'For I know the plans I have for you, declares the Lord, plans to prosper you and not to harm you, plans to give you hope and a future.'" Caroline patted Olivia's shoulder. "It's going to work out just fine. You'll see."

Caroline clicked across the dance floor, making her way to the sound system. A CD player and rack of dance CDs sat on a wall shelf in the far corner of the room. "Which grade of Al Gilbert technique would you like to start with?"

Olivia shuffled in Caroline's direction. "Grade Two would be good. I used Grade One at my previous teaching job."

Caroline pulled out the Grade Two CD, placed it in the player, and put the system on pause. "Grade Two builds on the foundation of Grade One," she informed. "For the most part, you'll be using Grades One and Two with the classes I've scheduled for you. I hope you don't mind teaching the younger kids."

"That sounds great," Olivia exclaimed. "I can't wait to get started!"

Caroline looked for any hesitation in Olivia's manner, but the girl remained steadfast in her conviction. She wondered how much credit went to Roseann and the recovery program at Angel's Wings, or whether it was God beginning to shine through Olivia's cracks. Whatever the reason, her assistant's new persona fit her like a comfortable ballet slipper.

"That's good to hear, because I know the kids are going to adore you."

That much, Caroline knew to be true. She also knew from experience that teaching young children could be a challenge. She hoped that Olivia was mature enough to handle teaching dance technique, choreographing routines, maintaining discipline, and satisfying persnickety parents. Practically speaking, she needed to fill the teaching position. So, for now, she'd have to give her protégé the benefit of the doubt.

"All right then," Caroline stated. "Let's jump in with both feet." She did a shuffle-jump-toe and threw her arms out front.

Olivia looked at Caroline and giggled. "You've got to be a little goofy when you work with kids."

"So true, sister." Caroline gave Olivia a high-five. "But on the plus side, it keeps one young at heart."

"You go, girl." Olivia snapped her fingers and waved her hand in the air.

Caroline pulled the dance notes from her choreography notebook and bopped Olivia lightly over the head with them. "Let's get to work."

Olivia drew to attention. "Yes ma'am." She gave her boss a salute.

Getting down to business, the twosome spent the next hour going over tap technique and outlining a typical class. As they tapped along with Al, their feet blocked out all other sound.

Noticing movement out of the corner of her eye, Caroline turned to see Zoe standing in the doorway dressed in a red satin number from Ralph Lauren. She gave her friend a wave and paused the sound system. "Hey there, glamor girl," she greeted as she and Olivia walked to the door.

Zoe wore a worried look on her face. "I hope I'm not interrupting, but this is the first break I've gotten in two days."

"Did you work yesterday?" Caroline questioned, knowing that Zoe usually reserved Sunday for God and family.

Zoe looked at Caroline and Olivia like they had purple polka-dots all over their faces. "Unfortunately, yes. Have you not heard?"

Caroline looked at Olivia. Olivia shrugged. She looked back at Zoe. "I was off the grid yesterday. Jason and I went shopping for glass door knobs after church. We didn't even watch T.V. What's happened?"

"I've just come from a news conference at the CCPD. A shooting occurred at the docks Saturday night. The body of a young man was found floating in the water at East End Marina Sunday morning. The police are calling it a homicide, and it's been a madhouse there ever since."

Caroline gasped.

Olivia's eyes looked like they were going to pop out of their sockets. She stared at Zoe in disbelief.

Caroline's gut did a spin. "Oh…my…Lord," she stammered. "Is it anyone we know?"

As Zoe kicked into reporter mode, she regained her composure.

"Thankfully no, but its little comfort knowing that someone has lost a life."

Curiosity rode roughshod over Caroline's better judgement and blended with her building apprehension. "Do the police know the victim's identity?" she asked.

Zoe leaned against the door jamb. "The police are not releasing any information right now. They know his identity, but wouldn't give me anything else."

Olivia's brow furrowed. "I wonder why he was here in Chandler's Cove."

Zoe fingered the turquoise eagle hanging around her neck. "There's no indication as to how long the victim had been in the states or why he was in Chandler's Cove, for that matter. Maybe the autopsy report will shed some light."

Confusing thoughts played badminton in Caroline's brain. She mentally reviewed what Zoe had said. A young man, not old. It was unlikely that the dead man was the man in the Greek fisherman's cap. She exhaled, realizing that she'd been holding her breath. Both ladies gave her a quizzical look.

"So—I guess he wasn't a local," Caroline surmised. "That's a relief."

Zoe gave her friend a stern scowl. "Who did you think it was going to be?"

Caroline knew that now was not the time to divulge her recent covert sleuthing activities. "Um...I...how would I know?" she stuttered. "It's just that we were at the docks Saturday night. And to think that a murderer could have been lurking about is frightening, that's all."

"Oh boy, that's *too* scary," Olivia breathed in a hushed tone.

Zoe grunted. "Caroline, what's in that curious red head of yours?"

"Nothing," she said, wide-eyed.

Zoe's eyes narrowed to slits. "Why don't I believe you?"

"I know what you're going to say. Curiosity killed Caroline—I mean *the cat*."

Zoe shook a red-tipped finger at Caroline. "Don't let those 'gut' feelings of yours get you into trouble," she warned. "I've got enough work to do without having to make sure you stay safe."

Caroline placed her hand over her heart. "I'll be on my best behavior. I promise."

Olivia stared at the two ladies like they were speaking a foreign language.

Caroline quickly changed the subject. "Where are my manners? Zoe, meet my new teaching assistant, Olivia Styles. Olivia, this is the editor of *The Village Times-Herald*, Zoe Castillo."

Zoe held out her hand. "How do you do?"

"Nice to meet you." Olivia shook Zoe's hand.

"Zoe's daughter, Isabella, is one of my best dancers," Caroline told Olivia. She looked at Zoe. "Maybe Isabella would like to assist Olivia with the preschool class?"

"I know that she'd love that. I'll see if—" Zoe's purse buzzed. Distracted, she retrieved her cell phone and read the text message. "I've got to get back to the paper. I'll call you tomorrow, Caroline." She gave a quick smile. "Good luck with your new job, Olivia." Waving over her shoulder, she breezed down the hall and out the door.

Olivia began massaging her temples with her fingertips. "Jeepers! What a day." She looked over at her new boss. "Are you okay, Miss Caroline? You seem upset by the news of the killing."

"I'll admit it's shocking. Nothing like this has happened since I've been in Chandler's Cove." Caroline's face darkened. "It's out of the ordinary, for sure."

Worry shaded Olivia's pretty face. "I agree. I hope the police find the killer soon. I don't know if I want to go to the boardwalk until this mess is cleared up."

Caroline walked over to the sound system and shut off the CD player. "It may sound trite, but we have to trust that God is in control." She headed back to Olivia.

Olivia linked her arm in Caroline's. "Miss Roseann has a great faith in God, too. I'm lucky to have both of you in my corner."

The pair walked arm in arm back to the office, took off their tap shoes, and gathered their belongings. They did not discuss the murder any further.

Caroline secured the studio for the night, remembering that she still needed to get cupcakes for dessert. Not wanting Olivia to walk across the square by herself, she invited her assistant to go to the bakery with her. Caroline bought five cupcakes and gave Olivia one to take home. Then, being overly protective, she drove Olivia to her car and watched as the young girl drove away.

As Caroline drove home, she revisited the events of the day, marveling at how quickly she and Olivia had bonded—almost like mother and daughter. Her brain abruptly shifted gears, remembering the murder on the docks. A vision of the man in the Greek fisherman's cap appeared in her mind's eye, and her pulse quickened. Who was her mystery man?

TWENTY

AS THE SUN set over Chandler's Cove Harbor, Nathan hosed the remnants of the day's catch off the aft deck of the *C.C. Princess.* The forensic team had completed their evidence gathering, and the charter fishing boats had been given the green light to go out on the water again. Nathan's group of six from Macon had arrived at the early hour of 7 a.m. for an 8 o'clock departure. They'd fished Nathan's usual spot thirty miles off-shore, which produced a bounty of Grouper, Amberjack, and Yellowfin Tuna. The distinct smell of fish still lingered in the air.

Nathan observed Captain Mac Nelson of the *Destiny* easing his 38-foot Hatteras into its slip. *What a strange fellow*, Nathan thought. Most of the captains on the docks were friendly with one another, but Mac usually kept to himself. Even so, Captain Mac seemed to always be around. He was either the hardest working captain on the docks, or he didn't have anything better to do.

Truth be told, Nathan had also been logging extra hours on the docks lately. The Chandler's Cove Annual Fishing Rodeo was set to begin Thursday night and would run through Labor Day. Fishing enthusiasts from all over the country would soon descend on the renowned fishing spot to try their luck at catching the biggest fish. Excited anticipation permeated the docks as fellow boat captains geared up for the event.

Reeling in his hose, Nathan scanned the dock for any sign of his new feline friend, but Tiger was nowhere in sight. Disappointed, he entered the cabin and crossed the room to the galley. Grabbing a cold beer from the fridge, he headed back to the salon, sat down on the couch, and chugged the calming brew.

Finishing the beer, he set the empty can on the coffee table and searched for the TV remote. Not spotting it on the table, he felt between the couch cushions, coming up empty. He hefted himself off the couch, ambled to the dinette table, and searched between the bench seat cushions.

On the far side, his fingers touched something hard and round. He pulled it out, switching on the wall light above the table to get a closer look. It resembled the gold doubloons that Captain Roy had used for the harbor coalition's raffle. Had the coin fallen out of Roy's pocket during one of his recent visits? Not likely. Roy always sat on the couch, not at the dinette table.

A glimmer of a memory tugged on Nathan's brain. Detectives Lobo and Kalani had occupied that seat when they were aboard the *Princess* on Sunday. Had either of them lost it during the interview? Something about that scenario bothered Nathan, but the reason presently escaped him.

Making his way back to the couch, Nathan spotted the remote on top of the storage cabinet by the door. He went over and picked it up, then returned to the couch. Tossing the gold doubloon on the coffee table, he sank down into the comfortable cushions and propped his feet up on the table. He then turned on the TV and placed it on mute.

As Nathan waited for WCOV to start their nightly news broadcast, his right eye began to twitch. Since the recent incident at the docks, his nerves had returned to high alert. An ominous pall had descended upon his soul, draining his joy. Uncertainty plagued him, and he felt helpless to shake the ever-present sense of impending doom. Could this be payback for his past mistakes?

Nathan thought about Caroline. Hurting her had been the furthest thing from his mind when he abandoned her for, what he thought was, a life of excitement and adventure. In hindsight, he could now see how young and foolish he had been. He regretted not listening to Roseann about taking that weekend out-of-town job. She'd assured him that they didn't need the extra money, but he had ignored her. Ultimately, the week-end affair that he'd developed with a co-worker had been the unforgivable sin.

It was now obvious to Nathan that his actions had produced catastrophic consequences. Roseann had punished him for his mistakes, and he deserved it. Though once he had made his decision, his fate had been sealed. That was when the darkness crept in.

Nathan wished that he could go back in time and undo what he had done. That was not an option, but he *could* move forward. Whatever the cost, he was now ready to own his mistakes. He hoped that it wasn't too late.

Desperate to make sense of the horror that was unfolding around him, Nathan took his mind back to the shooting in the Outer Banks. When he compared both cases, the similarities were uncanny. He made a mental inventory of the details. One—both men fit the same general description. Two—they had been killed with a gunshot wound to the upper body. Three—each murder occurred on a fishing dock in a coastal town.

Was this a coincidence or were the murders somehow connected? A connection seemed preposterous, but the situations were too bizarre for it to be a coincidence. Nathan instinctively knew that a connection was possible, even probable. And if the murders were connected, then what did that mean for his safety and anonymity?

Now that Captain Roy knew what had happened in the Outer

Banks, would he also believe that the two murders were connected? And what was with Roy's sudden suspicion of him? To be fair, Nathan knew that he was the most likely suspect in Roy's eyes, maybe in the police's eyes as well.

On TV, the cops were always looking for means, motive, and opportunity. He had been at ground zero on both occasions, so he had opportunity. Thus, it was feasible that he could have pulled off both shootings.

Frankly, Roy had been acting somewhat suspicious himself. He'd been on the docks the night of the shooting and his boat was docked close to the crime scene. That gave him opportunity. Nathan knew that Roy owned a handgun for protection, so he also had means. But what motive would he have for shooting a man unless it was in self-defense?

Roy denied any involvement in the shooting. And why would his friend kill a man on the docks knowing that the body would be found so close to *Roy's Toy*? Maybe he thought that the tide would carry the body away from the docks, but the storm thwarted his plans.

Nathan heaved a heavy sigh. What was he thinking? He knew that his friend wasn't a cold-blooded killer. But how well did one *really* know another person?

Nathan glanced at the TV on the wall. A close-up of Brenda King came into view. He turned on the volume as the flashy reporter introduced the Director of the Florida Bureau of Investigations, Special Agent Alonzo Prince.

"Agent Prince, I understand that you will be working with the Special Crimes Unit regarding the recent shooting at the harbor," she announced in her best reporter voice.

Agent Prince adjusted his black tie. "That is correct. I will be working with Detective Ronald Lobo and his partner, Detective Kale Kalani."

"Will you be taking the lead on this case, Agent Prince?" she continued.

"Let me begin by saying that this is a complex investigation. Detective Lobo will be the lead on the case, but the two agencies will be working in concert. CCPD Chief Mitchell requested extra resources to investigate and protect the community, but let me clarify that this is a team effort between local and federal partners." Agent Prince glanced to his left and the image of Ronald Lobo popped up on the screen. "I would now like for Detective Lobo to give everyone an update on the case."

Agent Prince stepped aside, and Lobo slid in beside Brenda King. "Detective Lobo, the CCPD rarely works with the FBI. In your opinion, is the department and the SCU equipped to handle an investigation of this size?"

"Thank you, Ms. King," Lobo began. "The CCPD and the SCU are making this case a top priority. As of today, all CCPD officers will be working 12 on and 12 off until we get a break."

The cameraman zoomed in for a close-up of Lobo as Brenda King pressed on. "Has the coroner released the official autopsy report yet, Detective?"

Lobo looked down at the paper in his hands, then continued. "The report was just released and the victim's next of kin has been notified. We can now tell you that the victim's identity is that of Juan Martinez, age 28 of Salento, Columbia. Mr. Martinez's family reports that he had been gone for two weeks, but they were under the impression that he was looking for work in another area of Columbia. They deny knowing that he was in the United States. One unusual aspect of the case is that Mr. Martinez had undergone recent surgery to remove one of his kidneys. It's speculated that this was the reason for the deceased being in the United States. Yet, there is no record of him legally entering the country."

The cameraman panned out giving a visual of Brenda King, Detective Lobo, and Agent Prince. The reporter addressed the special agent. "Agent Prince, do you believe that the victim had ties to a terrorist organization?"

Agent Prince stepped forward and spoke into Brenda King's

mic. "Let me calm everyone's concerns. At present, we've not found any such connection. This case has certain similarities to a shooting on the Outer Banks of North Carolina ten months ago. The FBI has been working on that case and was brought in to consult on this case, as well."

Brenda King glared at Agent Prince. "With a gunshot wound to the chest, this is an obvious case of murder. So, do you believe that the prior shooting in North Carolina and the recent shooting in Chandler's Cove were perpetrated by the same gunman?"

"At present, I cannot confirm or deny that question, but it's a possibility. The Koke County crime lab is currently running a ballistics test on the bullet recovered from Mr. Martinez. We are going to compare it to the bullet recovered from the victim in North Carolina to determine if the same weapon was used in both shootings." Agent Prince looked at the stoic face of Ronald Lobo. "Detective Lobo, do you have anything you would like to add?"

The mic appeared in front of Lobo. "I would like to say that the safety of the entire community is of the utmost importance to us. Law enforcement is utilizing all its resources to find every piece of evidence. We are looking into digital media such as cell phone records and emails, as well as human intelligence which will hopefully lead us to a motive, or other connections. But this takes time. The crime team appreciates your patience, and we ask that if you see anything suspicious, please don't hesitate to call the SCU day or night."

Brenda King thanked the police officials and looked back into the camera. "If anyone has information about either case, please call the number at the bottom of the TV screen. This is the number for the Special Crimes Unit."

As the news program went to a commercial, Nathan placed the TV on mute. What would Stan have to say about the recent development in Chandler's Cove? Surely, he must know about the shooting by now and could shed some light on Nathan's predicament. Regardless, Nathan needed to hear his old friend's voice. He took out his cell phone and dialed Stan's number. The call went to voicemail, so he left a brief message asking Stan to call him back.

Remembering that Jim was due in this weekend for the fishing rodeo, Nathan looked up his number and dialed it. No answer there either. Recalling that it was Jim's usual night to shoot pool with some of his fishing buddies, Nathan left a message and disconnected the call.

Should he call Captain Roy? Negative. Roy had a sunset harbor cruise scheduled tonight. He thought about having another beer and waiting for Roy to return, but he was tired of feeling isolated and alone. What he really wanted to do was try the new coffee shop on the square and not be afraid of being recognized.

Melancholia had invaded Nathan's thoughts and he wondered if this was how it felt to be slowly losing one's mind. "Where's your peaceful place now, Roy?" Nathan screamed into the silence.

Dropping his head back, he closed his eyes, allowing the rhythmic ebb and flow of the ocean's current to relax him. He drifted into a dream-like state, no longer on the *C.C. Princess*. A dense fog now surrounded him, and he couldn't find his way. Navigating through the murky gloom, he stumbled on a rock and fell to the ground.

The fog dissipated, revealing a triple-braided cord that stretched across a bottomless abyss. From the depths of his soul, a small voice called out. Nathan's only way of escape lay on the other side of the tightrope. Ignoring the intense fear growing within him, he stood. Placing one foot onto the thick sinew, he took a step.

A pain shot through Nathan's bad leg, and he bolted upright on the couch. Shaking the daunting dream from his head, he forced himself back to reality. Was he being shown a way out of the darkness?

Grabbing the remote and empty beer can, Nathan shut off the TV and made his way to the galley. He threw the can in the trash and turned off the light. Darkness had descended upon the harbor and the dim lights from the docks guided his way to the cabin door.

Picking up his cap and keys, he exited the *Princess* and stepped into the desolate night.

Hearing footsteps on the wooden planks, Nathan turned in the direction of the sound. A shadowy figure wearing dark shades and a ball cap stalked up the ramp. Unable to discern the person's identity, Nathan stood still in his tracks, waiting for the stranger to leave. Alone again, he made his way to his F-150.

Fog had rolled in, reminding him of his vision of the tightrope in the mist. Taking in a deep breath of sea air, he stepped forward into the night. The brilliant beacon of the Koke Island Lighthouse illuminated his path. Fear began to melt from his mind and, as it exited, it was swallowed up by the light. Baffled by this mysterious feeling, Nathan hoped that his spiritual friend could shed more light on this enigma.

TWENTY-ONE

Wednesday Morning, Sandpiper Shore

CRAVING A MORNING SUNBATH, Roseann had phoned Callahan Manor bright and early, inviting the family to join her at the beach. Jason was at work, but Caroline, Evan, and Max happily agreed. At 9:00 a.m., they piled into Evan's Scion and went to pick up Roseann.

Arriving at the beach pavilion, the group unloaded their beach bags and tromped through the deep sand to the lifeguard station. The lifeguard on duty escorted them to their beach umbrella and arranged the lounge chairs for maximum sun exposure. He chatted with Roseann for a moment before returning to his station.

After everyone applied sunscreen, Evan and Max grabbed their body boards and headed into the surf. Mother and daughter eased into the lounge chairs, making themselves comfortable. Caroline began watching the boys ride the waves, while Roseann closed her eyes and commenced with her habitual sun ritual.

As they sunbathed, Caroline gazed at the expansive emerald sea, absorbing its awesome beauty. She focused on the soothing sound of the roaring surf as it rushed to the shore. The synchronized white-crested waves rolled in and out, creating a sense of calm. She became one with nature, and it began to transform her restless soul. A spring of deep joy formed in the core of Caroline's being and spread through her body, tingling her hands and feet. Tears filled her eyes, and she let them roll down her face. Her spirit cried out, *"Be still and know that I am God."*

She continued watching the boys riding the waves, reflecting on the significance of God's promise. After a while, Evan and Max jumped out of the water and clumped back to the shade of the umbrella. They laid their body boards by the lounge chairs, grabbed their beach towels, and began drying off.

"We're going to get a snack," Evan said. "Want anything?"

"Get a couple of bottles of water for me and Nana, please." Caroline pulled her wallet out of her beach bag and handed Evan some cash, then he and Max headed up the wooden walkway to the pavilion snack bar.

The sound of voices roused Roseann from her repose. "Let's go cool off in the water for a few minutes," she prompted.

"That's a good idea," Caroline agreed, noticing that her fair skin had turned a vibrant shade of pink.

Roseann dug around in her beach bag and pulled out her watch. "It's just after 10 o'clock. We should leave in an hour or so. I have a hair appointment this afternoon."

"That's fine. I'm a lady of leisure today." A carefree smile etched Caroline's face. "It's great not having to rush anywhere or do anything for a change."

Mother and daughter walked to the ocean's edge, stepped in up to their knees, and splashed the cool salt water on their arms and legs. As they grew accustomed to the steady stream of diminishing waves, a tall swell rushed in and hit them square in the chest, splashing water in their faces. They were again reminded of the power and unpredictable nature of the sea.

After several more minutes, they sauntered back to their chairs, meeting Evan and Max coming back from the pavilion. Evan handed each an ice-cold bottle of water. Caroline took a couple of sips to remove the salty taste from her mouth.

Deciding to sit in the shade to dry off, they asked the boys to move their chairs under the umbrella. After repositioning the chairs, the two sea otters snatched up their body boards and headed back out for round two.

Grabbing her beach towel, Caroline wiped the salt water off her face and sat back down. Roseann appeared relaxed and happy, so Caroline thought it would be a good time to ask her what she thought about Aunt Flo and Walt's budding relationship.

"I'm glad that Aunt Flo and Walt seem to be enjoying each other's company," Caroline began, "but since she's going home at the end of the summer…"

Roseann sighed. "I've urged your aunt to go slow with Walt, but I can't tell her what to do." She got that far-off look in her eyes. "Once upon a time, I rushed into a relationship, and look what happened."

Caroline placed her hand over Roseann's. "I know that my biological father hurt you, and I'm thankful that you found Grant, but Aunt Flo has to live her life the way she sees fit. We can't stop her, but we can support her."

"I see the way Flonnie glows every time she talks about Walt, and I suppose I'm a little jealous," Roseann admitted. "But I *do* want my sister to be happy again." She lowered her voice. "I want to be happy again, too."

Caroline gave Roseann's hand a squeeze. "And you will, Mother. God's timing may be unpredictable, but it's always perfect."

"Of that, I have no doubt," Roseann affirmed. "That's what I've been trying to get through your brilliantly smart, but thick head, dear."

"Touché, Mother," Caroline said, letting go of Roseann's hand. "You're a study in contrasts, but your reasoning is amazingly sound."

Caroline swept her gaze across the sea, spotting the boys, then looked back at Roseann. Now that her mother had opened the door to a painful part of their past, she wanted to walk through it. She gauged Roseann's receptiveness to the million-dollar question she was about to ask. Now seemed to be the right time. Gaining confidence, she moved full speed ahead. "Since you brought him up, let's chat about my biological father. Why did he leave?"

Roseann's head snapped in Caroline's direction, a look of surprise on her face. "You don't beat around the bush, do you?"

Caroline shrugged. "I *am* my mother's daughter, after all. And since we're being honest with each other, I thought that now would be as good a time as any." She glanced at the ocean, keeping track of Evan and Max.

Roseann took a lengthy sip of water, then another, finally settling back in her lounge chair. It appeared that this was going to be a long story. Caroline shifted into a more comfortable position and waited. She'd waited her entire life for this story, so a few more minutes wasn't going to make a difference in the outcome.

Roseann cleared her throat. "It was not my intention to be secretive about your father, but I was trying to spare you any unnecessary pain. You were only four years old when the troubles began, and I'm not sure how much you remember about that time."

Caroline confessed that she didn't remember much about her life before age five.

Roseann nodded and continued. "You'd been sick off and on for a year before your fifth birthday, so the January you turned five, you had your tonsils and adenoids removed."

"I remember that," Caroline stated. "After the surgery, my throat burned like it was on fire." She placed her hand over her throat and grimaced. "All I wanted to eat was ice cream."

Roseann grinned. After a brief pause, she resumed her recollections. "Before the surgery, Nathan had an opportunity to work every Saturday at his firm's office in Hilton Head. The manager there was trying to impress his high-dollar clients. Your father was likable and had a solid work ethic, so he was the manager's first choice for the job. Mind you, he would still have to work a 40-hour week in Savannah." She paused to take another sip of water. "Naturally, it concerned me. He already worked long hours and rarely got to spend any quality time with you or me."

Caroline took her mind back in time. "I have to admit that I don't remember much about my relationship with Nathan." Her father's name coming from her lips sounded strange to her ears.

"That's understandable," Roseann replied. "After Nathan took that part-time job, Sunday was the only day he was home." She propped an elbow on the lounge chair's arm and rested her chin on her hand. "Now that I think about it, you and I went to church many Sundays without him, but there were always excuses. Lunch dates with coworkers. Golf dates with clients. Catching up on work at the office. Anything to keep him out of the house."

Caroline sensed agitation growing in her mother's spirit. "How did you cope with a young child all by yourself?" she asked, beginning to see her in a different light.

Roseann's attention shifted to a fishing boat on the horizon. "I did what I had to do, but it didn't feel like coping. You were my sunshine back then, and you still are." Her voice cracked.

Caroline's gaze ping-ponged from the boys playing in the surf, to Roseann, then back to the boys. Guilt crowded her thoughts. "I suppose there's been a few times when I was not the easiest person to get along with." She considered her confession. "Well—maybe more than a few times." She frowned. "I don't know what comes over me sometimes."

Roseann gave a snort. "I do! It's your Irish temper showing. You remember Granny Fi used to call you her little leprechaun."

Caroline gave a big belly laugh. "That she did. I sure could be a troublemaker when the mood struck me."

"Uh-huh. Like when it rained—or when the sun shined—or when it was cloudy…"

"Ouch! That bad, huh?"

Roseann cut her eyes at her daughter and grinned. "You said we were being honest."

"I'm a big girl. I can take it," Caroline admitted. "But enough about me. You inferred that Nathan was a workaholic. What else?"

"Workaholic would not be the correct word to describe Nathan back then. Philanderer is more appropriate." Roseann's expression looked as if she had bitten into an apple and found a worm in it.

Caroline gasped. "You don't mean…?"

"Yes—sadly, I do. He had an affair with a woman that worked in the Hilton Head office." Roseann spat the words out as if she was spitting out the worm.

A mixture of sadness, madness, and disgust hit Caroline all at once. She shook her head trying to make sense of what her mother was telling her. "Is that what broke up the marriage?"

"As soon as I found out about your father's infidelity, I asked him to move out. I was furious with him, and I didn't want my rage to affect you. Maybe that was the wrong thing to do, but he fractured our relationship, Caroline. I was in so much pain that I couldn't forgive him." Roseann's eyes pleaded for her daughter to understand.

Caroline put herself in her mother's shoes and tried to comprehend the predicament she must have been in all those years ago. In doing so, a barrage of questions began attacking her brain, and she desperately wanted to release them. *Was the break-up mutual? What happened after Nathan moved out? What about the woman that led him astray?* But now was not the time for any more questions. She'd forced Roseann to relive a very private, very painful time in her life, and now she needed to back off and give her some space.

"I'm sorry for your pain, Mother. You did what you thought was best for us. I understand that, but what I *don't* understand is why he abandoned me."

Roseann looked down at the sand. "I said some very hurtful things at the time of our break-up, but I've never understood why he chose to leave you." She shifted her gaze back to Caroline.

"What I *can* tell you is that your father stayed in Savannah after we separated. I'm almost positive he kept seeing that woman, but I never asked. Frankly, I didn't want to know. I just needed some time to process what he had done."

The hidden resentment Caroline harbored for her father began rising to the surface, and her anger level began rising along with it. "What kind of man leaves his child and never looks back?"

Roseann's face reddened. "A very irresponsible one! I gave Nathan every opportunity to do the right thing, even to the extent of setting up a weekend visitation schedule with the lawyer. Your father was agreeable to it, at first. He even quit working in Hilton Head, so that he could spend more time with you."

The wind off the water began to increase in intensity. Caroline looked up to see clouds gathering over the horizon. Reaching in her beach bag, she pulled out her cover-up and slipped it on.

Roseann wrapped her beach towel around her shoulders and pressed on. "Everything went smoothly for several months, but then Nathan started making excuses for not coming to get you. Some weekends he would show up and some weekends he wouldn't. There was no rhyme or reason to his actions. This went on for quite a while. When I confronted him about it, he said that he'd found someone else. At that point, I made the decision to get a divorce. Eventually, your father's lackadaisical attitude lost him the right to joint custody. Once the divorce was final, we moved to Atlanta."

Caroline looked into her mind's eye, remembering their move to Atlanta and Aunt Flo giving them a place to live. "I understand why we had to leave Savannah, but I sometimes wonder what might have happened if we had stayed." She crossed her arms over her chest and hugged herself tight. "It was always my childhood fantasy that my father would reunite with us. In the end, it didn't matter because I got my "happily ever after" without him."

"I wish that things could have worked out differently," Roseann confessed, "and sometimes I'm sorry that they didn't." She searched her daughter's face. "After you gave up your dream of becoming a counselor, I thought that your broken relationship with Nathan might be the reason. Was I right?"

Caroline looked down at her feet, burying them in the sand. "I always said that it was because I wanted to be home for my family, but you might be right. Frankly, the thought of turning into my father scares me."

Roseann nodded sagely. "Be that as it may, I believe that we got the life God planned for us all along. It's been a happy one, hasn't it?"

Caroline's eyes filled with tears. "I've had a very happy life, Mother. I wouldn't give back one minute of my time with Daddy. I miss him too, you know." She dabbed her eyes with the end of her beach towel and gave her mother a keen look. "Have you ever thought about what happened to Nathan?"

Roseann looked back at the ocean. "I must admit, there have been times over the years that I wondered where Nathan was or what he was doing." She shrugged. "But my life was filled with so much happiness that I thought it best to let sleeping dogs lie."

"Deep down, that's the way I've always felt, but sometimes my heart is so heavy it's like a part of it has turned to stone." A lump formed in Caroline's throat, and she struggled to speak. "I wish I knew how to make it light again."

"It all begins with your Heavenly Father," Roseann reminded her. "If it's his will for us to see Nathan again, then that is what will happen. The only way to free your heart from this burden is to forgive your earthly father for what he has done."

Confusion creased Caroline's face. "I don't know how to do that, Mother."

"Go to the Lord, Caroline. His love can soften even the hardest of hearts."

"Did you finally forgive Nathan?" Caroline asked, rather baffled.

"It took a while, but your step-father helped me see that I couldn't move forward until I let go of my hurtful past."

Caroline marveled at the strong, yet sensitive woman sitting next to her and silently thanked God for giving her such a wise mother. Looking heavenward, she noticed that the clouds had blown over and that the sun shone high in the sky. She pulled out her cell phone and checked the time.

Scanning the seascape, Caroline found Evan and Max riding the crest of a wave. She stood up and walked toward the shoreline, motioning for them to come over. Water-logged and covered with sand, the boys picked up their body boards and headed in her direction. "It's time to go, guys," she informed them. "Nana has a hair appointment this afternoon."

Reaching the umbrella, the boys dried themselves off with their beach towels and wrapped them around their waists. Caroline and Roseann rolled up their towels and shoved them in their bags. They took one last look around the chairs, making sure they weren't leaving anything behind, then walked to Evan's car. He dropped Roseann off at her condo, then headed back to Callahan Manor.

On the ride home, Caroline mentally replayed her conversation with Roseann. Would she ever be able to forgive Nathan? The task seemed impossible under her own power, but she knew that, with God, all things were possible. She sighed, visualizing the long road ahead. *Baby steps, Caroline. Baby steps.*

TWENTY-TWO

Thursday Late Afternoon, Chandler's Cove Harbor

NATHAN COVERED the two leather helm chairs on the open flybridge of the *C.C. Princess* and peered out over Chandler's Cove Harbor. From his elevated vantage point, he had a perfect view of the boardwalk. Preparations for the annual Chandler's Cove Fishing Rodeo were underway.

Nathan watched as busy boardwalk vendors set up their booths. All would be staying open late, and many were having sidewalk sales. The restaurants would be selling samples of sweet treats, salty snacks, or anything that could be eaten in a cup or on a stick. A newly installed zip-line would be thrilling kids of all ages. Crafts such as sand art, face painting, and Lego building would also be available.

At one end of the boardwalk, a popular swing band would be performing on the main stage, while local D.J., Music Man Dan, would be rockin' and rollin' at the other end. A podium and microphone sat at the center of the activities, and Mayor Barfield would give his usual kick-off speech right after sunset.

A recent shift in the ocean tides had moved the oil spill away from the harbor, so participation in the fishing rodeo would be at a record high. The annual event signaled the close of the summer season in Chandler's Cove, and tourists were already arriving, like schools of fish, to take advantage of a few more days of fun in the sun. After Labor Day, the summer vacationers would travel back to their own corners of the world, giving Chandler's Cove a brief reprieve before the annual migration of the snowbirds.

The late afternoon sun burned bright over the harbor. Nathan pulled a handkerchief from his jeans pocket and dabbed his sweaty face. He shoved the handkerchief back into his pocket and winced. His hip had been bothering him all day. Time to go home and take a load off.

Nathan estimated that he would have just enough time to make his escape before the crowds swooped in. He climbed down the port side ladder that connected the flybridge to the aft deck. Stepping onto the deck, his cell phone began to ring.

Nathan ambled into the cabin and wrestled the phone from his pocket. Stan's name appeared on the caller ID. Excited, Nathan sat down on the couch and pressed the talk button.

"Hi, Stan. I'm glad you called," Nathan spoke into the phone. "I've been wanting to talk to you." He told him about the tragic murder on the docks.

Stan stopped Nathan before he could finish, stating that he was already in the loop. Relieved that his friend was familiar with the case, Nathan questioned him about the possibility of a connection to the murder in the Outer Banks. Stan explained that he couldn't discuss specific details about the case, but he did confirm that the two murders were connected. He explained that ballistics tests on the bullets recovered from both victims pointed to a common police firearm. Thus, they were now looking into the possibility that the shooter worked in law enforcement.

As luck would have it, Stan's department would be collaborating with the CCPD to catch the killer. Stan informed Nathan that he would be making a trip to Chandler's Cove the next day to follow-up on a possible lead. He promised to get together with Nathan before returning to the Outer Banks.

After a lengthy conversation, Nathan disconnected the call. He was looking forward to spending some quality time with his old friend and hoped that the murder investigation would not put a damper on their reunion.

Nathan looked outside. The sun was beginning to set. Scores of attendees were milling about the docks or making their way to the boardwalk. *Darn!* He'd missed his window of opportunity to leave unobserved, but the call from Stan had been more important. *I'll have to stay until the festivities get underway*, he thought.

As Nathan waited, his stomach growled. He glanced at his watch. It read 7:25 p.m. He walked to the galley fridge and looked inside. A can of tuna and a Yuengling variety pack occupied the scant shelves. He grabbed a bottle of Black and Tan and popped the top.

Beer in hand, Nathan sat down at the dinette table, isolating himself from the controlled chaos a few feet away. The solitary galley light illuminated the salon with a dim amber glow. Nathan took a sip of his beer and glanced out the window. The crowds were beginning to thin on the docks, and Nathan figured that he would be able to hear the mayor's welcome announcement from the *Princess*. He hoped to make his get-a-way while everyone enjoyed the festivities.

Nathan closed his eyes and leaned back in his seat. He wouldn't be stuck on the *Princess* right now if it hadn't been for Jim's bad luck. His fishing buddy had planned to dock his boat at the West End Marina today, and Nathan had promised to meet him when he arrived. He'd waited all afternoon for Jim to call, wondering what had happened to his friend. After several hours, Jim finally phoned explaining that his Dodge Ram 3500 had broken down in Southern Alabama. Presently stranded in Andalusia, he hoped to be in Chandler's Cove by Friday evening.

Nathan opened his eyes and glanced at his watch again. Mayor Barfield was 15 minutes late with his speech. He wished the mayor would hurry up and get the show on the road. Standing, he walked into the salon.

Having grown quite familiar with his surroundings over the past several months, Nathan began having the strange sensation that something was off. Uneasiness swept over him and darkened his mood. Becoming antsy, he paced the floor like a caged animal. *Why am I so agitated?*

Nathan peeked out the window again. Shaking off his uneasiness, he analyzed his situation. People were still heading to the boardwalk. The mayor must be waiting for the crowds to settle down before making his announcements. What else could it be? Surely nothing to worry about. Was this how it was going to be for the rest of his life? Always looking over his shoulder? Always anticipating the worst and seeing danger around every corner?

Nathan heaved a heavy sigh. Stan had confirmed his greatest fear about the two murders. Nathan had felt all along that both murders were connected. There were too many similarities for them not to be. Even though he'd been right, Nathan was not happy about the fact that a killer, who could possibly identify him, was roaming around the docks of his new home. He'd fled the Outer Banks to escape possible danger and now that danger had followed him to Chandler's Cove.

What were the odds of something like that happening? If the killer *had* followed him here, then why hadn't he confronted him yet? Furthermore, was the killer playing games with Nathan, or did he not know who was on the docks that deadly October night?

Nathan's head throbbed from thinking about all the possibilities. He sat down on the couch and leaned back, desperate to find a way to rid himself of the dreadful demons that haunted him. He had to hold on a little while longer.

Out of the stillness, a noise from the loud speaker startled him. Mayor Barfield was coming in loud and clear. He jumped up and looked out the window. It was now quite dark on the docks, save for the dim lights that crowned the dock pilings.

Nathan moved his eyes right and left, straining to count the number of people remaining nearby. *Good—only a handful.* He walked to the galley, rinsed out his empty beer bottle, and threw it in the trash. He turned off the galley light and exited the cabin. He stood at the back of the deck and listened to the mayor's speech.

Mayor Barfield cleared his throat and began his long-winded welcome. "Good evening, ladies and gentlemen, boys and girls. My name is Don Barfield, and I am the mayor of Chandler's Cove. I would like to welcome everyone to the 35th Annual Chandler's Cove Fishing Rodeo kick-off festivities. As mayor of this glorious town, I would like to thank all those who have worked long and hard to make this event a success. More importantly, I would like to thank all the visitors who have chosen to spend some of their valuable time with us. I hope that you will think of Chandler's Cove as your home away from home."

The mayor turned to page two of his speech and continued. "Having said that, I would like to quell any fears you may have about the safety of our town and cleanliness of our waters. To begin with, the oil spill in the Gulf of Mexico is currently being treated and has yet to show up in Chandler's Cove. Regarding the recent unfortunate incident on the harbor docks, local, state, and national law enforcement are working around the clock to keep the streets of Chandler's Cove safe and to find the party or parties involved."

Mayor Barfield banged his fist on the podium causing the mic to squeal. "Let me emphasize that there is no need to be afraid to go to the harbor. Fear is our enemy, and we must not let the enemy defeat us. Let me clarify that. As FDR once said, 'the only thing we have to fear is fear itself.'"

"Atta boy, Mayor" rang out from somewhere in the crowd.

Nathan tuned out the mayor's "to fear or not to fear" rhetoric and crept to the edge of the boat. He was about to step onto the dock when he spied four figures walking toward him from the far end. Nathan stepped back into the shadowy darkness. As the quartet drew closer, he could hear spirited conversation mixed with laughter. Caroline's laughter! He slipped back into the dark cabin and eased the door shut.

As the group passed, Caroline shot a searching glance at the *Princess*. Nathan held his breath. Not until his daughter and her family were no longer in sight did he dare to breathe. What was Caroline up to? Had she discovered his identity?

Nathan was not sure what to think, but what he *did* know was that Caroline was getting very close to finding out that her father was in Chandler's Cove. That thought made Nathan's heart skip a beat. Could his daughter be in danger? One consolation, however, was that Roy now knew about Caroline and had vowed to help him keep her out of harm's way. Nathan owed her that much—and so much more.

It was obvious to Nathan that Caroline had a good life and a loving family, and he knew that he had no right to intrude upon that. His daughter was happy, and she was probably better off without him. But how could he know that for sure? What if she might want to know her biological father?

Nathan sat down and pondered the multitude of questions bombarding his brain. After a few more minutes, he decided it was safe to leave. Lost in thought, he opened the cabin door and stepped one foot onto the deck, nearly colliding with his spry friend.

"Evenin', Nate," Captain Roy boomed. "Expected yeh ta be gone for the day."

Nathan's eyes got as big as saucers. He swallowed hard, attempting to push his heart back down into his chest. "Geez, Roy!" Nathan spat out. "You scared the daylights out of me. I thought you were helping the mayor with the kick-off festivities."

Nathan stepped back inside, allowing Roy to enter. The colorful sea captain strutted into the salon with Tiger under one arm. "I'm done for the night," he replied. "I was headin' ta my truck an' saw yeh leavin'. I hope yeh don't mind I brought our furry friend."

Nathan turned on the light by the couch. "Not at all," he said. "Want a beer?"

"No thanks. I'm good. Sorry ta scare yeh, brother." Roy bent down and put the cat on the floor. Spotting a shiny object on the carpet by the coffee table, he reached over and picked it up. "Is this your gold doubloon from the raffle?" he asked Nathan as he sat down on the couch.

Nathan closed the window blinds and joined his friend. "No—mine had a different number on it. I found that one between the cushions of the dinette seat the other day. I thought one of the detectives might have lost it. They were sitting over there during the interview." The tabby jumped into Nathan's lap. He began stroking the cat's soft fur.

Roy pocketed the gold coin. "Don't recollect sellin' them one." He gave Nathan a shrewd stare. "You're keepin' the boat locked up tight when you're gone, I hope. There's a killer roamin' 'round the docks. Don't want nobody wanderin' aboard."

"I've been overly cautious since the shooting," Nathan assured him. "The *Princess* is secure."

"Oh, well. It is what it is, I suppose." Roy shrugged. "Did your buddy from the Outer Banks get settled in over at the West End Marina today?"

Nathan propped his aching leg up on the coffee table. "Jim's having mechanical issues with his new truck and will be delayed a day or so."

"That's too bad," Roy replied, "but it don't make any difference. The *big* fish don't come out till the end of the contest." He gave a hearty laugh.

"You don't say," Nathan said, feeling his body begin to relax. Was it the beer or the positive vibe radiating from his friend?

Captain Roy's eyes scanned the ill-lit room. "What yeh doin' sittin' in the dark?"

Nathan rubbed the back of his neck. "I hadn't planned on being here when the festivities began, but Stan called from the Outer

Banks and I got sidetracked. I figured that Caroline would be here tonight, and I was right." He shook his head, bewildered. "She walked right by the boat again. Do you think she knows something?"

Roy stroked his beard. "How could she, Nate? You've been careful not ta run into her, haven't yeh?"

Nathan put his foot on the floor and the tabby climbed out of his lap. "Probably not as careful as I should be, Roy." The cat circled around and settled in between the two men.

"Now that Caroline is so close, it's like there's an invisible cord connecting the two of us. Wherever she goes, I'm compelled to follow." Nathan furrowed his brow. "That sounds crazy, doesn't it?"

"Makes sense ta me," Roy said matter-of-factly. "You're her father. The two of yeh will always be connected. Can't get away from that."

Nathan felt conflicted. "So, you're saying that Caroline has been feeling the same pain that I've been feeling all these years?"

Roy's smile lit his eyes. "That's exactly what I'm sayin', brother. I do believe you're beginnin' ta see the light."

Nathan smiled back. "I guess I have a good teacher."

"Professor Armstrong at your service." Roy tipped his Panama hat and placed it back on his head. "So—tell me what officer Stan had ta say. Good news, I hope."

Nathan leaned forward, fingers clasped, elbows on his thighs. "Stan is collaborating on the case, but he couldn't share much information. He *did* say that both murders are connected, like I thought. On a high note, he'll be in Chandler's Cove tomorrow. I'd like for you to meet him, if he has the time."

"I'd be honored," Roy said, grinning. "Any friend of Nathan Beall's is a friend of mine."

Nathan's eyebrows shot up. "That's high praise coming from you, buddy. I don't think that I deserve it though."

Roy slapped his thighs. "Yeh need a higher opinion of yourself,

Nate. If yeh *think* you're in the gutter, you'll eventually end up in the gutter."

Nathan smirked. "Did you read that in a fortune cookie?"

"Yeah—got it from that place on the corner of Good Attitude Avenue and Buck Up Boulevard."

Roy and Nathan stared at each other for a moment, then had a good laugh.

Realizing that Mayor Barfield was no longer making announcements over the loud speaker, Nathan stood up and stretched his stiff joints. "I guess it's safe to leave now," he said. "The festivities should be in full swing."

Captain Roy followed suit. The tabby cat jumped off the couch and scampered to the door.

"I'm glad you came by tonight, Roy. I was hesitant to leave by myself."

"Me too, brother," Roy confessed. "There's been a heavy haze in the air since the murder. Can't put my finger on it, but I sense evil lurkin' 'round the docks."

"I know I'll feel safer when Stan gets here," Nathan admitted, turning off the interior light.

Both men joined the tabby at the door and exited the cabin, allowing the faint glow from the dock lights to help them navigate their way off the boat. As they walked up the ramp to their parked vehicles, they were unaware of a figure standing in the shadows, watching their every move.

At the far end of the docks, the killer sat in the dark, smoking a cigarette and contemplating his next move. He had to find out what the captain of the *C.C. Princess* knew. Had he put two and two together yet? Could he identify him?

Captain Beall had finally been alone on his boat tonight. He had hoped to ambush the fisherman when he left the *C.C. Princess*, but his friend had showed up, spoiling the plan.

He stubbed out his cigarette on the wooden dock plank and shook his muddled head. Had anyone seen him at the docks last Saturday night? And what had happened to the gold coin he'd taken from the dead man's pocket? He knew he should have fled the country as soon as the body turned up at the docks, but that didn't really matter now. If he tried to hide, the organization would find him. Their retaliation was never pleasant.

The man shivered—not from the cold, but from fear. There was nowhere to go, and no one to help him. He shook off the fear, knowing what he had to do next.

TWENTY-THREE

Friday Morning, Callahan Manor

EVAN AND MAX ROSE EARLY, ready for a full day of work. Max wanted to earn some spending money, and Roseann and Flo had honored his wishes with a list of chores for him to do. Evan had to work at The Jiffy Java, but he'd offered to drop Max off at Roseann's on the way.

Not as young as they used to be, the Thursday night frolic on the boardwalk had morphed into a Friday morning sleep-in for Caroline and Jason. Unfortunately, Jason's current client, Barry Chapman, had not gotten the memo. Their snooze-fest was cut short by an early morning call from the cantankerous client. According to Jason, Barry had been ultra-uptight for the past few days, and he was demanding some last-minute changes to the garage project ASAP.

After their unexpected wake-up call, they'd jumped out of bed and began their day. Since time was of the essence, Caroline let Jason have first dibs on the shower. Her company dancers would be performing a routine from their spring dance recital on Sunday, and she had an afternoon rehearsal at Leap of Faith.

In his haste to get to the job site, Jason had forgotten one of his tool bags. He called, catching Caroline as she was leaving Callahan Manor, and she'd promised to drop off the bag.

At noon, Caroline eased her Subaru onto Barry Chapman's short gravel drive and parked next to Jason's white Lincoln Mark LT affectionately nicknamed Great White. A brisk breeze tousled her hair as she exited the SUV with the tool bag. She looked up to see huge cotton ball shaped clouds, etched with shades of gray, littering the sky. A Bermuda High, the culprit for the sweltering summer heat and humidity, had recently entered the Gulf of Mexico, spawning a tropical depression. The weather forecast called for heavy rain and possible thunderstorms to arrive in the evening.

Walking to the garage of Barry's red-brick bungalow, Caroline's ears caught the sound of bird babble. She looked up to see two jet-black crows perched on a wire, their sights trained on her. She got the distinct impression that they were trying to tell her something. Her feathered friends stopped their synchronized cawing and gave her a beady-eyed stare. As if prompted by nature, the pair flew to a nearby tree. Were they warning her to prepare for the incoming storm?

Lost in thought, Caroline entered the garage through the side door and headed in the direction of loud hammering. She took a moment to savor the clean woodsy scent of fresh-cut lumber. For some unknown reason, she'd always enjoyed this olfactory delight. Jason called it her aromatherapy.

Noticing his wife, Jason stopped the noise. Caroline placed the tool bag on an adjacent workbench, strode over, and gave him a light kiss on the lips.

"Thanks for bringing my tool bag," Jason said, frowning. "Barry Chapman really chaps my hide."

"Why do you think he's being so hard to deal with all of a sudden?" Caroline asked.

Jason shrugged. "I don't have any idea, but he's been extremely agitated about something ever since the shooting."

"Maybe the guy's scared like most of the locals," she speculated.

He slipped his hammer in his tool belt. "Regardless of the reason, the job is almost finished, and that's all I care about."

Caroline looked around the room, admiring Jason's precision workmanship. Her husband never ceased to amaze her. "Everything looks great!" she declared.

Jason gave Caroline a one-armed hug. "You've always been my biggest fan," he affirmed, kissing the top of her head.

"You and me, baby—for better or worse."

Caroline looked at Jason's unflappable face. Eyes filled with love and wisdom looked down at her. Those determined eyes had seen her through ups and downs, good times and bad. But when she recalled their life together, the good times were all that she chose to remember.

Jason spun Caroline around and pulled her close. "And thanks for the moral support, too."

Caroline placed her palms on Jason's muscular chest and pushed herself back an inch. She focused on his expectant face. "I'll admit that I tend to bend with the wind, but I hope you know that my spirit is strong. You can always count on me."

"There's never been a doubt in my mind, and there never will be. Anyway, it's good to be bendable. You don't have to worry about breaking."

Caroline gave Jason a playful nudge. "That's me—Gumby."

"I guess that makes me your loyal steed, Pokey."

"Gumby would be lost without Pokey by her side," she said with a cheeky grin.

"It's a demanding job, but I'm up for the challenge," Jason said with a wink. "Speaking of jobs, I need to get back to this one." He reclaimed his hammer from his tool belt, retrieved a box of finishing nails from the workbench, and headed in the direction of his trim project.

Caroline followed behind him, spotting a pair of gun cabinets in the far corner of the room. Curiosity captured her attention, and she redirected her steps toward the towering cases. Approaching the locked cabinets, she looked inside. One cabinet held several rifles, while the other displayed an assortment of handguns. Engrossed in the detail of each weapon, she didn't hear Jason come up behind her.

"What's got your attention?" he asked.

"I was admiring your client's gun collection." The rifle case was full, and the handgun case was full minus one space. "It appears that one of Barry's guns is missing." Caroline pointed to the empty space. "See?"

"Barry took that handgun out of the case this morning, mumbling something about squeezing in some target practice before his meeting at the docks." Jason placed his hands on his tool belt. "He's a strange one, that's for sure."

"No doubt. It takes all kinds, you know." Caroline looked down at her watch. The 1 o'clock hour approached. "Good Gravy! I'm going to be late."

Making an about-face, Caroline power-walked toward the door, her heeled sandals clip-clopping on the smooth concrete. What she saw next stopped her dead in her tracks.

A stocky, skyscraper of a man with an axe in one hand and a handgun in the other blocked the threshold. The burly man gave Caroline a serious scowl, the kind of scowl that says, "Who are you, and what are you doing in my garage?"

Jason sprinted in his wife's direction, cutting The Incredible Hulk off at the pass. "Hi, Barry. Have you met my wife?"

"Hey, there," Caroline drawled.

Awkward silence followed.

Barry gave a slight nod, never cracking a smile, not even a half grin. He lumbered to the gun cabinets, placing the axe down long enough to put the handgun back in its proper place. Retrieving the axe, Barry headed back in their direction. Caroline and Jason scooted away from the door, giving Barry a wide berth. As Barry exited the garage, he mumbled something about chopping down a dead tree in the backyard.

Caroline's eyes followed Barry Chapman as he headed to the back of his property. *Better the tree than me,* Caroline thought with a shiver. "*That* was interesting," she whispered in wide-eyed amazement. "I'd hate to meet that guy late at night—on the docks—with his handgun in his possession."

Jason lowered his voice. "Sounds like you think that Barry could be the Chandler's Cove Killer."

"Don't joke," Caroline said under her breath. "I don't know about motive, but he's got means and opportunity. Don't you remember you saw him at the Seafood Festival the night of the murder?"

Jason tweaked her nose. "You make a good point, Sherlock, but I don't think that owning a handgun and frequenting the docks constitutes probable cause."

She giggled. "We've got to stop watching all those detective shows on TV. We're beginning to sound like our favorite crime-solving couple."

"Leave it to the professionals, Caroline," Jason lectured.

"Zoe said the same thing, and I'm going to tell you what I told her. I'm a dance teacher, not a detective." She tapped her bottom lip with her index finger. "But, in point of fact, Barry Chapman *has* been acting suspicious lately."

"Duly noted, darling." Jason turned Caroline toward the door and nudged her in that direction. "You better get going, or you'll be late for rehearsal."

Giving a farewell wave, Caroline clip-clopped out the door.

TWENTY-FOUR

SPRINTING TO HER SUBARU, Caroline noticed that nimbus clouds now covered the sky. The wind blew in sporadic gusts and played havoc with her hair. Jumping in the driver's seat, she flipped down the vanity mirror, and used her fingers to brush her wayward tresses back into place. She put the SUV in drive and made the short trip to Leap of Faith with two minutes to spare.

Caroline's company dancers were performing Sunday morning at the Seaside Community Church. Some of the dance moms were already parked in front of the studio. She joined them and rushed to unlock the door, offering profuse apologies along the way. Pushing the door open wide, she ushered the dancer's inside. They made themselves at home turning on lights and setting up the sound system.

Caroline grabbed her lyrical sandals from the shoe box in her office, sat down at her desk, and slipped on the skimpy leather shoes. The door chime jingled, and she looked up to see Zoe and Isabella coming through the door. Isabella gave Caroline a finger wave and a smile on her way to the dressing room.

Clad in a plain Jane pair of navy slacks, an untucked white

blouse, and tennis shoes, Zoe dragged herself into the office and slumped down in the chair beside the desk. She looked spent. It appeared that the demands of the newspaper and Isabella's substantial social calendar had finally caught up with her.

"I don't mean to sound critical," Caroline ventured, "but you're looking a little rough around the edges."

Sighing, Zoe threw her friend an exasperated glare. "This murder case has me working all hours of the day and night." She shook her head in disgust. "The police don't seem to be making much headway. And if they are, they're not giving me any pertinent information."

The sounds of *I Hope You Dance* trickled down the hall. The dancers had started warming up. Caroline figured that she could give Zoe a few more minutes before they pulled her into the rehearsal room. "What *are* they saying?" she asked.

Zoe leaned forward. "It's very hush-hush," she said, sotto voce. She played with the eagle *notch-kah* around her neck. "I'm getting the same tired quotes over and over. 'It's an ongoing investigation.' 'I can't answer that at present.' Or my favorite, 'The press will be notified when there's a break in the case.' In other words, butt out." Her voice escalated with every frustrating remark.

"Well...it's always darkest before the dawn," Caroline rationalized, realizing she sounded like a cliché.

"And the sun will come out tomorrow," Zoe rebuffed, glaring at her. "Thank-you, Annie. I feel *so* much better now."

The pair laughed. As Zoe vented, the pressure in the room dissipated.

"You need a break and some herbal tea," Caroline stated. "Let's meet at The Jiffy Java after dance rehearsal. Evan is working today, and Roseann and Flo will be bringing Max there when he's finished with his chores."

Zoe mustered up a smile. "That sounds like a plan. The downtime will do me good."

Caroline stood up and Zoe followed suit.

"Great! I'll call you when we're done, and you can meet me and Isabella there." Caroline gave her friend a hug and walked her to the door.

Zoe opened the door and paused. "Oh, by the way, the photo that Sergio took of Flo with her raffle winnings is in today's edition of the *Herald*," she informed. "Sergio made 8X10's of the photos he took at the seafood Festival. I took them to the police station in case they needed to see them, but I made an extra print for Aunt Flo. I'll bring it and some newspapers to The Jiffy Java this afternoon."

"What do the police need with the photos?" Caroline questioned, holding the door for Zoe.

"The photos were taken near the area of the docks where the body was discovered," she said, stepping out the door, "so they're hoping that Sergio captured something useful to the case."

Caroline nodded her head in understanding. Zoe waved good-bye and headed back to the trenches.

Caroline skittered in the direction of *I Can Only Imagine* as it played in the dance room. The girls had performed this routine in the spring and were reprising it for their Sunday performance. She popped her head in the door of the dance room. Her heart swelled as she watched the troupe flawlessly executing their choreographed movements. Each body flowed to the rhythm of the music, becoming one cohesive group. An aura of peace emanated from the girls as they danced for their Heavenly Father. What a thing of beauty! Caroline's eyes brimmed with tears of pure joy.

Once the dance routine had been run and re-run several times, the group took a break to iron out costume, hair, and makeup options. They took their job seriously, and Caroline enjoyed watching their decision-making process. After a successful couple of hours, the dance moms, one by one, strolled into the studio to catch the end of the rehearsal.

Caroline walked back to her office, grabbed the performance schedules off her desk, and began handing them to the waiting mothers. The dancers slipped on their street clothes and sauntered into the sitting room. Caroline summarized the details of Sunday's performance, then sent the mothers and daughters off to enjoy the sizzling summer afternoon.

Not seeing Isabella, Caroline walked down the hall and stuck her head in the dance room. She found Isabella practicing her turns. Her star student could execute a flawless double pirouette, but the triple-turn still eluded her.

Seeing Caroline at the door, Isabella begged for thirty more minutes of practice time. Caroline agreed, explaining that she would be in her office finishing up paperwork. She could keep an eye on Isabella from her viewing window.

Caroline headed back to her office and sat down at her desk, searching for her sandals. Spotting her slip-on sneakers next to the shoebox, she opted for comfort over fashion and picked up the sneakers as the front door chime jingled.

Looking up, Caroline saw Olivia entering with a grim expression on her face. Stepping into the office, Olivia greeted her boss with a half-smile. Her bonny glow was mysteriously absent.

Unaware of what could be bothering her protégé, Caroline silently asked God to send Olivia his peace. "Hi, Olivia," she welcomed as she slipped on her sneakers. "I wasn't expecting you today. Is everything all right?"

Olivia sat down at the desk and began wringing her hands. "I don't know what to do. I think I'm losing it."

"Tell me what happened," Caroline coaxed.

Olivia's eyes filled. She blinked, and big tears began rolling down her flushed cheeks. Caroline handed her a tissue, she dabbed her cheeks with it, then spoke.

"My parents came to town today to talk about my plans for the future. We were having a nice lunch at The Well, and I was explaining my living and working arrangements. Out of the blue, the two of them started arguing and telling me that I was too young to make my own decisions." Olivia forced herself to breathe. "They want me to make a choice, either come live in Pensacola or come live in Apalachicola, but I can't stay in Chandler's Cove." She burst out crying.

Caroline went over to Olivia and helped her stand. Olivia shook and cried, while Caroline held her tight. Once she'd exhausted herself, Olivia slunk back down in the chair and wiped her eyes with her hands. Sniffling, she attempted to speak. "I thought my parents would be proud of my accomplishment, but all they did was criticize and complain."

Caroline scooted her chair up next to Olivia's and searched her face. "We all have different ways of communicating our feelings, Olivia. Some people have a funny way of showing their love. Because of this, we often must dig down deep to discover the hidden love buried inside."

Olivia grabbed another tissue off the desk and blew her nose. "I don't want to live with either of them, Miss Caroline. I want to stay in Chandler's Cove and live with you."

At that point, it was all Caroline could do not to burst out crying along with her. She drew in a breath and lowered her voice to a whisper. "Deep down, sweetie, you know that your parents love you —and your Heavenly Father loves you, too."

A look of bewilderment spread over Olivia's tear-streaked face. "Is it possible that God could *truly* love me after all the mistakes I've made?"

Caroline took Olivia's hands in hers. They were cold to the touch. She began rubbing warmth back into them. "Romans three: twenty-three states, 'for *all* have sinned and fall short of the glory of God.' But our Heavenly Father did not abandon us because we sinned. He wants to save us from that sin. The Bible reveals God's unconditional love in John three: sixteen. The Scripture explains that 'God so loved the world that he gave his one and only Son, that whoever believes in him shall not perish, but have eternal life.' That's a mighty powerful love, don't you think?"

Olivia went silent for a moment. "I've been looking for that kind of love all my life. What can I do to receive it?"

Caroline smiled. "God's love is free for all who ask for it, Olivia. His son, Jesus Christ, is that gift. The Bible also says that if you declare with your mouth that Jesus is Lord and believe in your heart that God raised him from the dead, you will be saved." She looked into Olivia's mournful eyes. "Do you think you're ready to make Jesus master and savior of your life?"

Olivia took in a deep breath and closed her eyes, tilting her chin upward.

Caroline sat, allowing Olivia to process the message of hope she'd just shared.

After a full minute, Olivia opened her eyes and nodded her head. "After eighteen years of living for myself, I'm finally ready to give my life to Christ."

Caroline's heart swelled in her chest, and a rush of pure joy washed over her. She silently thanked the Lord for giving her the words that Olivia needed to hear, and for allowing her to share in her young friend's life-changing decision.

Holding her hand tight, Caroline explained that Olivia could make a commitment right then and there. She shared the confession of faith statement with Olivia and asked her to repeat it after her. Olivia repeated the words, "I believe that Jesus is the Christ, the Son of the Living God, and I am trusting Him as my Lord and Savior."

Caroline reached over and gave Olivia a congratulatory hug. "After eighteen years of waiting, Heaven is rejoicing in your decision!" The young girl's face beamed as if the light of the world shown upon it. Caroline explained the significance of baptism, and they prayed for God's guidance in Olivia's life.

Side-glancing at Isabella through her viewing window, Caroline found her sitting on the dance floor, stretching out her tired muscles. Caroline stood up and gave Olivia's back a quick rub. "I know that you're still worried about what to tell your parents, but God will be there with you every step of the way. All you have to do is ask."

Gathering her belongings, Caroline and Olivia exited the office. They stopped in the sitting room, and Caroline gave Olivia another hug. "My family will be praying for your situation, and for your parents, too. Please let me know if there's anything we can do to help."

Olivia walked toward the front door. "That's so nice of you, Miss Caroline. My parents aren't praying people, but maybe God can change their minds. I'll keep you posted."

The door chime jingled, and Olivia stepped out into the bright sunshine. With mixed emotions, Caroline watched her get into her little yellow Bug and drive away, hopefully not forever. God was in control of the situation, and she knew that in her heart. Now, she needed to have a little faith.

Walking back into the ballet room, Caroline rounded up Isabella. She turned off the lights and, like Elvis, they left the building.

TWENTY-FIVE

THE CLOCK TOWER struck its fourth chime as Caroline and Isabella entered The Jiffy Java. Business was booming, and the coffee shop was nearly full. Spying an empty table at the back of the room by the kitchen entrance, Caroline asked Isabella to grab it before someone else did. Isabella side-stepped through the crowd as Caroline scanned the room, making sure that Roseann and company hadn't already arrived.

Not seeing them, Caroline joined Isabella and pulled out her cell phone. She texted Zoe, letting her know that she and Isabella were at The Jiffy Java, then dialed Roseann's cell to let her know that she was done with dance rehearsal. Roseann confirmed that they would join them within the hour.

Looking around, Caroline noticed that Lucy Ledbetter had hired a couple of extra servers. She spotted Evan bussing a recently vacated table. He saw her and waved a quick hello, then went back to placing plates and glasses in a black bus box.

Caroline picked up two menus and gave one to Isabella. "I texted your mom. She should be here shortly." They began looking at the daily specials. "What are you going to have?" she asked.

"Probably chicken nuggets and a milkshake. That's what I always have."

"I like a girl who knows what she wants," Caroline teased.

Isabella flashed her pearly whites.

Caroline's eyes perused the menu, but her mind sat perched on her precarious situation. Yes, she'd told Olivia that God would work everything out, but uncertainty had crept back into her thoughts. After all the trouble she'd gone to getting an assistant, it looked like she might be back to square one. For her sake and Olivia's, Caroline prayed that would not be the case.

Temporarily shelving her troubling thoughts, Caroline returned to the menu selections as she decided between hummus or pimento cheese with pita wedges.

Lucy appeared next to Caroline, her face flushed. "Hi, ladies. How's your day going? Better than mine, I hope."

"What's up, Lucy?" Caroline asked.

"See the two guys over there?" Lucy discretely pointed her pen toward a couple of occupied barstools near the cash register.

Caroline cut her eyes in the direction she indicated. "The one with the black mane and the other with the pretty ponytail?"

She nodded in the affirmative. "I've about had it with those two."

Something registered in Caroline's memory bank. "They look familiar. Who are they?"

"They're detectives," Lucy said.

"Oh…yeah," Caroline replied, recognizing the men's faces from the recent TV news reports. "Detectives Lobo and Kalani, I believe." She whispered, "Murder investigation?"

Lucy nodded yes. "They've been sitting there for almost an hour taking up precious counter space." She huffed. "They haven't ordered any food, only water. Detective Peter Ponytail keeps hopping out of his seat. He goes outside, then comes back in and pops a stick of gum in his mouth." She shook her head. "What's up with that?"

Caroline tapped her index finger on her bottom lip. "I wonder if they've gotten a break in the case."

Lucy shrugged. "And Detective 'God's gift to women' Kalani,'" she indicated with a jerk of her head, "keeps hitting on me every time I walk by the cash register. Like I have time to talk today." She rolled her eyes.

Isabella giggled. "He likes you, Miss Lucy." She looked over at the determined detective. "I think he's cute."

"That may very well be, but I don't know him from Adam." Lucy shot Kalani a fleeting glare, then lowered her voice. "He could be trouble, for all I know."

"It's probably just harmless flirtation, Lucy," Caroline hypothesized. "He's not wearing a wedding band, is he?"

Lucy's demeanor changed. "No—but that doesn't mean anything nowadays." She tapped her pen on her order pad.

Caroline's eyebrows shot up. "So—you *were* checking out the Hawaiian hunk." Her head bobbed up and down. "Interesting."

Lucy's mocha complexion turned a nice shade of red. "I've got eyes, don't I?"

"Yes, you do. And there's no harm in looking." Caroline gave her a big grin.

"I say go for it, Miss Lucy," Isabella chimed in, sounding more like twenty-one than eleven.

"Has he asked you for your phone number yet?" the matchmaker in Caroline prodded.

"Of course not," Lucy sputtered. "I doubt he will. He's just preening in front of his partner."

Caroline studied the dark-haired detective for a beat. "If that peacock is smart, he'll ask you out. He doesn't look like a dodo bird to me."

That produced more giggles from Isabella.

Evan rushed by on his way to bus the just-vacated table next to them. Caroline asked him to place a RESERVED sign on it for the rest of the group when he was done.

She glanced at the door and spotted Zoe walking in their direction. "Here's your mom, Isabella."

Zoe joined them at the table. Everyone gave Lucy their beverage request, and Caroline ordered the pimento cheese appetizer, giving Zoe time to look at the menu. Five minutes later, Roseann, Flo, and Max paraded in and sat down at the table next to them, bombarding them with waves and greetings. Caroline slid off her stool and walked over to the trio.

"Hey, Max," she said, rustling his hair. "Why don't you go sit with Isabella? I want to talk to Aunt Flo and Nana for a few minutes." He plodded over and joined his friend. Pulling a twenty-dollar bill out of his pocket, he began telling her all about his workday.

Caroline gave both ladies a hug and sat down next to Roseann in Max's vacated seat. The ladies made small talk, while Roseann and Flo picked up menus and began perusing.

Lucy scooted to their table with Caroline's usual iced latte. "Detective Handsome and his partner just left," she whispered in Caroline's ear. "But he said he'd be back tomorrow. I guess he thinks that he can wear me down." She grinned. "Well, he can just keep thinking."

"Never say never," Caroline advised.

Lucy shifted her attention back to work. "Hi, ladies," she greeted Roseann and Flo. "Good to see you again. What can I get you?"

Caroline glanced over at the other half of their group. They munched on pimento cheese and pita wedges. "Let's have another one of those appetizers."

Lucy beamed. "Good choice. It's my own recipe. I hope you like it."

"It looks delicious," Roseann said with a smile. "We'll have sweet tea with lemon and a sprig of mint to drink, when you get a chance, dear. It looks like you're having a busy day."

"You said it, but I'm not complaining." Lucy threw them a quick grin and rushed back to the kitchen.

Evan brushed by with a dish towel in his hand. He stopped long enough to say hello to Roseann and Flo, then sped off to wipe down more dirty tables.

Zoe came over, carrying a folder. She handed the folder to Flo. "Here's a copy of today's *Herald*—hot off the press—and an 8x10 photo to go with it."

Flo opened the folder and retrieved the newspaper. Setting the folder aside, she opened the paper.

"Take a look on page five," Zoe said.

Flo turned to the page Zoe indicated. A wide shot of the three raffle winners with their treasure chests full of goodies occupied the center of the page.

Sheer joy spread over Flo's face. "Look, Sis!" she exclaimed. "I'm in the funny papers." She handed the newspaper to Roseann.

Roseann squinted her eyes at the photo. Her smile faded. She jabbed her index finger on the page several times. "Who is that man in the background?"

Flo picked up the crystal-clear 8x10 photo with the identical image on it. Her jaw dropped. Everyone took a closer look.

Caroline's eyes grew wide with amazement. "That's the man with the Greek fisherman's cap I've been seeing all over town."

Zoe looked at Caroline, then back at the photo. "Is that your mysterious stranger, Caroline? I know him. He's the captain of the *C.C. Princess*."

Caroline gave Zoe a questioning look. "*I* know that, but how do you know that?"

"Our family took one of his fishing charters a few months ago. He's relatively new on the docks. A very nice guy though."

Caroline shifted her gaze to Roseann and Flo, trying to discern their apprehension over this virtual stranger.

At the same moment, Lucy approached the table with their

order. As she set the drinks and appetizer down, she caught the look of confusion on everyone's face. "What's happened?" she queried.

Roseann and Flo went mute.

Caroline didn't know what to say.

Zoe clued her in. "It appears that there's some curiosity about one of the charter fishermen."

Lucy looked at the photo. "You mean the one with the Greek fisherman's cap?"

Everyone nodded.

"Who is it?" Lucy asked. "Someone special?"

Zoe fingered her necklace. "If I remember right, his name is Nathan Beall."

Roseann gasped. The color drained from her face as she wobbled on her stool. Caroline and Flo each grabbed an arm to steady her. Lucy snatched up a menu and started fanning Roseann with it.

Caroline's mouth went dry and her gut did a topsy-turvy somersault. She felt as if she'd just fallen through Alice's looking glass. "What did you say?" she choked out.

"Nathan Beall?" Zoe repeated, a perplexed look on her face. "I thought you didn't know the man."

"I...I...I don't," Caroline stuttered, struggling to gain her composure. "But my mother does."

Roseann placed her hands over her face and began to moan. Caroline shoved the iced tea glass in front of her and told her to drink. Flo looked heavenward and made the sign of the cross. Lucy kept fanning Roseann.

Zoe looked around the table. "Why is everyone so panicked?"

Roseann took a sip of tea and swallowed hard. "Nathan Beall is my ex-husband."

"And my ex-father," Caroline said.

Lucy noticed a line forming at the cash register. She stopped fanning and patted Caroline's shoulder. "Sorry, but I need to catch the register. Are you two going to be okay?"

Caroline forced a flat smile. "Go take care of your other customers—we'll manage."

Zoe glanced over at Isabella and Max. They stared at the group with blank looks on their faces. "I'll take care of Max and Bella, Caroline. You take care of your mother," she said, walking back to the other table to reassure the kids.

"What is *he* doing in Chandler's Cove?" Flo asked to no one in particular.

Roseann found her inner warrior goddess. She sat up straight and placed her tea glass on the table. "That's what I'd like to know," she breathed through gritted teeth. "And that's what I'm going to find out."

She stood up and straightened her skirt. "He's not going to come to *our* town and mess up our lives again. I'll not stand for it!" She yanked her purse off the back of her stool and flung the strap over her shoulder.

Caroline jumped off her stool and grabbed Roseann's arm. "Where are you going, Mother?"

Roseann's eyes turned cold. "I'm going to confront that scoundrel," she hissed, attempting to control her temper.

"But you don't know where he lives," Caroline reasoned with her.

"You heard Zoe. He's the captain of the *C.C. Princess*. I can find his boat if I go to the docks."

"I know where the *C.C. Princess* is docked," Caroline confessed. "I'll go with you." She kept holding Roseann's arm. She didn't want her mother running off without her. "You don't need to face him alone. He might be dangerous. For all we know, he's the killer that the police are looking for. He *was* on the docks the night of the murder."

"Listen to your daughter, Roseann," Flo ordered. "You're too upset to drive right now. Let Caroline Celeste take you to the docks." Her tone softened. "And for goodness' sake, calm down before you confront him."

Flo's words seemed to bring Roseann down a notch. She now appeared to be less of a flight risk, so Caroline let go of her arm. Her mother excused herself and headed to the Ladies' Room.

Caroline's head was spinning like a top; a myriad of thoughts bounced around in her brain. First, someone needed to watch after Max, while she and Roseann went off on their wild goose chase. Next, she needed to let Jason know where she and Roseann were going. Finally, she needed to give Zoe a good reason not to blow her top and put her and Roseann in restraints.

Caroline looked at Aunt Flo. "Can you take Max back to the condo? I'll have Evan join y'all there when he gets off work."

"Sure thing, sweetie. Don't fret. Max and I will go straight to Sandpiper Shore and wait." She stood up and placed a twenty-dollar bill on the table. "Better yet, I'll ask Walt to meet you there. Where's the boat docked anyway?"

"It's at the East End Marina," Caroline said. "Show Walt your photo. It'll help him locate the *C.C. Princess*. I'm going to text Jason and have him meet us there. Just to be on the safe side, give Walt Jason's cell number."

"Will do." Flo reached for Caroline's hand. "And, please be careful."

Caroline gave her aunt's hand a squeeze. "Yes ma'am. I'll do my best to keep Roseann from tearing up the docks."

Flo looked around the coffee shop. "I better go check on your mother." She headed in the direction of the restrooms.

Caroline stepped up next to Zoe, who had already paid the check. "Let me give you some money to cover me and Max."

"Nonsense. I've got it." Zoe gathered up her handbag and port-folio. "Do you think going to the docks to confront Captain Beall is wise?"

Caroline heaved a heavy sigh. "Mother's a ticking time bomb, and I need to defuse the situation before she blows up everyone and everything around her."

Zoe placed both hands on Caroline's shoulders and spun her

friend around, her expression transparent. "Caroline, I know that your emotions are running high right now. So, if you see your father, please count to ten before doing or saying anything that you might regret later."

Caroline placed her hands over Zoe's. "I promise to consult my Heavenly Father before confronting my biological one."

Zoe gave her a tight hug, then she and Isabella turned to leave. "And, *please* call me tonight. I'm going to worry until I hear from you." Mother and daughter breezed out of the restaurant.

Caroline looked at Max. "Nana and I have some business to take care of, so Aunt Flo is going to take you home with her until we can come get you."

A look of concern spread over her little man's face. She gave him a hug. "Don't worry," Caroline reassured him. "Everything's going to be all right."

"Let's pray, Mom," Max pleaded. "I want God to know where you're going, so he can send his angels to protect you."

Caroline fought back tears. She didn't want Max to know why she was afraid. They bowed their heads and asked God to protect them on their journeys and to bring them safely back together again.

As they opened their eyes, Evan appeared at the table. "Miss Lucy explained that there has been a *certain* development. What can I do to help?"

Caroline managed a smile. "Nana and I are going to the docks, and your father will be meeting us there. Aunt Flo and Max are going to Nana's condo. Could you go there after work? I don't want y'all at home by yourselves."

Evan nodded in understanding. "No problem. My shift ends soon." Caroline kissed Evan on the cheek, and he headed off to finish his shift.

Roseann and Flo joined Caroline and Max at the table. Caroline texted Jason, apprising him of the recent development, then the foursome exited The Jiffy Java. Threatening thunder clouds spanned the sky, and it looked like it could rain any minute. Caroline gave Max a good-bye kiss, and he and Aunt Flo headed to her station wagon, while she and Roseann headed to Caroline's SUV. Although still apprehensive, Caroline discerned an inner strength that had not been present before. Her Heavenly Father was with her. She had no reason to fear.

TWENTY-SIX

CAROLINE AND ROSEANN sped away from the square, running head-on into bumper-to-bumper rush- hour traffic. As Caroline merged onto Highway 98, a young driver, with one hand propped on the steering wheel and the other glued to her cell phone, squeezed into the half car-length space in front of them. The girl slammed on her brakes, narrowly avoiding a fender bender.

Roseann grabbed the dashboard. "That driver must be texting and driving," she grumbled, shaking her head in disgust.

Caroline's eyes narrowed. "More like dumb driving," she snapped.

Roseann remained silent.

"I guess I'm a little more stressed than I realized," Caroline admitted as she white-knuckled the steering wheel.

"Me, too," Roseann replied with a gush of breath.

Caroline forced a smile. "Never fear. The cavalry is on the way. Aunt Flo's going to call Walt, and he and Jason will meet us at the docks."

Roseann nodded. "That's good. Better safe than sorry."

Caroline glanced at the dash clock. The trip time from the square to Chandler's Cove Harbor usually took fifteen minutes, but with the fishing rodeo in full swing, she and Roseann would be lucky to get to the marina in thirty. As they putted down Hwy 98 at less than a snail's pace, Caroline wondered what was going through her mother's head.

Roseann sat quietly studying her nails. After several solemn minutes, she raised her head and fixed her eyes on the traffic in front of them. "I've been feeling a stirring in my spirit for the past few months, but I've shrugged it off as pre-birthday bash excitement." She sighed. "I'm wondering if the extent of my unease correlates with the length of time Nathan has been in Chandler's Cove."

"I wonder…" Caroline echoed.

Roseann slowly shook her head. "I guess our recent walk down memory lane has rekindled feelings that I didn't know still existed."

Caroline knew those feelings all too well. Her heavy heart ached with a pain that longed to escape the walls of stone surrounding it. "I'm sorry, Mother," she whispered, the words sticking in her dry throat.

"Don't be, dear." Roseann offered a brave smile. "I suppose you never forget your first love."

Mother and daughter pondered that thought as they headed to the docks.

Arriving at the harbor, Caroline circled the parking lot twice. Not finding an empty space, she drove to the neighboring entertainment complex and parked there. Exiting the Subaru, Caroline shoved her keys in the pocket of her Capri pants, and she and Roseann crossed the grassy verge that divided the two lots. A gusty wind breezed through the palm trees as they trekked to the East End Marina. Glancing skyward, Caroline noticed massive rain clouds hanging low in the graying sky, their bulging bellies blanketing the harbor.

Setting foot onto the boardwalk, she and Roseann navigated

through the crowd of pedestrians, making their way to the docks. They traversed down the dock ramp toward the designated slip in silence. Their synchronized footsteps drummed on the wooden planks and kept time with their pounding hearts.

Closing in on the *C.C. Princess*, Caroline pointed to Captain Beall's boat. Roseann froze in her tracks. She stood wide-eyed, staring at the vessel like she'd never seen a boat before.

Caroline attempted to fathom Roseann's next course of action. How would she handle the situation? Did she want to rush onto the boat full speed ahead, or slowly troll the docks, looking for any clue as to Nathan's whereabouts?

Fear and doubt clouded Caroline's mind, and she began questioning her sanity. What were they thinking coming out here by themselves? She wanted to run far away, but her feet felt like lead weights sinking in a deep pool of mixed emotions. She took Roseann's hand and held on tight.

"Lord, what should we do?" Caroline silently prayed.

"*Trust me, Caroline. Take the first step,*" the Lord replied.

"Come with me, Mother," Caroline coaxed. "It's going to be okay. No matter what happens, the Lord will be with us."

They walked toward the *C.C. Princess* and stopped in front of the aft deck, not moving a muscle, not uttering a sound. After all the hours she'd spent questioning the identity of the man in the Greek fisherman's cap, Caroline wondered why she was now afraid to take the next step.

Roseann broke the silence. "Let's *do* this," she said in a hushed tone, giving Caroline's hand a slight tug.

Caroline let go of Roseann's hand and scanned both ends of the lengthy dock. Not a soul in sight. "Do you think we should?"

Thunder rumbled in the distance. Caroline looked up. The clouds had darkened to an eerie shade of charcoal. For their sake, she hoped that the ominous vapor mass held a silver lining.

"We'd better do it now," Roseann urged. "The rain's coming."

They grabbed a wooden dock pile for support and heaved themselves onto the aft deck. The *C.C. Princess,* along with several of the surrounding boats, appeared to be as empty as a robbed grave. Roseann slowly, but deliberately, approached the cabin door and knocked three times. The sound echoed through the air. Caroline looked in both directions again, wondering if anyone had heard.

They anxiously waited for a response. Roseann knocked again. Still nothing.

Thunder boomed like a bass drum.

Hoping to avoid the impending downpour, Caroline suggested that they head back to the SUV, but Roseann had other intentions. She was a woman on a mission. Caroline knew that her mother wouldn't leave the docks until she'd positively identified the captain of the *C.C. Princess.*

Deploying plan B, Roseann exited the aft deck and marched down the port side finger pier. Caroline diligently followed. They reached the side cabin window, and Caroline craned her neck, hoping to catch a glimpse of someone inside. The cabin of the *C.C. Princess* was dark and devoid of movement.

"Do you see anyone in there?" she asked Roseann.

"There's no light on inside. I can't tell."

Caroline shifted her gaze up to the sky, then back to the boat. Bad weather and no captain. Uneasiness stirred in her gut. "No one's here, Mother. Let's go home. We can come back tomorrow."

Roseann finally saw reason. "I suppose you're right," she conceded. "I just had my hair done. It wouldn't do to get caught in the rain."

Caroline rolled her eyes. Only Princess Roseann would equate the inconvenience of a ruined hairstyle to the distress of finding an errant ex-husband. Proceeding back down the finger pier, they stepped onto the main dock, nearly colliding with a tall, male figure.

"Excuse me, ladies," the man said with a plastered-on smile. "I'm looking for the captain of the *C.C. Princess.* Do you know if he's on the boat?"

"I don't think so," Caroline responded, immediately recognizing the detective she'd seen earlier at The Jiffy Java. "Aren't you one of the detectives investigating the recent incident on the docks?"

Peter Ponytail held out his hand. "Yes ma'am. My name is Detective Ronald Lobo from the Chandler's Cove Special Crimes Unit."

Roseann gave the detective the once-over, then reluctantly shook his hand. "Does this have anything to do with the murder on the docks?"

Lobo grinned. "I'm not at liberty to comment on an ongoing investigation, but I *am* interested in speaking with Captain Beall again."

"Are you referring to a man in his sixty's named Nathan Beall?" Roseann asked.

"One and the same," Lobo stated, returning the once-over. "He's a person of interest in the case."

Roseann's brow knitted. "I knew it was Nathan in that photo," she muttered.

Lobo looked perplexed. "What photo are you referring to ma'am?"

"The photo of my sister that was taken right here on the docks the very night of the murder." Roseann pointed to the *C.C. Princess*. "Nathan was on *this* boat, and the lighthouse was in the background." She waved her hand toward the towering structure.

Lobo frowned. "I'd like to see that photo. It might reveal a key piece of evidence." He stepped toward Roseann.

Roseann's body stiffened. "I don't have it with me now. My sister has a copy, and your office should have one, too. I'm surprised you haven't seen it."

Lobo took a step back and forced a smile. "That's fine. Give me your sister's name and address and I can get it myself. It's possible we haven't seen this one."

Realizing her mistake, Roseann began to backtrack. "Perhaps I should let my sister know that you need to see the photo. I'm sure that she will be more than happy to bring it to the police station tomorrow."

Lightning flashed through the darkening sky, immediately followed by a peal of thunder. Blustery wind began to blow in forceful gusts, mussing Roseann's perfectly coiffed tresses. She grabbed Caroline's hand. "Come on, dear. We need to go before it starts raining."

They stepped forward, but Lobo blocked their path. Something about the detective's demeanor had changed. Caroline's gut did a cartwheel.

"I'm sure that you don't want to impede a murder investigation, now do you?" Lobo questioned, animosity rising in his voice.

"Certainly not," Roseann declared, her cheeks heating. "Excuse us. We're leaving." She stepped in front of Lobo, dragging Caroline with her. "I suggest you do the same, or you'll end up getting all wet."

Lightning flashed again, illuminating the lanky frame that loomed over them. Lobo dropped a firm hand onto Caroline's shoulder. "I hope that wasn't a threat, ladies. Because if it was, I might have to…"

Thunder roared like a lion, giving way to a chorus of footfalls on the wooden dock. The threesome jerked their heads in the direction of the noise, but Lobo maintained a strong grip on Caroline's shoulder.

Nathan hurried toward them, accompanied by two other men. Caroline recognized Captain Roy as the second man. The third man, whom she did not recognize, reached for the gun in his shoulder holster.

Shock registered on Lobo's face. He grabbed Caroline's arm with one hand and his shiny Glock with the other. He yanked her away from Roseann and thrust the gun in her side, holding her close. Fear gripped Caroline with frigid fingers and she shivered in its icy grasp.

Lobo glared at the group. "Stop right where you are, gentlemen."

The three men froze in their tracks. The third man rested his hand near his holster and spoke. "You don't want to do this, Ronnie," he cautioned.

Lobo pressed the barrel of the Glock into Caroline's ribs. "I can't go to prison, Stan. I'm a cop. They'll kill me in there."

"You were a gullible participant, buddy. We're not after you. We want the head of the operation." Stan lowered his hand off the holster. "Why don't you let her go? I'm sure we can make a deal."

"I wish it were that simple, but the truth is, I'm the one you're looking for." Lobo choked a laugh. "So, you see, I have everything to lose."

Caroline could feel the gun shaking against her side as Lobo spoke. She dared not breathe, fearing that it might accidentally go off.

Stan kept his hands where Lobo could see them and took a step forward. "You've got important names, dates, and locations that we need, detective. That's got to count for something."

"As you said, I'm a small fish. I'm worth nothing to you *or* them." Lobo's eyes turned dark and vacant like a shark. "This whole thing is bigger than you think. No...my best bet is to get as far away from here as possible."

Nathan inched toward Lobo. "I'll go with you," he bargained. "Just leave her here."

Holding Caroline close, Lobo took a step toward the dock ramp as huge drops of rain began to fall. A grieved expression came over his face. "I didn't want to do it, Stan, but I had orders. It was either them or me. I'm sorry, man."

Stan reached for his gun as Lobo aimed his Glock and fired. The shot reverberated in every direction. Stan dove sideways, but the bullet clipped him in the shoulder. Captain Roy caught Stan before he fell to the ground. Ripping a red bandana out of his pocket, Roy firmly pressed it on the fallen cop's wound.

Roseann screamed and lunged toward Caroline, hoping to pull her away from Lobo. The crazed killer shoved Roseann aside and began dragging Caroline up the dock ramp. Roseann lost her footing and fell backward. The last thing Caroline saw was Nathan rushing in and saving Roseann from toppling into the water.

TWENTY-SEVEN

THE TROPICAL DEPRESSION quickly morphed into a robust storm. Biting rain mixed with Roseann's tears and streaked down her cheeks. Holding her tight, Nathan's eyes searched the docks for Caroline, but she and the gunman were nowhere in sight. Trembling, Roseann pushed her ex-husband's hands away and slapped him in the face. On the verge of hysteria, she collapsed in his arms.

Nathan carried Roseann aboard the *C.C. Princess* and placed her on the couch. He immediately rushed back outside to help Captain Roy drag Stan in from the sudden downpour. As the three entered the cabin, Nathan explained the abducted girl's identity to Stan. He nodded his head in understanding.

As Roseann slumped on the couch rocking and sobbing, Nathan and Roy eased Stan onto the dinette bench. The injured cop retrieved his cell from his jeans pocket and dialed 9-1-1. Through shallow breaths, Stan gave the dispatcher a brief account of the shooting and of the abduction.

Wasting no time, Nathan ran down to the head and gathered up every towel he could find. A pain shot through his hip, but he ignored it. Bounding back upstairs, he thrust the towels at Roy.

Without delay, the experienced sailor applied pressure to Stan's bleeding wound.

In panic mode, Nathan threw on his yellow slicker and dashed to the aft deck. The billowing sea bounced against the sides of the *Princess,* tossing the boat back and forth. As Nathan struggled to stay upright, officers who had been monitoring the boardwalk activities arrived on the scene. Fire and rescue units followed.

Nathan ushered the paramedics onto the *Princess* and stood wringing his hands in anxious anticipation. Two paramedics placed Stan on a gurney, assessed his wound, and then applied a pressure dressing. A third paramedic began treating Roseann for shock.

As the medics wheeled Stan to the ambulance, he grabbed Nathan's arm. "You can trust Mac Nelson," he told him. "He's one of my men." Stan further stated that Detective Kalani would be in to talk to them shortly.

Outside, Kalani sat in the rescue unit waiting for a report. After the paramedics loaded Stan into the ambulance, he gave the detective a rundown of the situation.

Back on the *Princess,* Roy wiped up Stan's spilled blood, then sat down at the dinette table, watching as the paramedic took Roseann's vital signs. Nervous as a tabby cat on a hot tin roof, Nathan paced back and forth, from the door to the window, then back to the door, watching for any sign of the detective's arrival.

Out of the blue, the universe jarred Nathan's memory. He walked over to the couch. "Roseann, do you know how to reach Caroline's husband?" he asked.

Roseann gasped. "I forgot all about Jason. He was supposed to be meeting us on the docks. Do you think he got caught in the storm?"

"Let's not borrow trouble," Nathan said, steadying his voice. "If you have his cell number, I'll call him."

Roseann shook her head. "I don't have his number." Her voice cracked. "It's in my cell phone in Caroline's car." She closed her eyes and groaned.

"That's okay," Nathan assured her. "He'll be here when the storm lets up." As he spoke, a flash of lightning brightened the compact cabin. The light show was followed by a crack of thunder and a loud rapping at the door.

"Is that Jason?" Roseann asked in desperation.

Nathan shot across the salon and flung the door open. Detective Kalani entered and walked to the center of the room. Observing the frightened faces, his expression turned from suspicious to sympathetic.

"I'm sorry to interrupt, but I understand that Mrs. Callahan is your daughter," Kalani stated, looking from Nathan to Roseann. "Rest assured that the CCPD has issued a BOLO to all law enforcement agencies in the county, advising them to be on the lookout for Detective Ronald Lobo. Roadblocks are going up as we speak. He won't be able to leave town by car."

Roseann tried to sit up, but the room began spinning. She put one hand on her stomach and the other over her mouth. The paramedic shoved an emesis basin in her face. She closed her eyes, fighting back waves of nausea.

"Detective, you must protect my daughter from that madman," Roseann pleaded, her body trembling.

Kalani cleared his throat, looking from Nathan, to Roy, to Roseann. "What we need to figure out is where he's headed. I'm hoping that the three of you might remember something that can help me determine Detective Lobo's next move."

Nathan's hip began to throb. Limping over to the dinette bench, he sat down next to Captain Roy and began massaging the painful joint.

Roseann raised her head. "The maniac said that he needed to get far away from here." The paramedic stuck a needle in her upper arm. She jumped.

"I'm giving you a mild sedative to help you relax," the paramedic informed.

Kalani's questioning eyes searched the perplexed faces of the distraught sea captains.

Captain Roy removed his Panama hat and raked his fingers through his thinning hair. "Claimed ta be worth nothin'," Roy replied, shaking his head. "Could he be thinkin' of killin' himself?"

Nathan stared off into space for a second, then jerked his head to face Kalani. "He's *your* partner, detective. Don't you have any insight into where he might have taken my daughter?"

Kalani quirked an eyebrow and nodded. "I have a hunch, but I need to confirm something first." He pinned his gaze on the two fishermen. "Have either of you seen any unusual happenings at the lighthouse lately?" He waited for a response.

Nathan rubbed his chin and looked toward his friend.

Wonder creased Captain Roy's brow. "Matter of fact," he said, snapping his fingers, "I saw an unfamiliar boat headin' ta the lighthouse 'bout a week ago when I was comin' back from a sunset dolphin tour. Had a full boat, so I didn't think nothin' of it at the time."

"Can you describe the boat?" Kalani asked.

"It was white,—'bout a forty footer with a closed flybridge." Roy stroked his beard. "I remember it was registered in North Carolina 'cause I thought, 'now that's a coincidence.' Nate bein' from North Carolina, an' all."

Nathan's eyes lit with surprise. "What was the name of the boat, Roy?"

"Somethin' with sea in it." Roy placed a hand on Nathan's shoulder. "Sorry brother, the dolphins were 'specially playful that day. Guess I got distracted."

"Detective Lobo might be headed to the lighthouse," Kalani conjectured. "Let's hope that the storm has delayed his departure."

Kalani quickly calculated Lobo's options. If his hypothesis was correct, his partner would need a way to get to the lighthouse. He mentally checked off the detective's transportation options. Ronnie had a motorcycle, not a car. If he was going to use the motorcycle, he'd have to leave his hostage behind. On the other hand, if he needed a hostage, then he might try to escape in the girl's vehicle.

Kalani walked over to the couch. "Mrs. Whitmore, please describe your daughter's car for me."

Bleary-eyed, Roseann responded. "Caroline drive's a red Subaru Outback, and she's got one of those vanity license plates. It says 'TAP GIRL' on it. It's parked over by the entertainment center."

Kalani nodded. "Thank-you. That's very helpful. I'll get on this right away." He pulled out his cell phone and dialed the police precinct. He issued an all-points bulletin, accompanied by a description of Lobo's motorcycle, Caroline's SUV, and the boat in question. Every available cruiser was instructed to rendezvous at the lighthouse landing.

Ending the call, Kalani headed to the door. As he reached for the door handle, another knock bounced off the cabin walls. The detective opened the door. Jason and Walt stood on the other side, dressed in rain gear.

"Oh, Jason," Roseann cried, trying to stand, but the medication had already kicked in. She fell back down on the couch. "That's Caroline's husband," she wailed, bursting into tears.

Kalani gave a curt nod, allowing Jason and Walt to enter. The storm winds blew stinging rain into the cabin in angled gusts, tousling Kalani's jet-black mane. He shut the door and reentered the cabin. The newcomers placed their wet coats by the door and scanned the room. Nathan stood up and walked toward the door.

Jason's eyes rested on a familiar face. He acknowledged Captain Roy with a terse nod, then warily eyed Nathan and Kalani. Worry abruptly spread over his face. "Where's Caroline?" he asked in a clipped tone.

Kalani walked over to Jason. He held out his hand and Jason hesitantly shook it. "Mr. Callahan, my name is Detective Kale Kalani of the Chandler's Cove Special Crimes Unit." Jason's body tensed. "I regret to inform you that your wife was abducted about thirty minutes ago."

Jason's jaw dropped, not fully comprehending what he'd just heard. "What are you talking about, detective? My wife left me a message to meet her at this boat." His voice rose. "She has reason to believe that her father is here." Jason glared at Nathan. "That's you, I take it."

Nathan stiffly nodded.

Jason stomped over to the elder man. "What's your involvement in this?" He jabbed his finger into his father-in-law's chest. "If you didn't take her, then who did?"

"It's all my fault," Roseann whimpered. "I was the one who insisted we come here." Slapping her hand over her mouth, she grabbed the emesis basin out of the paramedic's hand and retched.

Walt stepped into the middle of the altercation and pulled the two men apart. He debated whether to call Florence but thought it best to wait until he had more information.

Detective Kalani approached Jason. "Please sit down, Mr. Callahan. Let me explain." Captain Roy rose from the bench and let Jason and the detective take the seat.

After several gut-wrenching minutes, Jason was up to speed. He searched the cabin in disbelief. Roseann lay on the couch with her eyes closed, clutching an emesis basin. Walt sat by her side, keeping watch. Captain Roy stood in the galley, lines of concern etched on his weathered face. Nathan hovered by the door, damp and dejected.

The paramedic finished his exam and handed Walt a detailed list of care instructions. He packed up his medical bag and stepped back into the storm.

Kalani stood up to leave. "I'm going straight to the lighthouse to look for Mrs. Callahan and a boat matching the description you gave me." He hurried to the door. Jason jumped up, following at the detective's heels.

Kalani stopped in the doorway. "Gentlemen, it would be safer if you stayed here," he advised. "I'll contact you as soon as I've canvased the area around the lighthouse."

The message fell on deaf ears.

Jason came nose to nose with the detective. Anguish pulsated through him. "If you don't want me going to the lighthouse, you'll have to arrest me!" he yelled. "We're wasting time standing here. Get moving or get out of my way." Jason grabbed his raincoat and pushed past Kalani, running out the door.

Kalani stepped onto the aft deck. He reminded Nathan of the risks of taking the law into his own hands, then followed Jason into the storm. He ducked his head, running through the blinding rain.

Dodging deep rain puddles and downed tree branches, Jason made a mad dash to his truck and slid inside. Gripping the steering wheel, he struggled to breathe, his body frozen in fear. In an instant, his whole world had changed. The light of his life was lost in the darkness. He closed his eyes and looked to the cross.

Heavenly Father, Caroline is in trouble and I am powerless to help her. Send your angels to protect her in the storm. You are her strength and her shield. I will trust in you. In Jesus Christ's Holy name, I pray. Amen.

With newfound courage, Jason put the truck in gear and bravely drove into the unknown.

Kale Kalani reached the unmarked squad car and slid behind the wheel. Adrenaline shot through his body, giving him a burst of energy. Now that the illegal organization's cover was blown, they would need to get out of town fast. Time was running out. He had to get to Caroline before they realized that she was expendable. The resolute detective looked heavenward, praying that he wasn't sending everyone on a wild goose chase.

Nathan was frantic. Danger and uncertainty lay ahead of him, but he had to do something. Caroline's life was at stake. Pushing his fears aside, he hobbled over to the couch, the pain in his hip intensifying with every step. He touched Roseann's shoulder. She stirred and looked up at Nathan with vacant eyes.

"I'm going to look for Caroline's car," Nathan told her. He took Roseann's limp hand and held it tight. "Don't worry. I'll find our daughter."

Tears formed in the corners of Roseann's eyes and dripped down her face. She squeezed her eyes shut and nodded her head. "Please be careful, Nathan."

Nathan leaned down and lightly kissed Roseann's forehead. "You rest now. I'll be back soon."

Before heading into the storm, Nathan asked Roy and Walt to keep an eye on Roseann. He promised to call as soon as he had news about Caroline.

Stumbling into the rain, Nathan sloshed to his F-150 and hefted himself into the cab. His emotions were off the charts. With shaking hands, he placed the key in the ignition. Not knowing which way to turn, he asked the universe to take care of his little girl. He couldn't lose her now.

Starting the engine, Nathan flipped on the bright beams and put the wipers on high. The gusty winds and pounding rain made visibility almost impossible. Summoning up the nerve, he eased the F-150 onto the flooded road and drove the short distance to the entertainment center parking lot.

From the covered deck of the *Destiny*, Captain Mac Nelson continued to watch the terrible drama unfolding around him. After hearing the gunshot, he had promptly called 9-1-1. He was thankful that the rescue units had arrived so quickly.

It shocked Mac to see his friend shot, blood spilling from his wound, and not be able to help. That was the trouble with under-cover work. He had to wait for further instructions. The detective had to protect Captain Beall at all costs.

Seven months ago, his job had been rather uneventful. Nathan had kept a low profile after relocating to Chandler's Cove, but, in recent weeks, the assignment had become increasingly difficult. Between the fisherman's need to reconnect with his daughter, and his daughter's curiosity, the safety of Nathan's entire family had been in jeopardy.

Mac's text alarm sounded. He read the message and prepared for action. With rain gear at the ready, he watched Nathan exit the *C.C. Princess* and amble to his F-150. Throwing on his raincoat, he followed several paces behind, not wanting to startle the panic-stricken captain. He jumped into his jeep and began tailing Nathan down the slick streets.

TWENTY-EIGHT

HEAVY PRECIPITATION BLANKETED THE MARINA, soaking
Caroline to the bone. Her teeth chattered as the blustery winds
sliced through her clothes like a knife. She could feel Detective
Lobo's gun jabbing her ribs as he half-dragged, half-pushed her
away from the deserted docks. Her heart pounded in her chest.

They skulked in the shadows, finally reaching the far end of the
boardwalk. Lobo jerked to a stop and scoped out his surroundings.
The Chandler's Cove entertainment center stood approximately
100 yards in front of them. It appeared that he didn't have a plan
but was being forced to improvise on the fly.

Lightning streaked the sky and bounced off Lobo's shiny Glock,
followed by a loud clap of thunder. The detective forced Caroline in
the direction of a covered area near the back of the building. They
zeroed in on the enclosure and hid behind a green garbage
container.

Training his gun on his hostage, Lobo pulled his cell phone from
his inside jacket pocket and dialed. The call connected, and Spanish
words flowed from his mouth.

Biting back tears, Caroline propped her back up against the

hard brick wall, thankful to be out of the driving rain, even if only for a moment. She tried to breathe, but her chest felt like it was in a vice. Feeling hope slipping through her fingers, she closed her eyes and silently cried out to the Lord.

Heavenly Father, I can't do this.

Yes, you can, came the soft reply. *You are not alone.*

With newfound courage, Caroline marshaled her thoughts, recalling her crisis intervention training. If she was going to get out of this situation alive, it was imperative that she keep a clear head. What had Lobo said right before dragging her away? She searched her memory bank, hoping to recall a pertinent piece of the detective's conversation with the man he called Stan.

"I'm the one you're looking for," Lobo had said. The revelation of his confession was beginning to sink in. Her captor was a brutal killer. Could she be his next victim? Caroline swept the thought from her mind.

Lobo had also mentioned something about needing to get far away from here. That must mean he was looking for a way to get out of town without getting caught. Did he want her to help him escape, or did he want to use her as a human shield? She shivered at the thought.

Her sudden movement startled the detective. He thrust the gun in her side and continued his unintelligible conversation. Caroline listened to the sing-song pattern of syllables bouncing off her eardrums, hoping to pick up a familiar word or phrase. Most of what she heard sounded like a babbly blur.

Caroline's ears pricked up when she heard *bote*—something, something—*ocho*. A boat was going to be somewhere at 8 o'clock. That must be how Lobo expected to escape. If so, what was her role in this impromptu plan?

The Spanish stopped and was replaced with a long rumble of thunder. The rain had lessened in intensity but continued to fall. Lobo disconnected the call and replaced his cell. He grabbed Caroline tightly around the waist and pulled her toward him. She could feel his hot breath on her cheek. He withdrew the Glock from her side but didn't put it away.

Lobo's lips touched Caroline's ear. "It seems my transport will be here sooner than expected. Ready for some more excitement?" He yanked her arm, jamming the gun back into her ribs. "You and I are going to take a little ride."

Bile rose up in Caroline's throat. She couldn't let that happen. She knew Lobo was desperate, so it was only a matter of time before he made a mistake. When he did, she'd make a run for it.

"Where's your car parked?" he hissed in her ear.

"It's not far," she stammered. "In the parking lot on the other side of the building."

Dragging Caroline along, Lobo skirted the perimeter of the entertainment center at an adrenaline-fueled pace. Rounding the corner, Caroline slowed her steps.

"Which one is yours?" Lobo shouted.

Caroline's eyes desperately searched the parking lot for any sign of life, but they seemed to be the only people dumb enough to be out in the storm. "The red Subaru over there," she choked.

Lobo pushed Caroline forward, but her feet felt as if they had melted into the pavement. Anger contorted Lobo's face and he tightened his grip on her arm. "Move!" he yelled.

Caroline shut her eyes and silently prayed to the Lord. *Jesus, you are in control. Give me strength. Protect me from harm.*

In that instant, God's almighty power soared on the wings of the wind, shielding her from the fray. Her soul seemed to separate from her body and an inner peace washed over her. She slowly opened her eyes. Lobo stood there with a blank expression on his face; the Glock rested by his side.

The detective's transformation was nothing short of a miracle. It was as if someone had suddenly slapped some sense into him. Caroline believed she was beginning to see the real Ronald Lobo, a scared, remorseful man who had let life drag him down the wrong path. Maybe she could use his fear to her advantage.

Lobo tugged at Caroline's arm, shoving her in the direction of the SUV. "We've got to go. The boat's coming."

Approaching the Subaru, Caroline pulled the keys from her pants pocket and held them out at arm's length. As Lobo reached for the keys, two sets of headlights blasted them with bright beams of light. Caroline dropped the keys and took off running in the direction of a tall trash container. Diving behind the waste receptacle, she inched her head out.

Lobo snatched the keys off the ground and bolted to the SUV. Holstering his Glock, he clumsily fumbled with the keys, finally unlocking the door.

Two men bolted from their vehicles and rushed in their direction. One had a gun in his hand; the other was Caroline's father. Nathan charged toward Lobo and punched him square in the jaw. Lobo stumbled backward and fell into the car door. Caroline's surroundings became a blur of slow-motion movements as she witnessed the horror unfolding around her, helpless to do anything to stop it.

"Stand down, Captain Beall," the other man ordered.

Nathan charged again and threw another punch, but this time Lobo was ready. Nathan's punch missed, and his momentum propelled him forward into the forceful fist of the dangerous detective. The punch hit Nathan in the temple, spinning him around. Nathan's leg buckled, sending him to the ground.

In a flash, Lobo entered the Subaru and sped away. The armed man rushed over to Nathan, pulled out his cell phone, and called 9-1-1. Caroline cautiously withdrew from her hiding place and stood gaping at her rescuer.

As the storm passed, the wind and rain decreased to a drizzle. Caroline rushed over to Nathan and knelt beside him. Pain etching his face, Nathan reached out his hand. Caroline clasped it and held on tight.

Nathan struggled to speak. "I'm sorry, Caroline. It's all my fault. Don't blame your mother…"

Sirens shrieked through the dense fog as an ambulance pulled up beside them. The rescue team jumped out and rushed to Nathan's aid. Caroline reluctantly let go of her father's hand, allowing the paramedics to do their work.

As the medics loaded Nathan onto the ambulance, Caroline attempted to pull her cell phone out of her pants pocket, but her fingers wouldn't work. On the verge of collapse, she stumbled over to a wooden bench under the covered entrance to the entertainment center and fell into the hard seat. Gentle rain sprinkled down as lightly as tears from Heaven. She searched for her world, but it had vanished.

After another attempt, Caroline managed to retrieve her cell and turn it on. There were several missed calls from Jason. She checked the time. Almost 8 o'clock. She wondered where Lobo was taking her SUV. Would he rendezvous with the boat, or would he turn himself in? Only God and the guilty man knew the answer to that. She hoped for the detective's sake that he would do the latter.

With shaking hands, Caroline dialed Jason's cell. After one ring, her husband's soothing voice echoed in her ear. She gave him her location, then shut off her phone and placed it back in her pocket. She didn't want to talk anymore. She didn't know what to say. Pulling her feet up onto the bench, she hugged her knees tight, letting the tears freely fall.

Detective Lobo sped down the rain-soaked streets, dodging cars and running red lights, making his way to Koke Island. His hands shook as he gripped the steering wheel. *Man, I could use a cigarette right about now,* he thought.

Lobo glanced at the Subaru's dash clock. Five minutes to get to the lighthouse. *Not to worry.* The transport boat would meet him there and shuttle him to the Columbian freighter waiting in international waters. Once back in Columbia, he could disappear in the jungles. It wasn't the future the young detective had planned, but it was better than the future awaiting him if he stayed in the states.

Lobo shook his head. His gambling addiction had changed his life forever. Why hadn't he gotten the help everyone said he needed? Stan and others had offered to help him see a new beginning, but he had refused, vowing to keep his habit under control. He had broken that vow.

Dollar signs had danced before Lobo's eyes when he'd been approached with the opportunity to make some "easy" money. The money began flowing like water, allowing him to pay off his gambling debts. That's when he should have gotten out, but greed consumed him like an eternal fire that would not be extinguished.

In the beginning, the operation had gone smoothly. All he had to do was connect buyers and sellers, and make sure that the donor entered and exited the country without any complications. True—the procedures were not sanctioned by the government, but the donor and recipient were always willing participants. To him, the illegal buying and selling of human kidneys was a victimless crime until that terrible night last October.

Lobo sped across the Inlet Pass Bridge in record time. Reaching the other side, he zipped into the left lane and made a sharp turn onto West End Marina Road, narrowly avoiding an oncoming RV. He spotted the distinctive black and white pattern of the Koke Island Lighthouse looming large at the end of the road. Only one more mile to freedom.

Lobo slammed his palm onto the steering wheel, chastising himself for not bringing the woman along. Now he had no hostage and no leverage. The plan, albeit improvised, couldn't have been any more straightforward. Grab the woman and get to the lighthouse. Everything was copacetic, until her father had intervened. How *had* the bumbling Captain Beall found him so fast? Had it been divine intervention or just dumb luck?

Lobo shook the silly notion of supernatural powers out of his head and turned his mind back to his escape plan. He was wary of what he would find at the lighthouse, but Stan was no longer a threat. He regretted having to shoot his friend, but it was the only way to escape arrest.

Kale Kalani was a different story. Lobo had disliked the detective from the start. Kalani was too smart for his own good. Shooting him would be a pleasure.

It was a sure bet that Kalani had already apprised the CCPD of the most likely escape scenarios. Lobo knew that his only hope of making a clean get-away rested on the chance that the clever detective had yet to discern his end game.

As Lobo approached the lighthouse, he slowed his pace. Stop signs stood on every corner and pedestrians were beginning to emerge from their dry shelters. The rain had stopped, but thick fog obscured his vision. He glimpsed the outline of the lighthouse in the distance, its beacon penetrating the eerie mist.

The West End Marina lay straight ahead. As Lobo neared the lighthouse landing, he was distracted by swirling red and blue lights and the shrill sound of sirens. Panicking, he jammed his foot on the accelerator, unaware of the Dodge Ram 3500 pick-up truck pulling out in front of him. He swerved to miss the truck and skidded off the dock ramp, crashing into the harbor.

TWENTY-NINE

TIME STOOD STILL as Caroline played out the surreal nightmare in her head. In a daze, she barely recognized Jason as he lifted her off the wooden bench at the entertainment center and put her in the back seat of his truck. He wrapped her in a blanket and held her tight as they waited for help to arrive. Minutes later, Roseann swooped in like an eagle protecting her nest, bringing the paramedics with her. They poked and prodded until Caroline screamed for them to leave her alone. At which point, a nice EMT administered a sedative and all her worries were gone with the wind.

Afterward, still on an adrenaline high, Caroline asked Jason to take her to the hospital. For some unfathomable reason, she wanted to check on her father. Not wanting to leave her daughter's side, Roseann insisted on coming with them.

Reaching the emergency room, they were informed that Nathan was being prepped for surgery. Desperately needing to make sure that her father was okay, Caroline demanded to see him. The understanding nurse told her to have a seat in the waiting area, and that she would come get her shortly.

As Caroline waited, a million thoughts whirled around inside her head. What would she say to Nathan? At the same time, conflicting feelings waged war upon her heart. Which one would win? She did not know.

Caroline fixed her eyes on the closed waiting room door that separated her from her father, anxiously waiting for it to open. After what seemed like an eternity, the door swung open and the nurse ushered her to Nathan's bedside. "Only a few minutes," she instructed before leaving the room.

Caroline's heart pounded in her chest as she looked at Nathan. Her spirit discerned that the man who lay before her was her father, but her mind and heart struggled to accept it.

Nathan reached his hand out and Caroline took it. "Thank-you for coming," he said in a hoarse voice.

Caroline stared at the bed sheets. Her mouth went dry and her stomach clenched. She knew that if she looked into Nathan's eyes, she'd lose her composure.

"Thank-you for saving my life," was all that she could say before the tears began streaming down her face. She let go of Nathan's hand and quickly swiped her cheeks with her hands.

Nathan shifted on the stretcher and winced. "My bad hip popped. Got to have surgery to fix it."

Caroline silently nodded. A sudden surge of guilt engulfed her. Was Nathan's injury her fault? Before she could respond, a man and a woman dressed in surgical scrubs entered the room and flanked either side of Nathan's stretcher. They informed him that it was time to go get his new hip.

Caroline looked at Nathan's expectant face. His crystal-blue eyes locked onto hers. "I hope to see you soon, Caroline," he said as the surgical team wheeled him out of the room and down the hall.

Knowing that Nathan was in God's hands, the threesome left the hospital. Caroline and Roseann were eager to give their account of the evening's events. Jason transported them to the CCPD, where they spent the next couple of hours being interviewed by Chief Mitchell, Detective Kalani, and Agent Prince from the FBI. When the three men were satisfied that Caroline and Roseann had no more information to give, they signed their statements in triplicate and left the station. Jason drove Roseann back to her condo, where they were mobbed by questions from Aunt Flo, Walt, and the boys. They took a few minutes to quell any concerns before heading back to Callahan Manor.

Driving home, a hollowness saturated Caroline inside; the same hollowness that had consumed her as a young child. Could it be that she feared her father might abandon her once more?

THIRTY

Sunday Morning, Seaside Community Church

STANDING in the atrium of the Seaside Community Church, Caroline was thankful to be safe and sound in the Lord's house this final Sunday of summer break. The annual Friend Day extravaganza was about to begin, and the sanctuary was packed beyond capacity. Members and non-members alike had come to take part in the faith-based community's time of collective worship. Leap of Faith was only one part of the anticipated celebration.

Still numb, but hopeful, Caroline ushered her dancers down the hall toward the church sanctuary. Reaching the side entrance, they stood in the empty vestibule, waiting for the pastor to announce their performance. The uplifting music of the worship team could be heard throughout the building. Caroline closed her eyes, letting the soothing sounds of *Amazing Grace* calm her searching soul. As the final chords resounded, she opened the sanctuary door a crack and peeked in. The associate pastor motioned them inside.

The dancers entered the sanctuary wearing purple chiffon skirts over glistening white unitards. Long strands of purple and white ribbon had been woven into perfectly shaped top-knot buns. Splitting into two groups, the girls circled the back of the sanctuary and placed themselves on the two aisles that divided the three groups of pews. Their tea length skirts flowed with every movement.

Jason had saved Caroline a seat in the first row, center section. She walked around to the front of the sanctuary and sat down next to him. Glancing over her shoulder, she spied Zoe and Sergio squeezed into the packed pew behind her. Roseann, Aunt Flo, Walt, Lucy, and the boys occupied the entire third row.

The senior pastor, Paul Yates, announced the troupe, then cued the music. As the soft sounds of *I Can Only Imagine* began to fill the room, the performers danced down the aisles toward the stage. They ascended the stage steps and positioned themselves in the form of a cross. One by one, they fanned out, creating a circular formation. The dancers spun, leaped, and twirled in perfect synchronization, honoring their creator with every graceful movement.

As the song neared its end, the dancers made their way to the rear of the stage. They formed a semi-circle around the baptistery. Above their heads, a massive stained-glass window in the shape of a cross hung over the water. Sunbeams shone through the multi-colored window and illuminated the dancers as they fell to their knees, raising their hands toward Heaven.

The music stopped and a chorus of "Amen" and "Praise the Lord" echoed throughout the sanctuary. The girls stood up and, with faces glowing, exited the stage. They made their way through the audience, finding their seats.

Caroline closed her eyes and prayed that the dancer's performance would be a blessing in someone's life. Savoring the moment, she opened her eyes and gazed upon the sparkling cross in front of her. As she reflected on the significance of Christ's sacrifice, the sound of rippling water arose from the baptistery.

Pastor Paul descended into the pool and held out his hand. A young girl with long honey-colored hair grasped onto his outstretched palm and inched down into the water. Caroline recognized the face. Her sweet Olivia was getting baptized!

Happy tears ran down Caroline's face as Pastor Paul introduced Olivia and announced, "I baptize you in the name of the Father, and of the Son, and of the Holy Spirit." Olivia held onto the pastor's strong arm as he immersed her in the water. Her head popped back up, and the room erupted into thunderous applause. The pastor led Olivia from the baptistery as the worship band played *There is a Pure and Tranquil Wave*.

After more songs and sermonettes, the worship service ended. Everyone gathered their belongings and headed to the atrium to congratulate Olivia on her decision. As they joined the newest member of their spiritual family, Caroline was introduced to Olivia's mother, who stood by her daughter's side, her proud face beaming.

After several minutes of hugs and words of encouragement, Olivia informed Caroline that she would be leaving tomorrow to spend a few days with her father. Her mentee had an important decision to make about her future in Chandler's Cove, and Caroline knew that special prayers were in order.

As the lunch hour approached, everyone waved good-bye to Olivia and her mother, then headed to their respective vehicles. Although closed on the Sabbath, Lucy had offered to open The Jiffy Java for a special Sunday brunch. She and Evan had prepared sandwiches, salads, and desserts for the occasion.

Driving to the coffee shop, Caroline received a call from Detective Kalani. He apologized for intruding on Sunday but hoped that he could ask her a few more questions. The last thing she wanted to do was relive her harrowing ordeal, but Kalani inferred that time was of the essence, and that her recollection of significant details about the event would soon fade.

As a surprise to Lucy, Caroline asked Kale Kalani to meet her at The Jiffy Java. She believed that Lucy was beginning to warm up to the sharp detective, and her gut told her that he felt the same way.

Jason would want to lecture his wife on the evils of minding people's business, but she'd deal with him later.

Within minutes, they arrived at the square and entered the unoccupied coffee shop. Lucy and Evan headed straight to the kitchen and began unloading the industrial-sized refrigerator. Roseann and Flo followed suit and offered a helping hand. Jason, Sergio, and Walt began rearranging tables and chairs to accommodate the large group.

Isabella popped up beside Caroline and planted a peck on her cheek before disappearing into the Ladies' Room to change out of her performance attire. She soon returned, dressed in hot-pink shorts and a Dance Diva T-shirt. Joining Max and Sam at the jukebox, the three began setting up a playlist of party songs.

Zoe grabbed Caroline's arm, pulling her away from the others. "How are you holding up?" she asked as they moved to the other side of the restaurant.

"I'm not sure. It's like I'm walking on a cloud, but when I least expect it, I'm going to fall through and land in the middle of a stormy sea. If it weren't for the good Lord and my extended family, I'd be in a deep, dark place right about now."

Closing her eyes, Caroline attempted to block out the cyclone of negativity that swirled around her—her abduction...her wayward father...her ruined SUV...her absent assistant...her dubious plans for grad school. Feeling the room begin to spin, she wobbled over to a chair and plopped down.

Zoe rushed over and began rubbing Caroline's arms. "Do you want to go to the urgent care and have a doctor give you something to calm your nerves?" she asked.

Caroline shook her head. "No—I'm exhausted, that's all. I just need to rest. I'll call the doctor in the morning and schedule a visit."

"Okay, but I'm going to be a monkey on your back until you do."

Caroline couldn't help but smile as she visualized her friend hanging around her neck. "That's us. A couple of chimps."

Zoe placed her hands onto Caroline's shoulders and began massaging her tight muscles. "The Lord won't give you more than you can handle, Caroline. Don't forget, he's right here with you."

"I know, but it doesn't help that he's dropped a big *man-sized* boulder in my path." Caroline's shoulders sagged as if someone had let the air out of her. "To make matters worse, Olivia will be gone for who knows how long."

Zoe took Caroline's hands in hers. "Let's pray," she said.

They bowed their heads and closed their eyes.

"Peace go with you," Zoe began. "God's quiet within the noise. God's hope within uncertainty. God's rest within the toil. God's presence within your soul. Peace go with you." Caroline breathed a hushed Amen as Zoe made the sign of the cross.

Taking in a deep breath, Caroline blew out the stress that had been building up over the past couple of days. On the plus side, she was still here, and God was on his throne. That thought put a big smile on her face. "Hallelujah!" she shouted. "It's a wonderful day to be alive. We should rejoice in God's greatness."

The assemblage snapped their heads in Caroline's direction.

Isabella flashed her pearly whites. "I've got the perfect song for you, Miss Caroline." She punched a few numbers on the jukebox and Mandisa began belting out *Overcomer*.

Caroline slid out of the chair and grabbed Isabella's hand. They began to boogie to the uplifting beat. Zoe, Max, and Sam joined in, while everyone else clapped and sang along. God's light filled the room, giving them strength to overcome the darkness.

THIRTY-ONE

THE FRONT DOOR of The Jiffy Java swung open, and Kale Kalani entered dressed in a navy-blue sport coat, white dress shirt, and tan slacks. He slipped off his green-tinted Maui Jim sunglasses and stood at the door. Everyone stopped what they were doing and eyeballed the debonair detective. Caroline glanced at Lucy, whose cheeks had turned from mocha to bronzed rose. Averting her gaze from the detective's smoldering stare, Lucy placed a tray of sandwiches on the food table and hurried back to the kitchen.

As the jukebox tune ended, Caroline walked to the party area and motioned for Detective Kalani to follow. She sat down at the table, and Kalani and Jason took the empty seats on either side of her. Sergio and Zoe kept the kids occupied at the jukebox, while everyone else scattered like rats leaving a sinking ship.

Kale pulled out his notepad and began firing away. Caroline dredged up Friday night's painful memories and answered his questions to the best of her ability. During the questioning, Roseann, Flo, Walt, Lucy, and Evan trekked back and forth from kitchen to table until all the food, drinks, and desserts had been set out. Once done, they slipped into waiting chairs, anxious to eavesdrop on the conversation in progress.

Kale informed everyone that Detective Lobo had confessed to the recent murder in Chandler's Cove and to the murder last October in the Outer Banks. He also explained how the two cases were connected.

"Both cases were similar in that they involved the illegal trafficking of human organs," Kale began. "The victims were from Columbia and had apparently donated a kidney prior to being murdered. The FBI got involved when no record could be found of either man entering the country legally."

Everyone blankly stared at the detective. Caroline had heard about such things happening overseas, but never in the United States. Eager to understand the whole story, the group began bombarding Kalani with questions.

"How common is the illegal buying and selling of human organs, detective?" Jason inquired.

"One out of ten organs that is transplanted comes from a trafficked human organ, kidneys being the most commonly traded."

Walt spoke next. "What's the reason behind this gruesome business?"

Kale placed his notepad back in his coat pocket. "Greed for the most part. It's a billion-dollar industry. The average recipient pays around 150,000 dollars for a kidney, while the donor receives about 5,000 dollars of that money. The medical staff and the transporters get a cut, but the one who brokers the deal, pockets most of the money."

Caroline looked toward the jukebox. Zoe and Sergio were engaging the kids in a lively game of charades. "Was Detective Lobo a broker?" she asked.

Kale nodded. "That is correct."

Aunt Flo had a puzzled look on her face. "It's strange that both men came from Columbia. Is that a coincidence or was it planned?"

Kale sat back in his chair, relishing the attention bestowed upon him. "Most donors come from impoverished countries in South America, Asia, and Africa, but Columbia has a higher than average number of young males who sell their kidneys as a way to escape debt."

"That's sad," Roseann responded. "Why is it called organ trafficking when donors agree to sell their organs?"

The detective linked his fingers together and placed his hands on his stomach. "In general, organ trafficking is seen as a victimless crime that benefits very sick people at the expense of others." He paused to clear his throat. "Donors are often deceived about the medical risks involved. They may be promised post-operative care, but that rarely happens. We believe this to be the case with the murder victims."

Lucy and Evan rose from their seats and began pouring drinks.

Jason raised his eyebrows. "Are you saying that this Lobo character refused to give the donors medical treatment after their surgeries?"

Kale raked his fingers through his thick mane. "From what I gather, donors are supposed to be sent home as soon as they're medically able to travel. It appears that the first victim had some sort of post-op complication or infection. According to Detective Lobo, the donor demanded additional medical treatment and refused to board the transport boat."

Lucy stopped pouring and turned to Kale, wide-eyed. "So—he shot the man in cold blood?"

Kale and Lucy locked eyes and a tiny grin formed at the corners of the detective's mouth. "Lobo claims that the shooting in the Outer Banks was accidental, and that he drew his weapon only to scare the donor into boarding the boat. The donor lunged at him, they struggled, and the gun went off."

"Is that why the operation was moved here?" Evan queried as he served the drinks.

"After the death of the donor in the Outer Banks, Lobo moved the operation to the Gulf of Mexico. That's when the stakes got higher. A member of the medical team was blackmailing him—demanding a bigger cut of the money." Kale took a sip of sweet tea.

"So why kill the second man?" Caroline wanted to know.

"The night of the shooting, Lobo and the donor were scheduled to meet the transport boat at the lighthouse at midnight, but the donor requested an earlier meeting. After the fireworks display, Lobo met the donor at the lighthouse. The donor demanded more money and threatened to go to the authorities if not duly compensated. An altercation ensued, and Lobo admits he finally snapped."

The aroma of Lucy's scrumptious edibles began permeating the air, drawing everyone's attention away from the detective's tale. One by one, the group began perusing the food tables and filling up plates. Caroline caught Zoe's attention, and motioned for her and Sergio to come get some food. Her friend rounded up the kids and herded them over.

Knowing Caroline's fondness for deviled eggs, Aunt Flo had placed an egg-laden tray on the table in front of her. Caroline's tummy rumbled, and she remembered that she hadn't eaten breakfast. Snagging an egg, she popped it in her mouth, savoring the creamy goodness. As she chewed, she noticed that Detective Kalani remained seated.

Swallowing the egg, Caroline asked him the question that had been bothering her ever since Friday. "Detective Lobo mentioned that he'd been questioning Nathan Beall. Is my father in any way involved with these killings?"

"Let me put your mind at ease, Mrs. Callahan. Captain Beall had nothing to do with either shooting. He was leaving the docks that night in the Outer Banks when Detective Lobo shot the first donor. Your father wasn't able to identify him as the shooter, but Lobo didn't know that." Kale swiped a chip from a nearby bowl and began munching. He washed it down with another sip of tea.

A line of concern creased Caroline's brow. "If my father was not involved in the organ trafficking ring, I wonder why he picked this particular time to show up in Chandler's Cove."

The detective's lips stretched into a smile. "Captain Beall mentioned the nature of your relationship, but you'll have to ask him that question yourself. If it's any consolation, it appears he regrets his past indiscretions."

Struggling to keep her emotions from exploding all over the nice detective, Caroline simply shrugged. "Don't get me wrong. I appreciate what Captain Beall did for me. I hate that he broke his hip and had to have replacement surgery, but sympathy is not the emotion I'm feeling right now."

Roseann glided to the table and slid into the empty seat next to Caroline. She addressed Kalani. "I've been wondering about the photo of my sister that was taken at the seafood festival. Do you know why Detective Lobo was so interested in seeing it?"

"Since Lobo and the donor were at the lighthouse around the time of the festivities, the detective was afraid that someone might have taken a photo of the two of them together," Kalani stated.

Roseann shuttered. "That whole ordeal was a nightmare! I never want to go through anything like it again."

Kale gave a perspicacious nod and stood up. He scanned the room and spotted Lucy in the kitchen. "If you will excuse me, ladies." He gave a slight bow and sauntered off in Lucy's direction.

Roseann looked at Caroline, her face brimming with motherly concern. She took her daughter's hand. Caroline had the sinking feeling that Roseann intended to impart some sound words of wisdom, but she was quite sure that she didn't want to hear them.

"I went to see your father at the hospital yesterday," Roseann stated. "After I swallowed the urge to beat the tar out of him, I listened to what he had to say." She paused and cleared her throat. "It's important you understand, Caroline. Nathan left the Outer Banks because he feared for his safety, but he came to Chandler's Cove for you, dear."

Roseann squeezed her daughter's hand, but Caroline refused to make eye contact. Roseann ignored the negative non-verbal communication and continued. "Once Nathan heard about the second shooting, he knew his life was in danger, but he stayed to make sure that no harm came to you."

"That's all well and good, Mother, but I'm not feeling it today." Caroline scowled, hot anger surging through her veins. "My heart still feels the pain of my father's abandonment." She shook her head. "Who knows? Maybe I'll feel differently tomorrow, but then again, maybe not."

"You have every right to feel the way you do. I've been thrown for a loop myself." Roseann's body gave a slight quiver. "It now makes sense why I've been feeling out of sorts for the past several months. Deep down, I must have known that Nathan was near. I guess I didn't want to believe it."

Jason came up behind Caroline and kissed the top of her head. He sat down next to her, noticing her flushed face. "What's wrong?" he questioned, frowning.

"I'm all right," Caroline snipped.

Roseann took that as her cue to leave. She sped to Flo and Walt's table and sat down. Jason opened his mouth to lecture but thought better of it.

As Caroline sat stewing in her own juices, wondering if her negativity toward her father would ever end, Detective Kalani reappeared from the kitchen with a big grin on his face. Wondering about the unknown man who had been with Nathan on the docks, Caroline motioned Kale over. He sat back down next to her.

Addressing the detective, Caroline asked, "Who was the man that Lobo shot on the docks before he abducted me?"

"His name is Stan Phillips. He's a friend of your father from the Outer Banks. He was the lead detective on the case up there. When Detective Phillips was investigating the death of the man your father found on the docks, he uncovered ties to an organ trafficking ring."

"It seemed that he and Detective Lobo knew each other," Caroline commented.

"Yes," Kale affirmed. "Detective Phillips worked a few cases with Detective Lobo in the Outer Banks, and he knew that Lobo had recently transferred to Pensacola. When Phillips realized that Lobo was consulting with the SCU, and that ballistics tests from both bullets pointed to a common police handgun, he began looking at Lobo as a viable suspect in both shootings. On a hunch, he came here to investigate Lobo further. Apparently seeing Stan on the docks threw Lobo over the edge."

Evan popped up at the table and spoke to Kale. "Miss Lucy is wondering if you can help us move some heavy boxes into her van."

Kale removed his sport coat, displaying a finely chiseled torso underneath his crisp dress shirt. "Duty calls," he announced as he placed the coat over a chair and headed back to the kitchen.

From where Caroline sat, it appeared that Lucy was warming up to Mr. Calm, Cool, and Collected. She grinned at the thought of a new beginning between her friend and the dashing detective.

Jason roused Caroline from her mental matchmaking. "You need to eat," he reminded. "Can I fix you something?"

"Thanks. That would be nice. I don't want to move."

As Jason proceeded to the food tables, Sergio joined Caroline and proffered a solicitous bow. "Carolina, I'm so sorry for your troubles."

Caroline inclined her head and looked into his kind eyes. "I appreciate your friendship, Sergio. You and Zoe are the best."

He took Caroline's hand in his. "I prayed to Saint Zachary, the patron saint of peace. Do not worry. All will be well for you." He gave her a broad smile and headed back to supervise the kids. Sergio was a man of few words, but with his charm and good looks, Caroline wasn't going to hold that against him.

Jason soon returned, balancing two plates piled high with food.

"I hope you're going to help me eat all this," Caroline said, eyeing the assortment of edibles.

Jason sat down beside Caroline and scooted his chair up next to hers. "It's all for you, darling. I already ate." He put his arms around her waist and pulled her in close. Caroline winced.

Jason loosened his hold. "Are you still in pain?"

"My side is sore from Lobo jabbing me with his gun," Caroline replied, rubbing her tender ribs. "I'll put some heat on it when we get home." She dropped her head on Jason's shoulder, breathing in the faint scent of his Burberry Touch cologne.

"What are you going to do about Nathan?" he whispered in her ear.

Caroline heaved a sigh. "I honestly don't know. My emotions are off the charts. I'm sad and mad and confused all at the same time. I can't think clearly. Now is not the time to make any decisions that could adversely affect my future."

Jason rubbed his prickly beard against her neck. "That's true. We'll tackle this together when you're ready."

Caroline smiled, thankful that she had such a wonderful, supportive husband. She closed her eyes and rested in his comforting arms. "Baby steps," she uttered. "Baby steps."

Caroline's tummy began to rumble again. She sat up, took a tuna salad croissant off the plate, and sunk her teeth into the mouth-watering sandwich. As she ate, a funny thought popped into her head and she shared it with Jason.

"I thought for sure that Barry Chapman would turn out to be the killer." Caroline chuckled. "He's such an odd duck."

Jason laughed. "That he is, but I guess we can stop worrying about him now."

"I wonder why he was acting so strange," she mused.

"Oh, I forgot to tell you. There *is* a Mrs. Barry Chapman after all, but the two of them are currently separated." Jason began rubbing his fingers across Caroline's back. "I guess that's why he's been so ornery."

Caroline continued to munch on her food, marveling in the joyous activity that surrounded her. "Will you do any more jobs for him, if he asks?"

Jason rubbed his chin. "I'll have to think about it. He sure gave me a lot of grief."

Caroline nodded in agreement. "But what a beautiful day *this* has turned out to be!"

Jason snuck a celery stick off his wife's plate. "Yes, it has, praise God." He bit off a mouthful and began crunching.

Everyone ate until they were stuffed, then ate some more. The kids finished eating and rushed to the jukebox to play more songs. Fat and happy, Caroline propped her feet up and breathed in the merriment as the kids sang and danced to their hearts' content.

Detective Kalani reappeared and approached Caroline and Jason. He handed her his card. "If I can be of further assistance, don't hesitate to call. I know it's tough right now, but it does get better."

Caroline shook the detective's hand. "Thank-you for your help. I'll keep that in mind."

Kale slipped on his Maui Jim's, grabbed his sport coat, and threw it over his shoulder. Executing a sharp about-face, the snappy detective exited the coffee shop.

"I'm not sure how to take Detective Kalani," Caroline said to Jason. "He's full of contradictions—but on the plus side, he's taken a shine to Lucy."

"It would appear so." Jason gave Caroline *the look*. "And I'm sure he doesn't need your help in the romance department."

Caroline gave him *the look* right back.

At that moment, Walt joined them, saving Jason from imminent reproof. The two men placed the tables and chairs back in their original positions. Caroline stood up, stretched her tired legs, and started snatching empty paper plates and cups off the tables.

Lucy and Evan escaped from the kitchen long enough to gather the empty serving bowls and trays. They zipped back to work washing the dishes and putting them away. With the surplus of tourists in town, they'd decided to stay and prep for tomorrow's breakfast crowd.

Tossing the final cup in the trash, Caroline slid over to Zoe's table and sat down next to her. The kids had cornered Sergio at the jukebox and were attempting to teach him the latest dance moves.

Zoe shifted in her seat and crossed her shapely legs. "Sergio and I are going to take the kids to the docks," she said. "They want to see which fisherman has caught the biggest fish today." Zoe's finely adorned foot began keeping time with the music. "I want *you* to go home and take a well-needed nap."

Caroline sparked a smile. "Thanks, friend. You're the best."

One by one, the happy group began making the rounds, saying their good-byes. On their way out, Caroline heard Roseann, Flo, and Walt mention something about going to see an evening movie. Sergio and the kids finished dancing and joined Caroline and Zoe at the table. Max gave his mother a good-bye hug, then Zoe and Sergio escorted the kids out the door. Before leaving, Caroline went to the kitchen to thank Lucy for the wonderful party and to tell Evan good-bye.

Exiting the Jiffy Java, Caroline and Jason joined the bustling activity on the square. As they strolled down the sidewalk, two Eurasian collared doves flew past them, landing on the rim of a nearby pot of multicolored purslanes. Caroline studied the pair as they watched the human interactions taking place around them, unruffled by the chaotic commotion.

"Are you feeling a little less blue now?" Jason asked, diverting Caroline's attention away from the beautiful birds.

"As a matter of fact, I'm feeling rather orange," Caroline replied, smiling from ear to ear. She hooked her arm in his and inhaled the sea-scented air, gaining her second wind. "I don't want to go home yet. Let's go car shopping, instead. A little retail therapy is just what the doctor ordered."

LUCY'S ZESTY PIMENTO CHEESE SPREAD

(1) 8 oz. bag of finely shredded cheddar cheese
$\frac{1}{2}$ cup crumbled feta cheese
$\frac{1}{4}$ cup grated parmesan cheese
(1) 4 oz. jar diced pimentos drained
$\frac{3}{4}$ cup chipotle mayonnaise
(1) tsp. Mrs. Dash Table Blend
Blend ingredients and serve with toasted pita wedges.

AUNT FLO'S DELICIOUS DEVILED EGGS

6 large hard-boiled Eggs
2 tbsp. Hellman's Organic Roasted Garlic Mayonnaise
1 tbsp. yellow mustard
1 tbsp. dill relish
$\frac{1}{2}$ tbsp. grated parmesan cheese
1 tsp. Mrs. Dash Table Blend
Paprika

1. Peel cooled hard-boiled eggs and cut them in half.
2. Place egg yolks in a small mixing bowl and egg whites in a slotted serving tray.
3. Add mayonnaise, mustard, relish, parmesan cheese, and Mrs. Dash Table Blend to egg yolks and blend together until mixture reaches a smooth, creamy consistency.
4. Spoon mixture into egg whites and garnish with paprika.

Yields: 12 deviled egg halves

BOOK CLUB DISCUSSION QUESTIONS

1. Many of the book's characters have come to Chandler's Cove for a new beginning. Can you recall a time in your life when you chanced a new beginning? What thoughts and feelings did you experience during this transition period?

2. Caroline Callahan is a middle-aged wife and mother who, after re-locating to a new town, is contemplating another major life change. Can you relate to the challenges that she faces regarding this new life experience?

3. Nathan Beall is a man who enjoys living life on his own terms. After all the time that has passed, do you believe it is possible for him to make the compromises necessary to reunite with his daughter? If so, what barriers might he have to overcome?

4. Olivia Styles is a new Christian with a difficult childhood. It appears that she will have to choose between keeping one foot in the past or taking a step into

an unknown future. What obstacles will she need to overcome with either decision?

5. Throughout the book, Caroline Callahan struggles with the idea of forgiving her biological father. What *baby steps* do you think she might need to take?

Made in the USA
Columbia, SC
23 June 2023

18445773R00150